Dream Big!

Bishop Takes Knig̲

Copyright © 2019 by McKenna Dean

MW01193961

Published by

REDCLAW PUBLISHING

Dedication

The saying goes it takes a village to raise a child, and I think that's true of producing a book as well. I know that this story would never have seen the light of day if not for the rigorous input of the lovely people in my crit group, who hold flames to my feet to encourage me to write a stronger sentence while at the same time shore up my flagging confidence.

The same goes for my wonderful beta readers, Pam, Margarita, Missy, and Michelle, who cheered me on and helped me realize I had something special with this story, as well as the fabulous MJ, who is the Continuity Queen and helped keep my timeline straight.

I dedicate this story to you guys. You're the best.

Chapter One

Having tea with Emmaline was my first mistake. Her insistence on taking me to lunch indirectly led to my botched interview, and that's how I wound up working for a super-secret agency.

Given how things turned out, it was far from my only mistake.

The day had dawned dank and dreary with the promise of snow in the air. Though the year was well into its third month, spring seemed far away.

We met at our old haunt, the Blue Moon. I had just enough bus fare to get to my job interview after lunch, so that meant I'd have to make do with a cup of tea and pretend to be slimming again. I hoped Em wouldn't hear my stomach growl. Since it wasn't possible to sustain life on the sheer odor of food alone, I'd have to drown my tea in sugar to avoid an unladylike faint. With luck, the sugar would carry me through lunch.

The first time I'd laid eyes on Emmaline Prentiss was at Bryn Mawr. When I entered my dorm room at the college, I'd discovered Em already entrenched, lounging in a lacy negligee while popping a chocolate cream between her pink, plump lips.

A fuzzy mule slipper hung off one foot as she bounced a leg. The other foot was bare.

The jiggling stopped when I walked in and set my suitcase down. I'd swept the small room with a glance, flabbergasted by the way my new roommate had converted a soulless box into a decadent boudoir. The study lamps wore frilly shades, and half a dozen bouquets lined one of the desks. The room smelled like a florist. Another pair of fluffy mules lay on their sides where they'd been kicked off, and an expensive mink coat spilled across the chair beside them. When my gaze fell back upon Em, her hard assessing stare seemed quite at odds with her brunette bombshell appearance. All at once her expression had softened, and she'd given me the most beatific smile.

She'd stretched out a hand with languid grace. I have no idea why I stepped forward to take her soft, white fingers in mine, but I did. I'd hoped she didn't expect me to kiss her knuckles. I drew the line at that. Not to mention, I might break a tooth on all those rings.

"I was worried when I saw you at first, but now I know we'll be such good friends." She had given my hand a little squeeze and then sank back onto the chaise lounge to select another chocolate from the open box. Since chaise lounges didn't come standard in dorm rooms, I wondered what piece of furniture she'd sacrificed to make way for it.

"Worried?" I wasn't sure what intrigued me more—that she might somehow have had concerns about my rooming with her or that something about my appearance had alleviated them.

Her eyes had opened wide with the same candor as her tone. "Well, you're just so lovely." At the time, I thought it was a well-practiced act, but it hadn't taken long to realize Em always spoke her mind. Perhaps because there was so little else to occupy it. "I mean, look at you," she continued. "You're a knockout. But that's okay. The men that go for you won't be the ones that go for me."

"Thanks. I think."

She'd set the chocolates down and hurried over to envelop me in a chiffon-laden hug. "Oh, don't be silly, dear. I'm Jane Russell and you're Katharine Hepburn. If she were a blonde, that is. You're elegance and smarts while I'm S.A., pure and simple. Two different audiences."

I blinked at her. "S.A.?" I repeated myself a lot around Em in those first days.

She'd laughed, low and breathy. "Sex appeal, darling."

I'd grinned back at her. It had been the start of a beautiful friendship, despite us having so little in common. As Em had predicted, we didn't end up competing for the same men. After four years, I had a degree in English Lit, which hadn't prepared me for anything in life, and Em had attained the coveted "Mrs. degree" that most of my classmates had pined for, even if they hadn't been willing to admit it.

Her invitation today was to celebrate the formal announcement of the engagement of Emmaline Prentiss to

Edgar Stanley Hardcastle III. Try as I might, I hadn't been able to come up with a good excuse for turning down her suggestion to meet for lunch. She had assured me she had Hardcastle 'in the bag' when we'd parted at the end of school, and the new ring on her finger meant that in the ten months since graduation, she'd had achieved her lifetime goal. I don't know what my lifetime goal might be, but at the moment, my attention was transfixed by the waitress walking past with a tray of mini-quiches, the pastry so light and flaky they melted in your mouth. Jean-Claude, the Blue Moon's pastry chef, once confessed to me that adding vodka to the dough was the secret to perfect crusts.

The idea of eating anything, especially something laced with vodka, sounded heavenly.

Our waitress appeared at our table, dressed in a perky pink uniform with a stiffly starched white apron. "May I take your order?"

Oh, if only. Managing somehow not to sigh, I said, "Just tea for me, please. Oolong. With sugar."

Em lowered her menu to fix me with a gimlet eye and then bestowed a bewitching smile upon the waitress. Unlike most beautiful women I knew, Em used her charms on both men and women alike. "Could we have just another moment, please?"

The woman almost curtseyed as she strove to oblige. "But of course, Miss. I'll be right back."

As soon as the waitress turned away, Em laid down her menu. "Darling, it's no use pretending with me. I saw you sniffing the air like a bloodhound when you came into the restaurant. So stuff your pride for once. Order what you like. Dear Eddie's paying."

That was the problem.

"I'm dieting."

Em's laugh was still charming and breathy. "My dear, if you get any thinner, you'll blow away like a leaf on the wind. Turn you sideways, and someone might mistake you for a playing card. Even your *shadow* is thicker than you are."

I couldn't help but smile at that one. "I highly recommend the 'no money, no food' plan of weight loss, by the way. Very effective."

"Yes, but the food here is to die for and I intend to eat. I can't very well do that if you're sitting across from me practically fainting from hunger."

"It's just a temporary setback." The image of the last can of soup at home in the kitchen cabinet flashed in my mind. That, and a packet of saltines, were all I had to live on until the next paycheck came in. Given the fact I'd been fired yet again, who knew when that would be? Still, pride is hard to abandon when you're a Bishop. When you were taught to believe honor meant something.

At one time, it did.

"I have an interview lined up this afternoon. After I leave here, as a matter of fact."

The Dragon Lady in charge of handing out potential interviews to those of us desperately hoping for work, any work, had given me a tight-lipped smile along with the slip of paper containing the directions to the agency.

"Maybe this one will do for you, Miss Bishop. It's a two-week assignment, so perhaps you can manage to stay through the contract this time. At least when you lose *this* job, it won't be anything out of the ordinary."

In return, I'd given her a smile dripping with honey. As I'd started to leave, clutching the directions in gloved hands and hoping the hole in the fingertip didn't show, she'd stopped me with her trilling little voice.

"Oh, and Miss Bishop? If you get fired or quit this position, I'm afraid we can no longer assist you. We *do* have a reputation to maintain."

As tempting as it had been to tell her exactly what I thought of her, I hadn't. My father had raised me better.

But I wasn't sure I could watch Em devour tiny sandwiches and delicate cakes with the same fortitude.

Em obviously thought the same. Like all predators, she excelled at sensing weakness. "If you have an interview this afternoon, then it behooves you not to pass out from starvation. You want to make a good first impression, right?"

She had a point. Besides, as she said, Eddie would pick up the tab. Good old Eddie. Though it wasn't as if Em didn't have the money. When we'd been roommates, we'd taken turns paying for each other's meals. We'd been on almost equal footing. What I'd lacked in outright funds compared to her father's wealth had been more than made up by my standing in the social register, at least in her father's eyes. The Mayflower antecedents. The long-dead great-great-great uncles who were signers of the Declaration of Independence. A few generals on the *right* side of the Civil War. To Em's parents I represented everything they'd ever wanted for their little girl and the one thing they couldn't buy: social standing.

Traveling the world with my father, I'd missed my presentation as a debutante until I was almost on the shelf, and my mother despaired of ever making a lady of me. She'd put an end to my globe-trotting days, insisting I attend her *alma mater* in the last ditch hope of turning me into a proper socialite and, more importantly, marrying me off to the highest bidder. Almost twenty-five when I graduated, I was considered long in the tooth by society's standards when it came to the marriage mart. I'd failed in that respect. Em had not.

Em's parents basked in second-hand glory as Em wore Edgar Stanley Hardcastle lll's enormous engagement ring on her finger, the only ring Em wore these days. When the sunlight caught the massive diamond, the flash could render anyone in striking distance temporarily blind.

From our recent phone conversations, there could be no doubt Em took her position as the future Mrs. Hardcastle as seriously as though she had been preparing for it her entire life. I suppose she had. She fully intended to put her days as the campus bombshell behind her and be the best wife Eddie could ever imagine—tending to his every need while feeding his fantasy of having captured the most alluring woman on the continent. She would fill her days with shopping, homemaking, and tennis matches at the country club. In a year or so, she'd produce a little Edgar IV.

I couldn't think of anything more incredibly tedious, but I was pleased for Em. She deserved whatever made her happy. She was one of the few people who hadn't either dropped me or turned catty and cutting after the death of my father. Her persistent friendship touched me.

Besides, who knew when I'd eat so well again? Pride was all good as far as it went, but it didn't fill your belly.

"By all means." I opened the menu again. "Let's eat."

We ordered a ridiculous amount of food, platters of all of our old favorites. I listened as Em nattered on about her wedding plans, her trousseau, and where they were going for their honeymoon—Paris, of course, though I would have preferred Tuscany or Corsica. I murmured at the appropriate moments and concentrated on the heavenly food, trying not to embarrass myself with little moans of appreciation.

Despite allowing Em, or at least Eddie, to be the benefactor of the feast, I didn't want her to know just how tight things were. The thought of Em insisting the staff box enough food to last me several days was mortifying, so I waited until she had made use of the ladies' room to stuff the sleeves of my coat with the rolls from the bread basket. I'd worn my Chanel suit for the interview to come. Though it was cold out, I thought I could walk out of the café with my coat folded over my arm, and no one would comment. I'd used this method of smuggling food out of restaurants in the past, and no one had caught me yet. The downside? A chilly journey lay before me on my way to the interview. Ah well, Mother always said a true lady never felt the heat or the cold.

I'd wrapped my napkin around several ham paste sandwiches to slip them into my purse when Em returned. As decadent as the pastries had been—and I hadn't been shy about eating them—meat was what I craved at the moment, it being rather scarce in my diet of late.

All of which meant I was a little distracted when Em spoke.

"I'm sure it will be a relief to you, but I'm *not* asking you to be my maid of honor."

"You're not?"

Emotions are a tricky thing. I'd practiced a little speech as to why I couldn't accept the honor in anticipation of Em asking me to perform that very same role, and here she was, saying the job would go to someone else.

"No. I decided to ask Eddie's sister, Milly, instead. She's such a mousy little thing. She'll enjoy the spotlight for a change."

"Are you sure that's wise? Mightn't she wish to make you look bad?"

Eddie's family hadn't exactly embraced Em. In the post-war industry boom, Mr. Prentiss had done well for himself with his various factories, and was wealthy enough to purchase an estate in the Hamptons and maintain a penthouse apartment in the city. He'd wanted nothing but the best for his precious daughter. That meant a university education at one of the finest colleges for women, though given the choice, Em would have been far happier eating bon bons and playing tennis six days a week. Although Em's family had money, it was *new* money, and while they belonged to country clubs, they weren't the *right* country clubs. Attending Bryn Mawr introduced Em to men who belonged to society's upper echelon, and she'd achieved one of her father's goals for her, marrying into a family with old money and prestige. I hoped he didn't realize the disdain with which society held him and his daughter.

"Oh, the dears no longer think I'm a gold-digger. Not once they realized how much Daddy's worth." A feline smile stretched Em's wine-red lips. As in the cat-got-the-cream smug. "Now I'm just a social climber. I've been working on Hardcastle senior, who thinks I'm an angel now. Of course, Eddie believes I can do no wrong."

Which just left the female contingent of the Hardcastle household up in arms.

"Much as they'd like me to show my vulgar roots, it *is* their dear Eddie's wedding, after all. The mother I won't win over until I have children, but with Daddy footing the bill for the ceremony, Milly is thawing out." Em grabbed my hand across the table and squeezed. "I know if I'd asked you, everything would have been simply *divine*, darling. You would have arranged things with deadly efficiency, and it would have been beautiful and elegant and so full of stinking class, people would've talked about it for years to come. Daddy would've wept with joy. But I don't think you would have enjoyed it much, would you?"

For all that Em had gadded about during her four years at the college like a mindless, gaudy butterfly, she could be remarkably astute when it suited her.

"You know me too well," I said. Under the cover of dropping my gaze into my lap at the admission, I transferred the ham sandwiches into my purse and closed the snap.

"Yes. I do." She sat back in her chair. A playful archness highlighted her expression as she continued. "I *do* expect you to be a bridesmaid. There's no getting out of that." She stopped me before I could protest. "Daddy's paying for this wedding. All expenses." She emphasized the word "all" and smiled. "You needn't worry about a thing. Now we just need to get you suitably situated."

She acted as though my current poverty was a temporary aberration, one I could cure with a simple engagement. In theory, she was right. I'd made my bed and so now had to lie in it, but I could change my mind if I swallowed my pride.

"Why don't you come out with us tonight? We're going clubbing. My treat. Everyone from the old gang will be there." She added with a mischievous smile, "Maybe some of your class will rub off on me."

"I don't know why you think it would after all this time."

Delighted laughter erupted out of her. "You see? Such an elegant, effortless put-down. You probably didn't even mean it.

And in your usual lovely, dry manner. I'll never master that, not in a million years."

Heat rushed into my cheeks. "You don't want to sound like my mother. Just be yourself and everyone will fall at your feet, the way they always do."

She preened a little before her frown showed she registered that the compliment was also a distraction. "You're changing the subject. You're already one of Eddie's set. Just pick someone and marry him. All your troubles will be over."

Not exactly. She was correct in one respect. Everyone in the upper social register knew Harry Bishop, of the Leesburg Bishops, who'd married the somewhat frail, but quite wealthy, Helen Cartwright. Harry Bishop, loquacious and charming, who'd had a coffee plantation in Africa and a stable of racing thoroughbreds in Maryland. Harry Bishop, who'd taught me, his only child, Henrietta, to ride anything with four legs and shoot like Annie Oakley. Harry Bishop, who'd gambled away everything he loved, and taken the easy way out with a bullet to the brain just a few weeks after my graduation. *That* Harry Bishop.

My mother had gone back to her cattle baron family out West. To my utter shock, less than three months after my father's death, my elegant mother had married a former beau from her debutante days. I refused to hide my sense of betrayal, nor, if I'm being entirely honest, my disgust. She had extended an invitation to join her in Wyoming, but I declined with some heat, and we were not on speaking terms these days. Sometimes I felt as though I never knew my parents at all.

"I tell you what, Em. If this job doesn't work out, what I really need is an introduction to one of your father's foremen. My deadly efficiency, as you so kindly call it, might be appreciated as an office or factory manager."

Though at first I'd rebelled at being pulled away from my beloved life of traveling with my father, I'd taken to university study like an orphaned duck introduced to water. I immersed myself in English Lit, finding kinship in women across the ages. I'd also taken advantage of the courses offered in political economy and women's industries. And thanks to my father, I knew what a well-managed business looked like, as well as one that was being used to launder money.

Pity I hadn't learned about these things before his death.

Em's lips pursed as though she'd bitten into a lemon tart when she was expecting chocolate instead. "Rhett, darling. If it were in my power, you know I would. But dearest, those jobs don't go to women."

"It's 1955. Women did those jobs and more during the war. There's no reason we can't do them now." I knew I could run a large factory better than I could alphabetize file folders. The problem was that filing was all I was being offered. Well, that wasn't entirely true. All too often, I received offers that had little to do with my skill at the typewriter and more with a presumptive knowledge of skills in the bedroom. Hence, my frequent need for a new job.

"Women only worked in factories until the men came home." Em looked as if she'd like add "idiot" to the end of her sentence.

"What about Tommy Stanford's father?"

"My dear." Em's eyebrows made a brief flight toward her hairline before she narrowed her eyes in speculation. "Don't you think he's a bit old for you? Tommy adores you and would make a far better match."

"Not as a *husband*." I glanced around before leaning across the table to hiss at Em. "What do you take me for?" With a sigh, I sat back in my chair. "I could run his stables and school his racehorses."

"Ah." Em's face relaxed as once more, as everything in her universe sank back in its proper orbit. "I'm certain you could, but you have even less chance of landing such a position than you do of managing a factory. But back to Tommy...."

"I'm not marrying Tommy."

This time, a single eyebrow arched upward. "Has he asked?"

"He wasn't serious. He was drunk at the time."

"My dear, that's the only time Tommy *is* serious. You should have accepted him."

"As amusing as Tommy is, I'm rather off drunkards at the moment. Besides, I can't marry someone for the sake of financial security."

"I don't see why not."

Like most people who didn't need money, Em had no real concept what it was like to live without it. I hadn't either, before I discovered I was dead broke. I could have taken the sanctuary my mother offered, but I didn't care for the price tag. I had a hard time believing her love of status and wealth hadn't been a huge factor in the decisions my father had made, even as he'd kept up the pretense that everything was all right. Aloud, I said I didn't blame her for my father's death, but in my heart of hearts, I did.

Em continued unconscious of her ignorance. "Women have been doing it for centuries. Not just for the money, but for power, too. Look at Cleopatra."

"You realize that didn't end well for her."

"Didn't it?" Em opened her eyes wide and then shrugged. "The point is, you shouldn't turn your nose up at the idea. Don't you ever want to get married?"

"Not to someone I don't love." I spoke with complete, uncomplicated sincerity.

"Oh, Rhett." Em gave me her genuine smile, not the sexy little moue she usually made. "I never would have pegged you for a romantic. Love is so over rated."

"So you don't love Eddie, then?"

She flicked her fingers in a dismissive little gesture. "Of course I do. We'll rub along together quite well. He'll worship me and I'll make him happy. But we're talking about you, not me. It takes no more effort to fall for a rich man than a poor one."

I laughed at this. I'm certain she quoted some celebrity, no doubt Marilyn Monroe. "I'll keep that in mind."

"Marriage is a contract one enters with good intentions. It helps if you like the other person involved, though." Em took a delicate sip of coffee. "Take Eddie and me, for example. I get the benefit of his family's place in society and everything that goes with it. And Eddie gets *me*." Wickedness curved her smile, a smile I envied, even if I had no desire to be Mrs. Hardcastle.

"I can see where liking the other person helps," I murmured against the rim of my cup.

Her next question came out of the blue. "Are you all right?"

I blinked. "Of course I am." Much better, in fact, than before the meal. I could almost feel the fog of hunger leaving from my brain.

She fidgeted with a fork before lifting her gaze to meet mine. "It's just that you've changed, whether or not you realize it."

"Having your father kill himself has a way of doing that to you." Let Em appreciate my lovely, dry comeback now.

I felt guilty for putting that rare frown on her face.

"I know it's a terrible thing to have happened, and I would be devastated if Daddy died all of a sudden—" she looked as though she might burst into tears for a moment, "—but it's not like you could have prevented it, you know."

"If I hadn't been so wrapped up in school…." The school I hadn't wanted to attend in the first place.

She waved me off with a flick of her napkin, which she then used to dab with care at her lips before speaking again. "Nonsense. It wouldn't have mattered if you'd been at your family's brownstone instead of in Pennsylvania. It's not like you were in Timbuktu, now was it?" She checked her lipstick in the deftly concealed mirror tucked in her palm, replaced the compact in her purse and then snapped the clasp shut in a moment of decision. "We're spending most of our time in the Hamptons right now. The apartment is empty, except on the rare occasions I come back to town for fittings and the like. Why don't you move in? Just until you get back on your feet. Martha would love having someone to take care of again."

Her generous offer made my eyes water for an instant, but hardened businesswomen don't cry, so I blinked back any signs of weakness. I could only imagine how their housekeeper would feel about my presence in the family's absence. And what if the entire family returned? It was one thing to room with Em in college, but I wasn't sure I could bear to bunk with her parents. Even if it saved on rent. "That's kind of you, but I couldn't."

"Couldn't or wouldn't? You know what they say about pride and falls, don't you?"

"No. What?"

A peal of laughter rang out. "I hoped you could tell me." Em patted my hand. "Promise me one thing, at least. If this new job doesn't pan out, and you're not marrying Tommy, please consider moving in before you're out on the street?"

"I promise. Anyway, impending marriage suits you better than it would me." If I sounded brisk, it was to dispel any sentimentality. "You look divine, as always, and I'll keep in mind your offer of the apartment and your advice on rich men. If this job doesn't work out, that is. Speaking of which, I should be going. It was lovely to see you, Em. We should try to get together again before the wedding."

"Of course we will. At the very least, there's the bridal shower, the bridesmaid's luncheon, and the rehearsal dinner...."

I nodded. I needed to get moving, or I'd be late for my job interview. As it was, I'd stayed too long, and walking to save the bus fare was no longer an option. I prayed they were running on time. I checked the position of my hat and put on my gloves.

Em signaled the waitress to bring the check and then fixed me with that imperious stare of hers. "What about Tommy?"

"What about him?" I stood, taking care to fold my coat over one arm so the bread wouldn't fall out of the sleeves. It took skill to tuck the sleeves in so that the rolls remained hidden, but then I'd had a lot of practice lately.

"Well, you'll need a date for the wedding. Tommy's part of the wedding party, and I know he's dying to find out where you're living these days. Shall I give him your number?"

I pictured trying to have a conversation with Tommy on the community phone in my building, wedged into the little booth at the bottom of the stairs while my landlady Mrs. King pounded on the door with her cane and yelled at me to hurry up.

I repressed a shudder at the memory of being trapped in Tommy's convertible, holding him at bay while he declared his drunken, undying love. "No, thanks. I have a date for the wedding."

"You do? Darling, spill the details." She reached toward me and her engagement ring caught the light again, sending little rainbows dancing across the white tablecloth.

"I'd love to, but I really must run. More later. Kiss, kiss." I blew a token of affection at her and dashed out the door before she could question me further about my fictional date. Darn it, I'd have to come up with a man or an excuse by the wedding. Good thing I had several months to solve that problem.

As I hurried out of the restaurant, a few flakes of snow tumbled in the surrounding air. A June wedding seemed an eternity away. A glance back at Em showed her accepting another cup of coffee instead of leaving as planned. She sat with such a feline look of appreciation, I couldn't help but feel a spurt of envy. The pane of glass separating us might have been as thick as steel, she in her world, and me in mine.

A world of my own choosing, I reminded myself. Since I'd rather have my fingernails pulled off with a pair of pliers than marry someone for the sake of getting married, it was off to the job interview for me. I'm sure Em felt the same about earning a living as a typist as I did about accepting Tommy's offer of marriage.

I hunched into the wind and turned away. Much as I loathed to spend the money, if I hurried, I could catch the next bus. With my head tucked against the cold, I strode to the corner. Ahead of me, a man stood waiting for the light, the collar of his coat turned up against the bitter weather. The light changed just as I reached him, and he stepped off the curb into the slushy street.

"Look out!" I grabbed him by the sleeve and pulled hard, causing him to stumble backward as a taxi rounding the corner almost clipped us both. The edge of his heel caught the curb, and he fell against me, knocking my coat to the sidewalk. He flailed his arms, turning in my direction, and I caught him mid-stumble before he took us both down. As it was, I ended up nose to chest with him. He smelled of pipe tobacco and damp wool.

I've always been a little partial to the scent of tobacco.

"Steady now." I held onto him to make sure he regained his footing on the slick pavement. With his fedora pulled down low, I couldn't see the color of his hair, but the day-old stubble on his chin suggested it was dark. He had the face of a beautiful, tortured angel, all planes and angles, with a thin, elegant nose. He could have been a priest or an artist, someone acquainted with suffering, but it was his eyes that struck me the most. A vivid, startling blue, they were almost electric in the gray light of the afternoon, but so sad it was as if they held the weight of the universe in them.

"Well, that would be utterly ironic, being run over by a taxi." He didn't explain his comment, speaking almost to himself. His clipped, yet polite accent marked him as British, not American. "I suppose I should thank you." This time, he met my eye. "Though I can't say you did me any favors."

Heaven knows what he thought of me standing there in the falling snow, studying his face like a lost Rembrandt. He glanced down where I still gripped his arms and then met my gaze with the lift of a decidedly opinionated eyebrow. Heat burned my wind-whipped cheeks as I flushed and let him go.

We both stared down at my coat lying on the damp sidewalk. When it became obvious he had no intention of picking it up, I stooped to collect it, just when he seemed to realize courtesy demanded he do the same. We bumped heads hard enough to make him mutter a curse, and he straightened, allowing me to scoop up my coat in a manner that kept the bread from falling out.

Those blue eyes glared at me from under the brim of his hat, but then faded into bleak indifference. I can't say that I liked the implication I should have let the taxi hit him. Stepping back, I took in his painful slenderness. I wasn't the only one missing meals these days. But starving or not, his attitude annoyed me. As long as you were alive, you could still put things right. I pulled a yeast roll out of one coat sleeve and slapped it up against his chest. "Cheer up, pal. I just stole bread from that restaurant back there for my breakfast tomorrow. You don't see me crying about it."

On reflex, he closed his hand over mine to take hold of the bread. When I was sure he had a sufficient grip on the roll, I pulled away and gave him a cheeky grin. Satisfied I'd done my part as a Good Samaritan, I checked the traffic and crossed the street through the swirling snow. After I reached the bus stop, I risked a glance back.

He stood where I'd left him, looking down at the bread roll in his gloved hand as the bus pulled up to take me away.

Chapter Two

With a belch of noxious exhaust, the bus trundled away from the parts of the city I knew well, far from the 5th Avenue stores and Broadway's marquees. A poster for *East of Eden* slipped by on a billboard, and I hoped it would still be in the theaters when I had the money to see it. I'd read the book by Steinbeck and wondered how they could distill the sweeping saga down to a single film.

With misgivings, I got off the bus at the stop closest to the address the Dragon Lady had given me. Sandwiched in between a shoe repair business and a pawnshop, the location in one of the rougher parts of town and the dinginess of the building itself were discouraging. Nothing on the door indicated I had the right place. Perhaps I'd made a mistake. I checked my directions again.

To my dismay, contact with the greasy napkin wrapping the ham sandwiches in my purse had caused the ink to blur the address, but I thought I could still make it out. I held the slip of paper by the corners to avoid ruining my gloves with oil. The note contained a street address with no company name, but since most of the surrounding businesses were shops, I had to be at the right place.

A spit of sleety wind rattled in behind me as I entered the building, chasing around my skirt to billow into the corridor. I

closed the door in haste, shutting out most of the natural light.
The hallway was narrow and dark, bordered on one side by a set
of stairs—the treads worn smooth in the middle—leading to the
second floor. The hallway wasn't much warmer than outside,
but at least there wasn't any wind. The wall facing the door bore
a small directory. Down the corridor, I could make out a door
not listed on the panel. The washroom, no doubt.

According to the directory, the second floor housed
offices for a lawyer and an insurance agent. The stillness in the
building suggested business wasn't brisk. My directions said the
organization I wanted was on the first floor. Only one firm was
listed at ground level.

Redclaw Security.

Odd name. A brokerage firm, perhaps? Or maybe a
different kind of security. It seemed unlikely anyone in this
neighborhood would hire private protection, or that someone
from my old way of life would hire guards from this part of
town. Though if I were perfectly frank, I wouldn't care to do
business with a broker in this seedy location, either.

I hesitated in front of the office. Should I knock? Or just
walk in? Nothing on the outer door confirmed I had the right
agency, and yet, Redclaw was the sole firm on this floor. Had
Dragon Lady sent me on a wild goose chase? The idea my
personal nemesis might crack an evil smile over my presumed
despair stiffened my spine. That and the fact it was so bloody
cold. Even if I'd been wearing my coat instead of carrying it, I
wouldn't have been warm enough. I dearly regretted hocking

the mink coat Father had given me for my last birthday. However I'd felt about wearing the pelts of dead animals, fur would have been welcome just then. At the very least, I could go inside the office and warm up a bit, even if the trip proved fruitless.

Pressing my ear to the door's paneling, I heard the indistinct murmur of voices. Chiding myself for my unusual indecision, I took hold of the handle with determination and opened the door.

A middle-aged woman seated at a desk looked up upon my entrance. A mass of faded red hair spilled out from an untidy bun, forming a messy halo around her head as she held the telephone to one ear and took notes on a legal pad. She acknowledged my presence with a narrow-eyed glance though horn-rimmed spectacles and continued writing. "Yes. I understand. Yes, sir. I'll get right on it. Go on, I'm listening."

For a place of employment, the room was disappointing. Along a windowless wall, two chairs covered in drab olive fabric bordered the sides of a small table littered with old magazines. Besides the receptionist's desk, there were two filing cabinets and a second desk, empty save for a covered typewriter.

As though she'd read my thoughts, the woman on the phone glanced up, her pencil pausing in mid-air over her pad. Our gazes met, and then she returned her focus to the phone call. "Very good, sir." She scribbled a final note. "I'll see that it gets done."

She replaced the heavy black receiver in its cradle, set the pencil down precisely in the middle of the pad, and dropped her chin to peer at me over the bridge of her glasses. It had the effect of making her gaze down her nose at me, even though I stood above her. A look of keen assessment lurked in those mild grey eyes. I was certain she took in the expensive-but-outdated suit and pegged me as unfit for the job.

"Hello." I'd hoped to sound calm and efficient, but I'm afraid the cold lent a slight chatter to my speech. "I'm Miss Henrietta Bishop. I'm here to see Mr. Jameson."

"There's no Mr. Jameson here."

"There isn't?" I peered at the smeared, handwritten note. "Oh, dear. I can't quite make this out. Perhaps I read that wrong."

"Do you mean Mr. Jessop?"

I masked the relief flooding through me. "Yes. That must be it."

"I'm Miss Climpson." She spoke with a primness that made me picture her at church, holding a hymnal and singing in a mournful way along with the rest of a tone-deaf congregation. "Mr. Jessop is in a meeting at the moment. You may put your hat and coat on the rack by the door. Please take a seat. He'll be with you shortly."

She pointed toward a row of utilitarian chairs by the outside wall. They looked as though they came straight from the bus station. I removed my hat and placed it on the small stand next to the entrance, but there was no way I could hang the coat without the rolls falling out. Besides, it was too chilly to set aside my coat. Not inclined to sit with my back to the cold brick, I took a seat closer to the door bearing the word "Private" in small gilt lettering near the radiator. I settled myself into the hard chair and removed my gloves, placing them and my coat on my lap.

Miss Climpson used the intercom to inform someone I was waiting for my interview. I couldn't decipher the response.

Behind her, on the other side of the filing cabinets, stood a second, smaller door. No doubt a storage closet. The additional desk stood in the middle of the room with a general air of abandonment. I remembered the Dragon Lady saying this was a short-term contract and I could see why. It didn't appear to be a thriving establishment.

Miss Climpson made several phone calls, but her conversations were so cryptic I couldn't determine their full nature. I got the impression she was directing people to locate certain things. Perhaps Redclaw was a private investigation firm, maybe even for insurance fraud. The thought cheered me up a bit, as the work might prove interesting.

After she finished her calls, Miss Climpson removed a large stack of reports from a basket on her desk and arranged them so she could view them as she typed, her fingers flying across the keyboard with a speed I'd never possess. She paused long enough to turn the pages of the reports. The clacking of the keys, combined with the musical sound made when she hit the return bar and the whirr of the rollers when she whipped out a completed page, was familiar and soothing, soporific, even. I shouldn't have eaten such a large meal before an important interview. As the heat from the radiator seeped into my bones, thawing out my hands and feet, I dozed off.

I jolted awake when the door to the private office opened, and the most extraordinary individual burst out. He stormed into the reception area, his trench coat billowing like a cape on a movie villain. He had hair like black silk, streaked with a single dash of silver at his forelock, and the beginnings of an early five o'clock shadow marked his jaw. His eyes glittered with a kind of repressed fury and were such a pale brown they seemed yellow. If I were a fanciful sort of person, I'd have described them as topaz.

I started to full alertness, my coat almost slipping off my lap.

Something in my blinking stare must have revealed my slight alarm, for he halted to glare at me, as if I meant to address him without permission.

I couldn't help it; I stiffened and leaned back when he swooped in closer. Without a word, he dropped to one knee, and scooped up the glove I hadn't realized had fallen.

He proffered it as though he were presenting me with a ring. "I believe this is yours."

It must have been a trick of light that made his pupils seem more like the vertical slits of a cat or a snake rather than round. Yet, when he lifted his head to smile at me, that impression vanished.

"Thank you." For reasons I couldn't explain, my fingers trembled as I accepted the glove, and I hoped he hadn't noticed. "I didn't know I'd dropped it."

I have no idea why, but I found him disturbing.

"You must keep your wits about you around here." His words were followed by a sardonic smile that sent an inexplicable shiver through me. "Otherwise, they'll eat you *alive*."

Rising with the exquisite grace of a dancer, he gave his coat tails a flick and left the office.

"Who was that?" I breathed, my heart thudding in my chest like a trapped sparrow.

Miss Climpson made a disapproving snort. "None of your concern."

She went back to her typing.

Miss Climpson's attitude was discouraging, but with any luck, she'd have no input into the hiring decisions.

Time passed. I didn't have to sneak glances at my wristwatch; the slow march of the hands on the clock behind Miss Climpson's desk gave me the hour. Another fifteen minutes had passed after the exit of the mysterious gentlemen when the outer door opened and a dark-skinned woman peered with trepidation into the room.

"Come in." Miss Climpson was much more welcoming to the newcomer than she had been to me. "Mr. Jessop has been expecting you."

The woman shot me a nervous glance before smoothing the hair under her hat and then hurried toward the private office. She waited, shifting from foot to foot as Miss Climpson announced her on the intercom and buzzed her through.

Annoyance grated like a tiny pebble in my shoe. My appointment had been scheduled for half an hour earlier, and yet Mr. Jessop continued to see other people before me. Business must be brisker than I'd thought, and I decided to take that as a good sign, despite becoming bored. Wishing I'd thought to bring a book, I poked through the back issues of *Life* and the *Saturday Evening Post*. Selecting a copy of *Ellery Queen's Mystery Magazine*, the edges of the pages yellowed and curling, I retired back to my chair.

I read *EQ* cover to cover as the hands on the clock moved another three quarters of an hour. During that time, the rabbity woman had left the private office in a rush, tossing a pained glance at Miss Climpson as she hurried out of the rooms.

Still, I waited.

Miss Climpson cleared her throat to catch my attention. "Mr. Jessop is likely to be some time. If you'd like to tell me the nature of your business with him...?"

Oh, no. Maybe she didn't know about the temp job. Maybe *her* job was up for grabs. She wouldn't get rid of me so easily. I thought of the long, chilly ride home with no one to greet me, where the evening hours with nothing to do stretched into eternity. The idea of leaving Redclaw without knowing if I had the job made my heart drop in a sickening free fall to my stomach. I went back to the reading table and picked up a copy of *Life,* leafing through it as I returned to my seat.

"That's quite all right." Maybe if I didn't make eye contact, Miss Climpson wouldn't tell me outright to go home. "I can wait."

Miss Climpson gave a loud sniff. I couldn't tell if the harsh sound indicated approval or disdain. Reassuring myself that her opinion didn't matter, I continued to flick through the magazine. I would stay until my interview or until the office closed. If Mr. Jessop left without seeing me, I would come back in the morning. Although the neighborhood was questionable, tucked in my purse alongside the ham sandwiches was a 0.25 caliber Baby Browning, and I am an excellent shot.

I read on.

The intercom buzzed, and Miss Climpson pressed a switch. "Yes, Mr. Jessop?"

This time, I heard his voice, sounding as if he were speaking through a tin can underwater. "Could you please step in here a moment, Miss Climpson?"

She hesitated, fixing me with a rather jaundiced eye. "There's still someone waiting to speak with you in the anteroom, sir. A young woman."

"There is? Does she have an appointment?" There was a pause before he continued. "Never mind. Send her in."

The fact he didn't remember he had an interview lined up didn't bode well for his management style, but I could deal with that. I'd worked in worse conditions.

"Very good, sir." Miss Climpson released the intercom switch and said, as if I were deaf, "Mr. Jessop will see you now." She held the buzzer as though blowing a raspberry at me as I entered the private room.

After the long delay and the hints from the mysterious client, I half expected to see an autocratic tyrant sitting on the other side of the desk. I'd envisioned an American version of Winston Churchill, gruff and jowly, with a fat cigar in his mouth. Mr. Jessop was more pug-like than a bulldog. He was stout, to be sure, but there was no piercing glare, no belligerence about him. Instead, his forehead furrowed with concern as he stood.

"I'm so sorry to keep you waiting, Miss, ah...?" He waved at the chair in front of the desk, another relic no doubt obtained from a Salvation Army meeting room. "Please, be seated."

The inner wall held more filing cabinets, several with drawers bursting at the seams with protruding papers. A large map hung from a roller on the wall between the filing cabinets, the type teachers pulled down before a geography lesson. Colored pins dotted the map's surface, connected in many instances with narrow black twine and looking somewhat like a web created by a drunken spider. Small, handwritten notes festooned the entire display.

A sideboard stood along the outer wall stacked with several bottles of alcohol, a set of tumblers, and a humidor. A large bookcase loomed behind the desk, with books and papers crammed in every available space. Folders balanced precariously on the corner of Mr. Jessop's desk, topped by what appeared to be a Slinky, of all things, though I'd never seen a gold-colored one before. My fingers itched to put the room in some kind of order, but instead I closed my hands around my purse and rested them on my folded coat in my lap.

The overhead light shone off Mr. Jessop's bald pate. A narrow rim of dull brown hair remained on his head. Had he been wearing robes instead of a crumpled suit, he could have passed for a Benedictine monk. He settled a pair of pince-nez on his nose and steepled his fingers together, resting his hands on his desk. "How may I help you?"

I handed him my resume, along with the sealed envelope from the Dragon Lady containing my references, hoping both had been spared contact with the ham sandwiches.

He extracted the folded paper from the envelope, frowning as he perused the page. With a furrow still creasing his forehead, he laid it on the desk before him. "I'm afraid I don't understand."

My pulse thrummed in my ears as doubt struck me again. Had I come to the wrong place after all? "I'm here about the temp job."

His brow cleared, and he leaned back in his chair. "I'm afraid there's been some mistake. We're not hiring at this time. And if we were...." He shrugged. "We have our own resources for employment."

No! I'd sat here for ages waiting for this meeting. If I was at the wrong address, I'd missed my interview long ago. Even if

I could figure out where I should be, the fact I hadn't shown up on time was enough to strike me off as a potential employee. And the Dragon Lady had made it clear she wouldn't give me another chance. "Are you sure you're not hiring? Your office seems busy for just one receptionist."

Mr. Jessop's smile was sympathetic, but firm. "I'm sure."

As he shifted in preparation to rise and see me out, I spoke rapidly. "I can type forty words a minute."

"You realize that is somewhat below average, yes?" He wore the pained expression of a man attempting to be kind without being crushing. Now that there seemed to be no hope of employment, he appeared to be the perfect boss.

"Yes, sir, but if you'll check my resume, you'll see I've worked for many of the top firms in the city."

He picked up the single sheet of paper and peered at it a moment before lowering it again. "But you didn't stay at any of these jobs. Why is that, may I ask?"

I gave him my stock answer. "Many of the positions were temporary. In some cases, I felt my skills could be better utilized elsewhere."

He lifted a disbelieving eyebrow and tapped the Dragon Lady's letter. "Mr. Billingsley of Haversham's Insurance claims you broke his hand."

Damn the Dragon Lady. I should have read her letter before deciding to share it. "Unfortunately, Mr. Billingsley's hand was where it shouldn't have been at the time."

Mr. Jessop's lips twitched. "And Mr. Steinbrenner's foot?"

The instep is a very sensitive part of the body. A well-placed high heel can disable a man. And if you open your eyes wide and apologize profusely, it's possible to make it look as though your actions were merely clumsy instead of intentional. Even if your intent was self-protection. "That was an accident, sir."

He placed my resume on top of the letter from the Dragon Lady and pushed both across the desk toward me. The action threatened the stability of the stacked files on the corner. The Slinky shimmied, but though I sucked in my breath, nothing toppled.

"Miss Bishop, I'll be frank. Your shorthand is described as passable, though not always accurate. Nearly every company that hired you states you have excellent organizational abilities, and you are both efficient and thorough with your assignments. But your reasons for leaving some places of employment aside, most of your previous employers spoke of an unseemly forwardness and a general inability to know your place."

My face burned.

He continued without seeming to notice. "You're right. We're quite busy here at Redclaw, more so than we expected when opening the firm. It's more than one person can do to answer the phone, collate information, type up reports, and so on. At some point we'll need someone to deal with the routine paperwork, thus freeing up Miss Climpson to handle the more critical assignments."

I leaned forward at his slight encouragement. "Yes, sir."

"When we're ready to hire, however, we'll need someone with a specific skill set. One you don't seem to have. Our work here is of a sensitive nature. I'm afraid we can't help you, Miss Bishop."

I thought of the time Em had stayed out past curfew, and then had the nerve to sneak Tigh Brannaugh into our rooms overnight, or when Professor Helmsley made a pass at me in the chemistry labs and it was his word against mine, or the most embarrassing moment of them all: Tommy's drunken proposal. I knew when to keep my mouth shut and when to speak up. "I'm very discreet. Ask Mr. Steinbrenner."

Mr. Jessop offered a gentle smile. "That may be. It's not personal, mind you. We have our own pool of candidates from which to choose. I appreciate your time, Miss Bishop. Good day."

Desperation made me persist. "I have skills that aren't on any resume. I've faced down a lion's charge in Africa. I shot a rattlesnake at point blank range while it was attacking my boot. I ran a coffee plantation in Kenya. I managed a racing stable in Maryland." I told the truth on all points, though the last two were somewhat subject to interpretation. As in, I'd been more of an observer than an actual manager. After all, I'd been a mere teenager at the time. Still, I knew I could do the job, though, if given the chance.

If nothing else, I now had his attention. His brows beetled together as though he suspected me of embellishing my history more than I already was. He flicked a quick glance at the map behind him on the wall before reaching for my resume again. "Have you ever been in Nevada?"

What an odd question during a job interview. "No. But my mother's family is from Wyoming." I couldn't see how that could help my cause, but I tossed it out there, anyway.

Mr. Jessop eyed me for a long moment before shaking his head. "You appear to be a remarkable young woman. I'm sure you'll be an admirable addition to the right agency. But you aren't what we are looking for here at Redclaw."

"I can fly an airplane."

I could. Nothing could compare to flying over the soaring beauty of an African veldt. Although, I hadn't flown since my mother insisted it was time to stop "gallivanting around the world with your father" and demanded I return to the States to take my place in society. Still, once a pilot, always a pilot, I say.

Mr. Jessop raised an eyebrow at that, and his gaze turned in thoughtful consideration again. He then seemed to come to his senses and shake off that appeal. "I'm sorry. I wish you well, Miss Bishop."

He placed my resume back on the referral letter and eased both toward me again. This time, the stack of papers on his desk shifted, sliding into the other items balanced there. I caught the Slinky as it undulated off the corner of his desk into my hand. The metal felt surprisingly warm. I replaced it with care and looked up to see Mr. Jessop staring at me with his mouth hanging open.

I smiled. "Good reflexes."

"Indeed." He gave a little cough, stood up and motioned toward the door with a flourish of his hand.

I had no choice but to stand as well. When I picked up my resume and letter of introduction, I noticed a glob of some pink rubbery substance stuck to the bottom of my papers. I thought it was chewing gum at first, but then I realized it was more like that stuff kids played with. Silly something. I couldn't remember the name. Frowning, I tried pulling off the offending goo, but it clung like rubber cement. I managed to stretch it into a ridiculous string and had to roll it back up again before I could peel it off. Once freed from my papers, I pressed it into a ball and half-flung it to Mr. Jessop's desk.

Looking down on the ball of putty, the imprint of the first line of my resume visible on its surface, I had the oddest impression it moved a little toward me. Impossible. I shook off the delusion. Crushed by disappointment, I put my coat on without thinking. The bread rolls I'd hidden up my sleeves shot out and bounced across the floor.

Mortified, I dropped to my knees and chased after them as they rolled away like mice evading a cat. "The bakery was out of bags," I lied. "I'd folded them in my jacket to protect them from the weather, but forgot they were there."

Mr. Jessop said nothing, but his brow crinkled in pained compassion. "Is there anything you'd like to share with us, Miss Bishop?"

I shook my head, refusing to dignify the implication I'd stolen bread. Which, of course, was true, but I had no intention of admitting it. What else could he have meant, anyway? I collected the rolls along with my dignity and made to leave. As my hand landed on the doorknob, the intercom buzzed. When I glanced back over my shoulder, I saw a blinking red light on the phone.

Mr. Jessop lifted an index finger to indicate I should wait, and picked up the phone, dialing a single digit. The rotary on the phone whirred as the number connected. He spoke into the receiver. "Yes, sir?"

A long pause ensued, during which time I strained to hear what the caller might say, but to no avail.

"But, sir!" Mr. Jessop shot me a look, only to turn his back and speak into the receiver in a lowered voice. "We know nothing about her."

Whatever the person on the other end of the phone had to say, it didn't make Mr. Jessop happy.

"Very good, sir. Right away, sir." Mr. Jessop hung up the phone with an ill-concealed sigh. "It seems Ryker would like you to start on Monday."

"Ryker?" That made little sense. Wasn't Mr. Jessop in charge?

"The head of Redclaw. He's decided to hire you, at least for now."

"Thank you, sir." The realization that Mr. Ryker, whoever he may be, had to have been monitoring the interview dampened my overwhelming relief. "I won't disappoint you."

Mr. Jessop raised both eyebrows and pursed his lips. "That remains to be seen."

He crossed over to a framed print of a 1952 Oldsmobile that hung by the filing cabinets. To my surprise, the painting swung to one side at his touch, revealing a wall safe concealed behind it. After he turned the dial too fast for me to follow, the tumblers clicked into place and he opened the door.

He took out a sheaf of papers and an envelope. Retiring to the desk, he indicated I should take my seat again.

"Ryker would like you to have an advance on your salary. I assume that would be acceptable to you?"

I blinked as he opened the envelope and counted out more bills than I'd ever seen offered for a secretarial position. He set the stack of cash to one side of his blotter.

"Yes, sir."

"You will, of course, have to sign a non-disclosure form." He dipped his pen into an inkwell and held it out to me, even as he shoved the papers in my direction.

A single drop of ink threatened to spill from the nib of the pen, like blood from the tip of a knife.

I didn't hesitate. "Of course," I said, accepting the pen.

After I signed the form, I ventured to ask a question. "Why did your boss hire me?"

Mr. Jessop's smile was a cross between a wince and a grimace, and yet I sensed some hidden speculation behind it. Or perhaps I was imagining things. "He thinks you're plucky. Ryker likes your spirit."

With that, I would have to be satisfied.

Chapter Three

The first few weeks at Redclaw Security proved uneventful. Once I'd been there longer than my temp job would have lasted, the fear of being fired at any given moment faded.

Every morning, Miss Climpson and I arrived at the same time. Since I hadn't been given a key yet, I waited behind her in the foyer while she opened the office. Most days she carried a stack of newspapers with her, some still damp with fresh ink. Once, when it looked as though they would spill out of her arms, I helped her carry them inside. In addition to the *Times* and the *Washington Post*, she collected copies of some of the more notorious tabloids, including the *Enquirer*, and even an issue of *Ripley's Believe It or Not*.

After I started the percolator each morning, slowly awakening the senses as the rich scent of coffee filled the office, Miss Climpson would sit down at her desk and scan the papers, clipping out odd articles and placing them in a file.

At the end of each workday, I emptied the trash. Try as I might, I couldn't tell the significance of what Miss Climpson chose to clip out versus what remained behind.

In time, on seeing the work assigned to me met her expectations, even if my typing barely passed muster, Miss Climpson unthawed enough to be pleasant. Our conversation

never strayed beyond the weather or the business of the day, but that was fine with me. Anything other than outright hostility I could manage.

I noticed Miss Climpson still kept a close eye on me. No doubt ready to swoop in should I make a mistake.

Clearly, she delegated to me mindless tasks—the necessary minutia of running a business—no matter how boring. I typed blank contracts, filed paperwork, inventoried supplies, and took messages, while Miss Climpson met with both clients and people that I came to realize were other employees. The rabbity woman, whose name was Betty Snowden, came in every few days, always looking as if she expected someone to pounce on her at any moment and devour her whole. Her style was neat and fashionable, and I was tempted to ask her for shopping tips, but even the act of shaking my hand seemed to terrify her.

Most of the other staff members popped in and out without more than a glance in my direction before asking for Miss Climpson or Mr. Jessop. We didn't advance beyond the "smile and nod" stage of office relationships. There seemed to be an invisible barrier between me and the other staffers. I wasn't sure why, but it was a little depressing. However, I'd gotten used to being on my own this last year. I didn't need to be friends with my coworkers.

While I never again saw the mysterious stranger with the pale golden eyes, another young man came in now and then. Rick Russo's dark eyes flashed with an inner secret—either amusement or passion—it was hard to tell. He favored a battered rain coat and always looked in need of a shave and a haircut. Like Betty, he seemed uneasy in my presence and preferred dealing with Miss Climpson. Sometimes I'd catch him in quiet conversation with Betty, teasing a real smile out of the shy woman. I couldn't help but think they'd make a cute couple.

I knew from my filing they were both on the payroll in freelance positions, and that whenever they showed up, Miss Climpson entered into a flurry of activity. More than that, Redclaw had decided I didn't need to know.

I never saw my boss, the all-powerful Mr. Ryker, though I did wonder at the fact his employees referred to him by his last name only, as if he were some celebrity performer, like that piano player on television. For the most part, I forgot Ryker even existed. It was easier to think of Mr. Jessop as the man in charge, even though I knew that wasn't the case. Mr. J was pleasant and comfortable, and we rubbed along together well enough. I knew there were secrets within the firm I wasn't privy to, but the pay was outstanding and the work well within my capabilities. I was content to let any concerns slide for the moment, at least until I was a well-established employee. My gut feeling told me the business was on the up-and-up, even if the exact nature of the dealings seemed very much hush-hush. Based on my previous experiences with my father's business partners, I could tell when the books were being cooked or if something crooked was going on.

I didn't get that impression at Redclaw, though clearly, the work was of a highly confidential nature. On the surface, the firm functioned as a glorified lost and found service. I'm being a little facetious, but that's what the bulk of the inquiries seemed to entail. Finding missing relatives. Restoring lost items, typically heirlooms. Old, musty, and often hideous things where one had to assume the value was sentimental.

Sometimes, the firm provided security for private parties or special events. That clientele appeared well-heeled and reeked of old money, though I never recognized any of the faces or names from my own circle. In contrast to the rare wealthy client, a steady stream of odd-looking people came in and out during office hours, many clutching satchels or briefcases to their chests. When they entered, they eyed the room as warily as a gazelle approaching a watering hole. Miss Climpson rushed those clients straight into Mr. J's office. I never even saw their paperwork.

But they often left empty-handed.

Once, when Miss Climpson was out of the office, someone dropped off an ornate carved wooden box with a heavy padlock. When I took the item to store it in Mr. J's office until his return, I swore something alive moved within. I said as much to Miss Climpson when she came back from lunch, in case she needed to attend to whatever it was right away. She fixed me with an odd look before hurrying off to deal with the matter. I caught her staring at me on and off the rest of the afternoon.

After such visits, there were often new pins added to the maps on Mr. J's wall. Since the pins were clustered around specific locations, I made a habit of checking the newspaper files in the library on the weekends, looking for stories connected to the locations in question. More than once, I found mention of strange happenings. Miss Climpson's cuttings now took on new significance.

I went to work. I came home. I had money for food and the kind of little extras that make a girl happy. I saw the James Dean movie, and was impressed by this new actor's emotional performance. I chatted with Em about her wedding plans, and entered the dates of the bridal shower, bridesmaid's luncheon, rehearsal dinner, and wedding into my calendar. I bought a bottle of *Fifth Avenue Red* nail polish and some new outfits for work, but for the most part, socked my money away in case things got tight again. In the evenings, I read library books and mended my stockings.

Now and again, if truth be told, I thought about the beautiful, sad man I'd bumped into on the street the day of my interview. I wondered who he was, what he was doing, and why he'd said I hadn't done him any favors by preventing him from getting hit by that car. Sometimes, before I drifted off to sleep at night, I'd entertain myself with stories about him.

There was a slight possibility that I imagined myself in those stories as well. I admit it. I was bored. Once you've flown at dawn over the Serengeti, or galloped a promising

Thoroughbred on the track at Belmont, the life of a secretary, even at a mysterious firm such as Redclaw, was a bit tame.

I suppose I could have continued along these lines indefinitely, had it not been for the day of the mechanical spider.

I'd gotten into the habit of going out for lunch three or four days a week. My finances, while nothing compared to what they had been prior to my father's death, now lent themselves to meals at the local diner. I would order the blue plate special (eating half and boxing the rest for dinner) and indulge in the occasional slice of pie. Miss Climpson and I arranged our schedules so someone always covered the reception desk, though I suspected she advised certain people not to call during her absence.

One day, I'd just returned from lunch. With a nod to Miss Climpson as she left on her break, I sat down to finish typing the morning's notes. A soft skittering caught my attention, and I broke off from my work to listen.

After a long pause, during which I heard nothing but the faint hissing of the radiator, I shrugged and went back to typing. A few minutes later, the noise came again, the *ticka-ticka-ticka* of claws on tile, or scales brushing together.

The hair on the back of my neck rose.

I don't scare easily, but some sounds you never forget. The dry paper rustle of a rattlesnake, complete with the characteristic final shakes as the rattle dies away. The angry hum of a swarm of hornets boiling out of a hive. The chuffing of a lion in the dark close to your position. These sounds scream, "Danger!"

This noise had the exact same effect on me.

I glanced around the office. I still heard the sibilant sound, but had trouble locating it. Without pushing back my chair, I peered under my desk.

There it was, a scant six inches from my foot. It had a large ovoid body, about the size of a small egg, and too many legs to count. I stifled a reflexive jerk backward, but was unable to contain the involuntary sound I made. A less than kind person might suggest it was a shriek, but I assure you; it was a mere gasp.

The problem remained what to do about the shiny creature.

On my desk sat a tall drinking glass filled with pencils and pens. These I poured out on the desktop. Taking a file folder in one hand and the glass in the other, I wheeled my chair back with my feet. The thing under the desk scurried away in alarm at the movement, faster than I'd been expecting. Hurrying around the corner of the desk, I saw it sitting in the middle of the room, two of its forelegs waving ominously as it faced me. Clapping a glass over the creature and sliding the folder beneath it wouldn't work as long as it faced me with such aggression.

I glanced at my purse sitting on the corner of my desk. Nestled within, as always, was my trusty little gun. I thought perhaps Miss Climpson might take exception to my shooting up the office, but I seriously, if briefly, considered it.

I eyed my brand new suit jacket hanging on the back of my chair. I wasn't able to afford anything as nice as the Chanel or Dior as I had in previous years, but the new clothes were serviceable and up to date. I flinched at the thought of perhaps ruining something I'd just purchased, clothing meant to last me a long time. Still, alone in the office with a giant spider, sacrifices would have to be made.

I set down the glass and folder and picked up my jacket instead. I made a wide, cautious circle around the creature which shifted in a flurry of legs to continuously face me. That unnerved me. As much as I abhorred the idea of making myself the slightest bit vulnerable, I slipped off one of my shoes and held it at the ready as I approached with the jacket. My exposed toes, sheathed in a cheap stocking, curled in self-defense as I moved with uneven steps toward the spider.

When it scuttled toward me, I tossed the shoe. The creature tracked the movement as one of my best pumps landed almost on top of it, and in that moment of confusion, I leapt forward with my jacket. I pounced on the shiny arachnoid, bundling it up, even as I worried about it stinging me through the cloth.

The moment I gripped the spider, I gained another piece of information that didn't make sense. When I clamped down on the creature in the folds of my jacket, I felt a hard body. Harder even than one would expect from a shell. After unfolding one edge of the cloth, I dumped the spider onto my desk and clapped the glass down as it righted itself.

It ticked around within its little prison, tapping on the glass with silver legs. I could now examine it in safety, marveling at both its construction and its lifelike movement. How odd. It wasn't a real spider, thank goodness, but mechanical. Whatever spring or motor propelled it was strong enough to rock the glass from side to side in an attempt to tip its prison over. I became alarmed enough to stack a dictionary and some other heavy books on top of the glass. I watched the spider out of the corner of my eye as I retrieved my shoe and tried to focus on the typing once more.

From time to time I'd run across the odd toy when assisting Mr. J in his office, like the Slinky, part of his incomprehensible filing system, that he used to designate important papers, or the putty I'd accidentally picked up the day of my interview. He had little tin cars tucked away in drawers, and once a toy metal throwing disc had fallen off the bookcase on top of my head. Sometimes while dictating, he liked to play with a Yo-Yo. He said it helped him think. But I'd seen nothing as advanced as the spider now tapping the walls of my water glass.

A malevolent aura clung to it like no toy I'd ever seen before, and its presence didn't make me feel any better about it running loose in the building.

It was almost time for Miss Climpson to return from lunch when the outer door sprang open and Rick Russo blew in.

"Hello, Bishop." He glanced over at Miss Climpson's desk. "Climmy not back yet?"

"Any minute now." I continued with my laborious typing. I suppose Russo was handsome in a dark, Italian way, but I didn't feel a flicker of interest in him. I was starting to think Tommy's "Ice Queen" designation for me was correct.

Russo came over to my desk to peer at the spider under the glass.

"Ho now, what's that?"

"I'm not sure. I found the ugly thing when I came back from lunch. I thought it best to keep it contained until I could ask someone about the horrible little beast."

When he straightened, Russo gave me a strange little smile. "You're an odd duck, you know that, right?"

Concentration broken, I gave up and gave Russo my full attention.

"What do you mean?"

"Something like that would give most girls the heebie-jeebies. Here you are with the thing trapped under a glass, coolly going about your business."

"I thought about burning the building down, but decided it would be counterproductive to retaining my job."

He gave a short bark of laughter, which seemed to surprise him almost as much as it did me. "You'll do, Bishop. You'll do."

I'm not sure why that rather backward compliment pleased me, but it did. I sensed compliments weren't something Russo gave out often. Or maybe it was because, although I no longer had nightmares about losing my job, I still felt like an outsider at Redclaw.

The door opened again, and Miss Climpson entered, turning bright pink on seeing Russo by my desk.

"Mr. Russo." The emphasis she laid on the 'mister' implied some sort of hanky panky between us, which was ridiculous. "I wasn't expecting you so soon. You—"

As rouged as her cheeks had appeared before, all color fled and her lips thinned to the point of invisibility when she caught sight of the spider under the glass. She pressed a hand to her chest, her stubby, ink-stained fingers splayed over the squirrel trim of her winter coat. Her mouth formed a perfect little O of shock. "How did *that* come to be here?"

Her accusatory tone annoyed me, as though I'd broken into the private office and released the little bugger of my own accord.

"This?" I pointed at the glass with the eraser I used to correct typos. "I found it under my desk when I came back from lunch. You didn't notice it?"

If she'd been pink before, Miss Climpson turned an alarming shade of puce now. "I should say not."

"Then you don't know where it came from?"

She hesitated just long enough for me to see her formulate the lie. "I imagine it's one of Mr. Jessop's mechanical toys. You know he collects them."

I reached for the glass. "Well, then. If it's a toy, there's no reason not to let it out."

"No!"

Russo and Miss Climpson spoke in unison, holding up hands like synchronized swimmers to stop me. They exchanged a somewhat guilty glance, and then Russo withdrew from my desk. By distancing himself from me, it had the effect of suggesting he'd chosen to side with Miss Climpson.

"Perhaps we should just keep it contained until Mr. Jessop returns. I'm sure he would be sorry to lose something of such fine, er, workmanship." Miss Climpson grimaced a smile and took Russo aside. She spoke to him in an agitated whisper. I couldn't make out their conversation, and he left soon afterward. Miss Climpson unlocked her desk drawer and pulled out a small red ledger, making several notations before replacing it and starting on a new client folder.

"Oh my," Mr. Jessop said, upon returning from his meeting and spying the spider still confined on my desk. "What's been going on here?"

He listened with frowning concentration as I relayed what had happened, worrying his lower lip with his teeth as he did so. Then, with only a brief glance at Miss Climpson, he went into his office and came out with a small metal case. "I'm going to hold this open at the edge of the desk, Miss Bishop. If you would be so good as to sweep the, er...device within?"

He opened the lid and pressed the case against the lip of my desk. I slid the glass containing the spider to the edge and shoved the device over with a swift movement. He pulled the box back and snapped the lid shut, beaming in relief. "Well, now. That's taken care of. Thank you, ladies."

And with that, he went back to his office, holding the case aloft as though it held a jar of nitroglycerin.

I won't say the experience led to my snooping afterwards. After all, I would do nothing to jeopardize my job. But I paid more attention to things when I took something in to Mr. J, and I was alone in the office most days when Miss Climpson took her lunch break. If the circumstances of my father's death had taught me anything, it was not to make assumptions about anything in my life and to always look for a second set of account books. While I needed this job, I would never again ignore the warning signals laid before me.

Even if I didn't fully understand them.

My casual observations and mild snooping around made me certain of one thing: I didn't work at an ordinary office. There were too many reports that never crossed my desk. I might never have learned more about Redclaw other than what my employer wanted me to know, had it not been for another disturbing incident.

It happened a couple of weeks after my run-in with the mechanical spider. Spring battled with the last dregs of winter to make a full appearance, and after waking to a cold rain, I'd decided to bring some soup in a Thermos to work instead of taking my lunch out. On previous explorations of the building that housed Redclaw, I'd discovered an unlocked, empty room on the second floor. I'd just borrowed the latest Agatha Christie from the library, and while I *could* have eaten at my desk, I preferred to get out of the office for a while and read in peace. When it came time for my lunch break, I collected my Thermos and book and went upstairs.

The former occupants had stripped the office of everything save a dilapidated chair, either forgotten or deemed not worth moving. By positioning myself near the window, I could prop my Thermos on the sill and read while I had my soup. The room was chilly but quiet, and I lost myself in the story of the disappearing scientist. I'd long ago figured out the key to solving the typical Christie mystery, but she spun a good tale and I enjoyed the process of everyone *else* figuring out who the villain was.

Deep into the tribulations of the main character, a young woman with nothing left to lose, I heard the outer door below open and shut. The sound reverberated in the empty room, jarring me out of the story. When no footsteps came up the stairs, I realized it must have been another one of Miss Climpson's personal clients, and I went back to the book.

A moment later, I heard a dull thud.

I couldn't place what had made that noise, and that bothered me. It might have been nothing, and had it not been for the business with the mechanical spider, I might have gone back to my reading. I'm a great believer in trusting one's instincts. My gut never steered me wrong. Right then, my gut sent up a red flag. I closed the novel and left it beside the open

Thermos, steam still rising from the open container. Uneasy, I collected my purse and crept down the stairs.

Outside the door to Redclaw, I paused. A glance at my watch told me I still had at least a half hour to go on my break, something most of the 'special' clients would know. Pressing an ear to the paneling, I heard the *thunk* of slammed drawers. The movement within had a sense of anger and haste that was out of character for Miss Climpson.

I opened the clasp on my purse and felt for the comforting presence of the Browning. With my free hand, I tuned the knob and burst in, already speaking. "Wouldn't you know, Climmy? I forgot my lunch money."

The man at Miss Climpson's desk whipped around at my entrance, his lips curling into an ugly snarl. I'd seen that expression once before when I came across a leopard defending its kill. I halted, letting my eyes go wide and my mouth fall open in an expression of clueless surprise, the one I'd witnessed so often on Em's face when she played the innocent.

"Oh, my," I breathed. "You startled me. Miss Climpson must be in the ladies' room. May I help you find something?"

I did my best to look vacant and accommodating, even as my fingers closed around the Browning. Someone had wrenched several of the file drawers open, and folders stood in an uneven row where a hasty search had pulled them up. I saw one of Miss Climpson's shoes sticking from behind the desk. I forced my gaze to remain on the face of the intruder instead of letting them register on Miss Climpson's prone body.

The feral expression on the man's face faded into a genial smile as he did his best to smooth out his anger at my presence. "You must be the new girl. Yes, Miss Climpson had to step out for a moment. But I'm here on urgent business and can't wait. Perhaps you can help me." He swung around the desk with the confident grace of a predator that knows no fear.

Every hair on the back of my neck stood straight up. He kept coming.

My father taught me a long time ago that if you wanted to take out an attacking animal, you aimed for the head or the legs. Body shots, while an easier target, might not disable something bent on killing you in time to save your life. When the intruder kept walking toward me with that smarmy smile on his face, I lifted my purse toward his head.

My voice was steady, for which I was proud. "I wouldn't do that, if I were you."

"Or you'll do what, little lady? Throw your purse at me?"

I detest being called 'little lady'. I also don't believe in letting the bad guy know your every move. So I said nothing and kept my purse trained on him.

Something about my silence and posture registered with him anyway, and he let out a throaty growl, the likes no human could ever make. When he lowered his head, I could have sworn something flashed in his eyes, momentarily gleaming gold. His fingers curled into angry claws, and I realized with a start they were *becoming* claws. With a gasp, I glanced up at his face. Gray fur sprouted along his cheekbones. His shoulders seemed to expand, stretching the cloth of his raincoat tight against them. When he bared his teeth, his canines were considerably longer than they should have been.

As he sprang forward, I adjusted my aim to his kneecap and fired. The gunshot rang in the small room, as did the shriek of agony from the intruder as he went down clutching his leg. Brilliant scarlet blood oozed through his fingers as he rolled about on the floor, gasping and moaning.

The eyes he lifted toward me blared red with anger. They also weren't human.

To my horror, the intruder placed bloody hands on the floor and pushed upright.

I shucked off the ruins of my purse from around the Browning and held him in my sights. "If you take so much as a deep breath, I'll shoot you again." I hoped I sounded confident, and that he didn't notice the trembling of my hand. What had I gotten myself into? And could a mere bullet incapacitate whatever species lay before me? Already, the flow of blood from his leg had stemmed, and he pulled his feet underneath him as though preparing to spring at me.

The sound of footsteps pounded along the corridor. Someone must have heard the gunshot. But friend or foe?

The door flew open, and a man stood in the entrance. I swung my weapon toward him. "Stop right there. Identify yourself."

The stranger in the doorway took one look at the intruder on the floor and then brought his gaze back to the gun in my hand. His face broke into the most ridiculous smile. "My dear Miss Bishop. You may call me Ryker. I'm your boss."

Chapter Four

Well, that was embarrassing.

Almost shooting my boss, that is.

Ryker wore his dark brown hair swept back from his forehead and a beard and mustache neatly trimmed to frame his jaw line. With a dash of silver at his temples, he looked like a reformed pirate. Certainly the way he took over reminded me of a captain on the command deck of his ship.

In the aftermath of Ryker's arrival, things began happening in short order. After telling me to maintain my cover of the intruder with my weapon, Ryker checked on Miss Climpson. To my relief, he pronounced her stunned, but coming around. Then he pressed a button under the edge of her desk, causing a greenish light to bathe us all in a sickly hue. After a bit, there was a faint odor as well, like the air after a lightning strike. Ryker then told me to stand down. I lowered my weapon but remained on alert. The prisoner howled in dismay and began sobbing incoherently.

"I don't like it, either." Ryker's voice lacked any trace of sympathy as he glared down at the prisoner. "But we can't have you changing on us. I'm surprised and disappointed in you, Billy. You of all people should be on our side."

Billy? Something other-than-human went by the name of Billy? It boggled the mind. That, and the fact my employer knew the intruder.

Had I imagined Billy's hands turning into claws?

Ryker grabbed the man by the arm and hauled him to his feet with surprising ease, seating our 'guest' with little care for his comfort in the nearest chair. My boss moved with the studied elegance I associated with fencing; I pictured him with a foil in his hand. He reminded me of the mysterious golden-eyed stranger in the office on the day of my interview—there was a similarity of grace there. Instead of swooning at Ryker's forceful handling of the situation, however, I felt frustrated once more by not knowing the whole story, of being an outsider.

"Side? You think you've chosen a side?" The prisoner, unaware of my musings, bared his now human teeth in a sneer. "It's going to come down to us against them, Ryker, and you know it. Sooner or later, us against them."

"So you thought you'd steal from Redclaw?"

"Do I have to spell it out? These things, these incredible tools, they're meant for us. To give us the advantage over *them*. You're collecting them and locking them away. It's stupid."

Ryker shook his head. "You have no idea what these devices are capable of. No one does. That's what we're trying to figure out here."

"Yeah, well, some people think Redclaw shouldn't be making all the decisions," Billy said with snide bravado, which faded when Ryker turned a burning glare on him.

"You're working for Rian, aren't you?"

I didn't know who Rian was, but I knew I never wanted to be on the receiving end of such a look from my boss.

"I didn't say nothing!" Billy's sharp voice rang with anger, and perhaps a touch of fear.

Ryker stared at him a moment longer and then turned to me. "Miss Bishop, if you'd see to Miss Climpson? I'll handle our prisoner."

A whine grated in Billy's voice. "What are you going to do with me?"

"I don't know. Perhaps de Winter will have some thoughts on the matter."

"Hold on, now. You don't have to bother the Council over this little business, do you?"

"If you've seriously injured Miss Climpson, I'll deal with you myself." The chill in Ryker's voice left no doubt his manner of dealing with Billy would be highly unpleasant. But then he shrugged. "As for bringing de Winter and the Council into the matter, you've left me little choice."

Whoever this de Winter fellow was, the thought of his involvement in the matter turned Billy pale. I moved away to check on Miss Climpson, who stirred feebly.

In due course, I had her sitting in the most comfortable of the visitor chairs with an icepack purchased from the local five and dime resting on the goose-egg lump she had on the back of her head. A hot cup of tea, laced with a shot of Mr. J's brandy, brought the color back into her cheeks. She fixed a glare on Billy as soon as she could focus her eyes. If looks could kill, she would have drawn and quartered our good friend Billy on the spot.

Ryker telephoned Russo, who arrived with a young man I'd never seen before. Where Russo was dark, the newcomer's freckles and flaming red hair spoke of Irish descent. The two men stood guard as Ryker went into Mr. J's office and came out with a set of manacles that gave off a faint green glow. Billy put up a bit of a protest, struggling to avoid having his wrists cuffed, but the fight went out of him as soon as the cuffs were on. After Russo and his helper led Billy away, Ryker flipped the switch under Miss Climpson's desk and the lighting in the room returned to normal.

A sense of pressure in my head that I hadn't fully realized yet, receded, the more noticeable for its absence.

Mr. J came bustling in, worried and anxious for Miss Climpson's wellbeing. Ryker let him fuss and tut-tut for a bit, and then asked him to make sure nothing had been stolen or damaged. Miss Climpson offered to help, but Ryker ordered her back into her seat.

Ryker fixed his gaze upon me. "Miss Bishop. A word with you in my office, please."

I followed him out into the corridor and down the hallway, past the restroom facilities and to an unmarked door I'd assumed was a utility closet. Inside was a small office, much smaller than I would expect for the head of the firm. At the same time, an authentic Persian rug carpeted the floor and a heavy mahogany desk gleamed in the overhead light. Which made the Magic 8 Ball sitting on the corner of the desk a bit incongruous.

Once again, I wondered how Ryker had observed the workings within the main office, and where he'd been during Miss Climpson's attack.

Ryker, who'd gone over to a sideboard similar to the one in Mr. J's office, glanced back over his shoulder when he heard me mutter, "Damn."

"Problem, Miss Bishop?"

"I just realized I put a bullet hole though my favorite purse."

Ryker's unexpected laugh startled me; a sound rich with true amusement. "What I like most about you, Miss Bishop, is that you seem more upset over the ruined purse than the person you shot. Do have a seat."

I placed my clutch on the desk and took the guest's chair.

"May I offer you something? Some tea? Or perhaps you need something a bit stronger?"

To my utter embarrassment, my voice quavered when I spoke. "Tea would be lovely."

"Ah." Ryker set down the decanter he'd just picked up and opened a drawer in the sideboard instead. "Reaction setting in, I dare say. The best remedy seems to be chocolate."

He peeled back the paper wrapper of a Hershey bar as he approached and held it out to me.

It was all I could do to refrain from shoving the candy whole into my mouth and leave smears of chocolate around my lips. Instead, I managed a lady-like nibble, eyeing my boss as he took his seat behind the desk opposite me.

Ryker leaned back in his chair and tapped his fingers together. On closer inspection, he was older than I'd thought. Besides the touch of silver at his temples, tiny lines formed around his brown eyes. "I imagine you have questions."

I nodded. "Several. What will happen to Billy?"

He blew air softly through his lips. "He will have to answer for his crimes."

"But not to the police."

Ryker shot me a sharp glance. As I continued to eat the candy bar, a slow smile creased his lips. "No. Billy violated certain, ah, community laws. He will appear before those leaders."

I nodded. Billy had mentioned the Council. "Like the Freemasons? A secret order?"

"Something like that."

Approval seemed to simmer in Ryker's eyes, although I wasn't quite sure what brought it about. If I had to guess, some underlying amusement resided there as well. Determined to show nothing but complete composure, I folded the paper around the rest of the chocolate and laid the bar beside my purse on the desk. "So you won't involve the police? Despite the shooting?"

"No. And you needn't worry about his recovery. He'll be fine."

I lifted an eyebrow at his presumption. "I shattered his kneecap."

At the very least, Billy would need surgery. Or would he? Billy had seemed quick to rally until Ryker had turned on the green light.

"Ah, yes. Your concern for our lunchtime intruder does you credit. Rest assured, Billy will receive whatever treatment he needs. And our people are fast healers."

Our "people"?

"Sir, was it my imagination, or did this man start to...?" I wasn't sure how to complete my sentence. Perhaps I was guilty of reading too many pulp magazines. They made a nice change from the classics, but they had a sad tendency to influence my dreams. Could they affect my waking thoughts as well?

No, I know what I saw.

Ryker didn't make it easy for me, merely lifting his own questioning eyebrow.

"Just as he was about to attack me, his nails became claws and his face sprouted *fur*." Before Ryker could call me crazy or tell me I was imaging things, I said in a quiet but firm voice, "I saw him change."

"Ah. I was hoping you hadn't noticed that." With a heavy sigh, he went back to the sideboard and poured whiskey into two tumblers, returning to the desk to hand one to me.

I hesitated before accepting the glass. Given my father's fate, more than most people, I had good reason to avoid alcohol. Yet, whiskey seemed like a better choice than tea right now, especially since tea didn't seem to be forthcoming. When Ryker had taken his seat again, I continued, "I also noticed when you pressed the switch under Miss Climpson's desk, you seemed confident Billy no longer posed a threat. Did you turn some kind of dampening field on him? What did he want? Was he after the mechanical spider?"

My questions caught Ryker as he took a sip and he choked. Setting the glass down, he looked at me with mild astonishment. "My word, Miss Bishop. In another century, they'd have burned you at the stake." À propos of nothing, he added, "What do you go by? Henrietta?"

My eyes narrowed. In my experience, you couldn't trust bosses who asked for personal information. "My friends call me Rhett," I spoke each word with careful deliberation.

He nodded. If he sensed my wariness, he had chosen to ignore it. "Very nice, indeed. It suits you." Something of my expression must have registered with him because he held up a hand. "Please believe me when I say I have no designs on your person. It's just that I feel you're wasted in a secretarial position, and I don't want to keep 'Miss Bishoping' you. Unless, of course, you prefer it."

"You may call me Bishop, if it's easier."

He seemed delighted by this. "Like I would Russo or the others? Except for Miss Climpson. She could never be anything other than that." He leaned forward with a conspiratorial smile. "At least to her face."

I coughed to conceal a small laugh. No one called Miss Climpson 'Climmy' in her presence. In fact, I'd chosen to do so when confronting the intruder solely to alert Miss Climpson I was aware something was wrong, had she been able to hear me.

Ryker picked up his tumbler again, staring into its amber depths. "How would you like to be a field agent, Bishop?"

He hadn't answered my questions, but his offer was intriguing.

"I suspect I would like it very much, as long as it doesn't involve sitting in front of a typewriter. What does a field agent do and does the position come with a raise?"

He chuckled at that. "Well, you may have noticed we're on the lookout for certain unusual artifacts."

I took a sip of my whiskey. It burned going down but left me with a warm, steadying glow. Dutch courage, but I'd take it. "Artifacts and people."

"Yes. Two different sides of the same issue. Ever since the war, the world has changed at a rate faster than many of us can adapt to. Some people wake up to find their entire lives turned upside down. New technology is being discovered, some of which is incredibly dangerous. My colleagues and I are a small but dedicated group of people trying our best to keep our world safe as these new challenges appear."

"Do you think they have something to do with the world-wide use of atomic weapons?"

Ryker's brows came down over his eyes. "What makes you say that?"

I set my tumbler on the desk, lining it up alongside my purse, the chocolate, and the Magic 8 Ball. "The map in Mr. J's office pinpoints the locations of many of the atomic weapons test sites. The lines of string identify areas in which some of these artifacts have been recovered by Redclaw. An astonishing number of artifacts are found near areas of nuclear activity."

He looked confused, so I added, "I made a point of looking up the areas in question to see if there was anything distinguishing about them. The one consistent factor was their proximity to a nuclear detonation."

Ryker's expression went blank for a moment, and then he took out a small gold case. With slow deliberate movements, he struck a match and lit a cigarette. He took a deep drag, blowing smoke out through his nostrils before speaking. "I'm glad to see my instincts about you were right. Mr. Jessop was against hiring you at first, you know."

I swallowed hard. I didn't want to know if werewolves or vampires or alien body snatchers surrounded me. At the same time, I couldn't afford to operate in ignorance. The last time I'd turned a blind eye to events taking place around me, I lost everything in the world that mattered. "Because I'm not like you."

"Yes, and no." His voice was gentle. Smoke wreathed his head as he chose his words with care. "Whether or not you realize it, you have shown tendencies we normally associate with members of our community. Some of the technology has responded to you, which only happens to people of a certain genetic makeup. We think it's possible you may have a recessive gene."

With that, Miss Climpson's obsessive interest in my work habits took on a different meaning. She hadn't been waiting to see if I'd make a mistake as much as observing me in case I showed a flair for handling the technology.

Ryker met my eyes as he continued smoking, almost as if he could read my thoughts. For all I knew, he could.

"Redclaw has a big task ahead. Locating these devices before someone gets hurt, helping people adjust to the changes that have come into their lives, and helping them find family who have gone missing. Also, keeping the tech out of the hands of people who would use such information and power against others, including, sometimes, our own government."

"When you say people who would use this technology against others, you mean ordinary humans pitting themselves against the ones who have somehow mutated since the use of atomic weapons?"

He gave a slow nod, as though he were giving himself time to craft a response. "We don't think of it as mutation as much as coming into our real selves, but yes. Right now, our numbers are small. We need the help of smart, resourceful people such as you. The only typing you'll do is the filing of your own reports. What say you, Bishop? Are you in?"

I didn't know how to respond. Logic would dictate that I support the side of humans against the unnamed 'others' Ryker described. But Ryker seemed to suggest I wasn't as human as I thought. Besides, I've always had a thing for the underdog.

Giving my boss a wry smile, I picked up the Magic 8 Ball and rotated it back and forth in my hand. It was heavier than I expected and, like some other objects I'd held at Redclaw, generated an odd warmth in my hands. I closed my eyes and thought about Ryker's offer and then opened them as I rotated the ball so the advice printed on the floating triangle within appeared in the small window.

Trust your instincts.

I had to smile at that. Pretty sage advice for a kid's toy. Looking up, I saw Ryker eyeing me. One eyebrow lifted, prompting me for my answer.

Was there ever any doubt I would say no? I set the toy back on the desk and held out my hand. "I'm in."

Ryker shook my hand with a smile and then removed a file from a drawer on his side of the desk. He held it out. "Excellent. I have your first assignment."

I opened it. To my utter surprise, attached to the sheaf of typewritten pages within was a small black and white photograph of the man I'd run into that day outside The Blue Moon. The man I hadn't been able to stop thinking about. "Sir?"

"Meet Peter Knight. A former atomic scientist who has dropped out of sight. A British ex-pat who came over during the war to work with the government but has now gone missing."

My heart sank at the sight of the photo. Though my impression of the man on the street was fleeting, I was sure this was the same person. The same elegance of bone structure, the same hard line of his jaw. Even though the image was in black-and-white, the photo captured the clear intensity of his eyes. But if Redclaw was interested in finding him, then he must be nothing like I had imagined. "So he is… one of you then?"

I couldn't say "us." Not yet. I was still reeling from the revelation I might have the gene.

Ryker frowned, stubbing out the remains of his cigarette. "I don't know, though it seems unlikely. As far as we can tell, the shifter gene is present in not quite ten percent of the population at this time. But the person best suited to evaluate and catalog the technology has decided against helping us. Which means Redclaw has to look outside its usual pool of applicants for someone with the same scientific background. The full resources of Redclaw are at your disposal, naturally. If you find him, we'll take over from there."

I'd do more than find him. I'd bring him in. I'd prove to Ryker—and Redclaw—he was right to hire me.

Chapter Five

I refrained from telling Ryker I'd seen the missing man described in the file. It made sense to keep my mouth shut about perhaps knowing where to locate Knight until I could prove I could find him again. If I discovered his whereabouts soon, I'd appear brilliant. If I said I could find him but failed, I'd look incompetent.

Ryker led the way back into the hallway. The notion of a missing scientist reminded me of the book and Thermos I'd left upstairs, and I excused myself to retrieve them, Knight's file tucked under my arm for further perusal later.

When I returned to the main office, Ryker was holding court there. Miss Climpson, looking far more alert and energized than I would have expected for someone throttled and bashed over the head, sat in her usual spot. I wondered about the switch under her desk and its function. I also wondered if my boss had conveniently taken me into his office for other reasons besides a confidential chat.

Mr. J was coming out of his office when I entered the room.

"As near as I can ascertain, sir, nothing is missing." The look he cast Ryker seemed to imply more than just his bare statement, given the marked waggling of his eyebrows toward his private office.

"Good. That's what Russo said as well, but it never hurts to have additional confirmation."

I made my way to my desk and put my book and Thermos along with the Browning in the bottom drawer. I laid the file beside the typewriter and took my seat.

Ryker glanced around the room, taking in the presence of everyone there with a gaze that contained an air of satisfaction. Once again, he reminded me of a pirate, this time standing on the deck with arms akimbo, about to address his crew.

The crew of three.

"I've decided we're underutilizing Bishop's skills here."

Miss Climpson winced, presumably because she disagreed with his decision, though it could have been at the dropping of "Miss" as Ryker addressed me. Hard to tell with Climmy.

I said nothing.

Ryker continued, "I've promoted Bishop to field agent. I believe she has what it takes."

"Sir." It was a single word of protest on Mr. J's part. I knew Ryker could put his foot down and his employees would give in, but for this to work, it needed more than "because I said so" from the boss.

I cleared my throat. I found it impossible to refer to the uncanny change I'd seen Billy undergo or insinuate any of them could do the same, and so I danced delicately around the subject. "I realize there's more to this agency than meets the eye. Please believe me when I say I'm not interested in anyone's personal life. I'm here to do a job. One I think I could do quite well."

Mr. J and Miss Climpson traded worried glances.

Ryker observed the exchange and decided to put me on the spot. "What would you change around here, Bishop?"

Oh, Lord.

"Well, for one thing, if you're known to have items of value, you must do more about security here than what's currently in place. You can't always rely on Miss Climpson or myself to stop a determined intruder. And, if I may be so bold to point out, that blow to the back of her head could have killed Miss Climpson."

"Really, sir!" Mr. J puffed up with indignation. "We agreed that maintaining a low profile in the neighborhood was paramount to our success and safety. With all due respect, what Miss Bishop is suggesting—"

"Is correct. Hiding in plain sight might have worked before, but now the cat is out of the bag. Our anonymity is no longer protecting us. There are people who know who we are and what we're trying to do. See to it, Reggie. I want guards here at all times."

Reggie? After the initial shock, I realize it suited Mr. J. I wondered if there was a Mrs. J, and if she was normal like me or something...different. Because, as plain as the nose on my face, I stood on one side of normal and my coworkers stood on the other, even if I could influence the weird technology Redclaw retrieved. What that 'other' entailed, I didn't want to think too much about right now. At last, I was being offered the chance of work that excited me in a way I hadn't felt since my mother decided it was time for me to become a lady. Was I going to quibble about little details as to whether or not my colleagues were entirely human?

"Sir." Miss Climpson spoke for the first time. She cut her eyes toward me and then fixed them on the boss. "I know you believe Miss Bishop has the qualifications to be a field agent." She hesitated and glanced in my direction again. "Certainly her performance today would support that. But the stakes are high for all of us."

I stood up. "Miss Climpson. You have little reason to trust me. I realize there are secrets within this firm you feel are too great for me to know. But I also understand what it's like to belong to a set group within society and become an outcast. I know what it's like to become a social pariah, to lose both my standing and security. Whatever secrets you're hiding, I won't betray your trust."

Miss Climpson turned a wan smile toward me. "I'm sure you believe that, my dear. But belief is not proof of action when push comes to shove. Not to mention, we have far more to lose than you."

Ryker cleared his throat. "I trust Bishop." The authority in Ryker's voice made Miss Climpson's shoulders sag. "I've assigned her the task of locating Peter Knight."

Mr. J's face fell, and his mouth opened. "But sir—"

Ryker made an abrupt chopping gesture with his hand. "We've been over this before. We need someone with Knight's skills to analyze and assess the artifacts coming in each day."

Mr. J made as if to speak, but a single, sharp glance from Ryker was enough to quell him. "I know who you're going to suggest, and that's impossible. That particular individual has set himself up in opposition to Redclaw's mission."

Miss Climpson's face crumpled like tissue paper. For a moment, I thought she might cry. Ryker's thunderous expression arrested me, however. His brows, normally an elegant line over his eyes, beetled together in a ferocious scowl. He looked as though he might spontaneously combust. Whoever Mr. J thought would be a better choice than Peter Knight was someone they all knew. Someone who disagreed with Redclaw's mission. Maybe even someone who'd betrayed them.

Ryker wiped all traces of fury from his face as he turned to me. "That's settled then. Bishop, come with me. I'd like to test a theory."

Based on the look his staff members shot each other, it was far from settled, at least as far as they were concerned. Ryker ignored their consternation and strode toward Mr. J's office, expecting me to follow in his wake.

I did.

Inside the inner sanctum, Ryker didn't hesitate, but made for the bookcase on the far wall.

I'd been in that office dozens of times and had shelved books without thinking. Ryker pulled a series of books forward from their slots and replaced them so fast I couldn't track the sequence. When he completed the last move, the bookcase swung open, revealing a large room on the other side. The light within was brilliant, like that of a hospital or laboratory.

He paused at the threshold. "There's a subterranean complex in here. For now, it's where we're storing artifacts of immense and inexplicable energy. You were right. Something about the advent of atomic weaponry woke a power that's been lying dormant on this world for centuries, perhaps even millennia. In the wrong hands, these artifacts could be lethal. I'm trying to get them off the streets, but also determine what they do. That's where I hope Dr. Knight's genius will prove invaluable."

As tempting as it was to ask about the person who could have done Knight's job but refused, I suspected Ryker wouldn't give me any more information than I already knew. My heartbeat pulsed in my ears as I gathered my courage enough to ask the damning question I could no longer put off. "This newly awakened power. It isn't just limited to artifacts, is it?"

Ryker nodded. "That's right. Redclaw also exists to help people deal with the changes that have come over them against their will. What you saw with Billy. Some of us can transform into animals and other creatures."

What other creatures were there besides animals? Not knowing how to respond, I simply nodded.

"We call ourselves shifters." One of Ryker's eyebrows rose in an eloquent arch. "Are you all right there, Bishop? You seem to be breathing hard."

I forced my respiration rate to slow. "Quite fine, sir. I'm just, er, absorbing the information."

Ryker laughed. "You don't have to 'sir' me. I have a good nose for people, Bishop. I knew I could count on you."

When someone says something like that, your goose is cooked. You either fulfill their trust or betray it.

Small wonder Mr. J and Miss Climpson worried about me being included in on the secret.

Also, I couldn't imagine *not* calling Ryker 'sir.'

Ryker entered the well-lit room. I followed.

The room appeared to be some sort of cramped workspace. Shelves bearing an assortment of glass containers containing odd specimens lined the walls, much like an old biology lab or natural history museum. As if that weren't strange enough, there were also several cardboard cutouts from the movies stacked against one wall. John Wayne scowled at me alongside a grinning Gene Kelly, while James Mason was almost unrecognizable in his Captain Nemo costume.

A bench in one corner seemed devoted to electrical equipment, with a series of cathode tubes connected by extensive wiring positioned next to a small device no bigger than a face powder compact. The table in the middle of the space could have come from Santa's workshop. On it, tools and bits of mechanical devices lay in scattered disarray. My fingers itched to put it in order—a sewing kit would do nicely for containing the small pieces and prevent inadvertent loss. At the far end, a huge metal door with a series of bolts barred the other exit from the room.

At first, I thought the chaos represented construction. Only then did I recognize an artifact Russo had brought in a few weeks ago: a small triangular shaped object with a raised centerpiece. It now lay half-open like a clamshell. Not so much construction then as investigation.

Beside the clamshell object lay a slender silver-barreled device that looked like a ray gun from a Buck Rogers serial. I began breathing a little faster again. How much of what we called science fiction was actually science fact?

A slight movement out of the corner of my eye made me swing my glance around to spy my old friend, the mechanical spider, clicking around inside a glass box.

"What do these things do?"

Did I imagine Ryker made a small sound of frustration? "Good question. Some we can readily identify." He indicated the ray gun. "Others, not so much." He shot a dark glance at the spider before turning his gaze back to me. "The technology is often beyond our own understanding, particularly when it comes to the energy sources. That's why I want Knight to come on board. Some of our investigations suggest the power might be atomic-based."

I moved a step back from the table. "Are they safe?"

He shrugged. "In terms of radiation? According to our information, yes. Most of the artifacts are well-shielded, though damage can result in leakage. But the devices themselves can be dangerous in the wrong hands."

I noted a thick folder of newspaper clippings sitting at the end of the table. Miss Climpson's interest in the weird and bizarre items of news made sense now.

"Sir, how did Redclaw get started?" Though I swept a hand toward the room, I meant more than just the collection of artifacts of inexplicable design.

"Imagine, if you will, the fear and confusion when people with a history of radiation exposure began changing. Most were terrified. They had no idea if the ability to shift meant they were dying or if they would turn into animal form and be unable to change back. Not to mention, what their friends and family might do to them out of lack of understanding." A sad smile flickered over Ryker's features. "You won't have heard of it, as there isn't yet an American translation, but last year, the Japanese made a movie about a monster called *Godzilla*. It's a deep sea creature transformed by hydrogen bomb testing, which then wreaks havoc on Tokyo. While it's just a movie, it hits far too close to home for many of us. Many people in the shifter community fear this is how the rest of the world will view us—as monsters that need to be destroyed."

I nodded, while suppressing a little shiver of unease. *Shifters*, as they described themselves, seemed to operate under a different set of rules. A mostly human being, such as myself, might be in over her head.

"Soldiers came home from the war afraid to tell their wives about their strange new abilities. As more atomic testing took place, new shifters emerged. In addition, the dumping of radioactive waste in local communities triggered latent shifter genes, even as many without those genes succumbed to the terrible effects of the callous handling of such dangerous materials. At the same time, mysterious devices were also being discovered, sometimes with disastrous consequences." Ryker walked the length of the room, gazing at the various objects in passing, pausing to touch one here and there before speaking again.

"There have always been a few shifters among us. Some you've heard stories about, I'm sure. Dragons, werewolves, and the like. Always in small numbers, the stuff of mythology and legends. Stories to scare small children." His gaze lost focus and turned inward, almost as if he was listening to something only he could hear, before he took a sharp breath and continued with brisk determination. "Anyway, for ages the older shifters had their own Council. Now we were seeing different species of shifters—lions, tigers, and bears, if you like. Were these mysterious artifacts connected in some way? Timing would suggest so. As the numbers of new types of shifters rose, the Council created Redclaw, with its mission being to collect and contain the artifacts from the general population and assist in the unique matters pertaining to the shifter community. Not everyone has agreed with this decision, but it is the will of the Council."

He picked up a metal disc etched with strange symbols and flipped it through his fingers several times before laying it down once more. "No, I'm not telling you everything, Bishop. I can see the question in your eyes although you're doing your damnedest to hide it. I'm telling you what I think you need to know. We're not the only ones seeking artifacts and trying to figure out what they do. There are other people out there who believe they have equal right to this technology. They may well be right, but there are also criminal networks and corrupt governments who crave the power such devices can wield. I believe as the Council does, that we need to keep such technology out of the hands of people who would misuse it."

I opened my mouth to speak, but squashed the urge. It wasn't my place to lecture my boss about absolute power and its ability to corrupt those who hold it. Ryker might be an honorable man, but could the same be said about every Redclaw employee? Or for that matter, anyone who succeeded him in the future?

"Not everything we've discovered is dangerous, however. Some tech has proven useful. Even decorative." Ryker opened a drawer and took out a small box that could have passed for a jewelry case and lifted the lid. Inside, several enameled pieces lay on blue velvet packing. He selected a red and black ladybug and smiled as he held it out to me. "I want you to wear this."

I took the ladybug. It looked like an ordinary piece of costume jewelry. "What does it do?" I pinned it to my collar.

"Just as we're not the only ones looking for this technology, there are others out there looking for Knight." The corner of his mouth quirked. "I know you can take care of yourself. But every agent gets one of these, in some form or another. The pin is a kind of emergency signal. If you press on it, we'll get notified you're in trouble and you need assistance. We can zero in on the frequency and determine your location."

"How many of these artifacts do you have?" The steel door at the other end of the room looked sturdy enough. I wondered where it led.

"Many. Find me Peter Knight and I'll give you both the Grand Tour."

"Aren't you taking a risk letting me in on your—I mean, Redclaw's—secrets? It's plain to see the others aren't happy about your decision, nor of the decision to bring Knight on board."

I fancied Ryker's nod was a touch rueful. "I took the biggest chance when I didn't turn you away on the spot the day you showed up by mistake for an interview. Even then, however, you showed indications the artifacts might respond to you."

I thought back to my first visit to Redclaw, and my so-called interview with Mr. J. At first, I recalled nothing out of the ordinary, but then I remembered the way the Slinky had poured into my hand, and the fleeting impression that the Silly Putty had moved in my presence.

As supernatural abilities went, manipulating a child's plaything was disappointing, to say the least. Ryker, however, had more to say. "Once I decided to hire you, there was always a risk that someone as intelligent as you would figure out that Redclaw and its employees were...different."

To put it mildly.

"You showed a distinct level of resourcefulness and coolness under pressure the day the artifact got loose in the office." He pointed at the mechanical spider in its small glass prison. "And again today, when Miss Climpson was attacked. And you signed a non-disclosure agreement. Are you saying I *shouldn't* trust you?"

"No." My face reddened at the unaccustomed compliment for my actions. "But I see their point. Mr. Jessop and Miss Climpson, that is. They—all of you—have a lot to lose if you trust the wrong person. And you seem determined to add another...outsider...to the ranks."

"We must assess Dr. Knight's character prior to asking him to come on board, it's true. But I've often found people who've lost everything are more inclined to hold their own counsel. Isn't that so, Bishop?"

His words weighed on me in a manner that made me wonder if he'd done a background check on me at some point.

"Perhaps." I frowned as a slight whistling sound reached my ears. "Do you hear that?"

Ryker frowned too, looking about. "Hear what?"

"A high-pitched whistle." I walked around the worktable, trying to pinpoint the origin. As I came abreast of the silver gun, the sound intensified. "May I?" I asked, indicating the weapon.

A look of faint apprehension skimmed Ryker's features before he smoothed it away. "Of course. Though as a rule, I'd caution you to be careful with any artifact you run across. The vast majority of the technology we've recovered only responds to those with the shifter genes. That's not a universal characteristic, however, and the potential to hurt yourself or others is great if you don't know what you're doing." He waved his hand toward the weapon.

I picked it up. The small gun fit into the palm of my hand as though made for it, looking more like a toy than anything that might inflict damage. Recalling some of the artifacts I'd handled before, I recognized its innate warmth. It reminded me of the Magic 8 Ball. "It almost begs me to fire it." I laughed as I admired the gun.

"Unfortunately, it doesn't seem to have much range." Ryker pointed out the cardboard cutout of John Wayne dressed as a cowboy from one of his many Westerns. I wasn't sure which one. I noticed tiny pinholes in the cutout, and lines marked on the floor in chalk that marked distance. Now the existence of the movie cutouts made sense. "You must be close to your target to have any effect."

According to the marks, I was nowhere near close enough to hit John Wayne. Ryker watched with an irritating air of amused benevolence, resting his hands at his waist. With a sly grin in his direction, I refocused on the target and pulled the trigger.

An intense red beam of light shot out of the barrel and pierced John Wayne through the eye. Ryker's gasp covered my own surprised intake of air. Pretending a nonchalance I didn't feel, I said, "Maybe you just need someone who knows how to shoot."

Ryker's thoughtful study startled me when I turned to face him. "It's more than the ability to aim a weapon. You were at least fifteen feet from the target, farther than anyone else. It's as I thought. You must have the shifter gene, too."

I'm pretty sure I'd know if I could turn into a werewolf or not. Though maybe that's what every other shifter said before it happened to them. Without warning, an image of my mother leaped to mind, staring down her patrician nose with horror and dismay at her daughter, the shifter.

No. Impossible.

Ryker's eyes narrowed as he tapped his lips with a finger while continuing to speak, almost as though to himself. "Not the full gene, no. But possibly a partial recessive. The genes must be widespread throughout the human population, but not everyone's was strong enough to be activated—unless it requires a higher dose of radiation...."

I waggled the gun, inviting him to take it.

He shook his head, a slow grin breaking out on his face. "Try it again."

I stared at the little gun nestled in my palm. Using the tip of one finger, I traced some almost imperceptible carvings along its grip. A row of tiny lights appeared, the topmost glowing red. "There seems to be some settings here." I showed Ryker what I meant.

Both his eyebrows lifted. "That's a first. See if you can change them."

I pressed one of the other buttons, and the red light went out. A blue light showed up next in line.

A speculative gleam glowed in Ryker's eyes. "I wonder—?"

Without warning, he lifted the lid on the container enclosing the spider. With astonishing speed, it scaled the side of the glass and skittered out along the table. "Shoot it, Bishop."

I didn't hesitate. I aimed at the spider, now hurtling toward me. Instead of the tightly focused red beam of before, wavering rings of blue pulsed out of the gun's barrel. It took longer than I liked for them to reach the spider, but when it did, the mechanical device shuddered and collapsed, going limp.

Ryker swooped in and picked up the spider with a delighted grin, giving it a little shake that made its legs flop loosely. "Outstanding. I wonder if it was an EM pulse or a stun mechanism of some other means. And will it work safely on living creatures? We must test it. See, this is why we need someone like Knight here."

With great care, he placed the spider back in its container and secured the lid. After checking the clock on the wall, he took out a small notebook, removed the band that held it closed, and jotted down some notes.

I couldn't explain it, but I wanted the gun. I *needed* it. I slipped it into my pocket.

"Our expert in genetics won't be in until next week, but when Dr. Botha gets here, I'd like you to come back here for testing. I suspect you'll be in great demand down here in the labs." Ryker replaced the band on the outside of the notebook and left it on the table. He must have caught the guilty apprehension in my eyes and misinterpreted it for anxiety, for he added. "It won't hurt. Provide a blood sample, handle some artifacts, that sort of thing. We need to establish baselines for what it takes to use the technology. Anything we learn is useful."

He smiled as he tapped on the glass container holding the spider. Without looking at me, he said, "I imagine it will relieve the other staff members to know you have more of a stake in maintaining Redclaw's confidentiality agreement than previously thought."

Indeed. Maybe not as much of a reason as someone who could turn into a wolf, but a reason just the same.

I waited for him to say something about the gun, to offer to put it away, but he didn't. Noting that the mechanical spider was twitching, he checked the time again and made another entry in his notebook. Pleased satisfaction radiated from him as he indicated I should precede him back into Mr. J's office. All at once, I was out of time to confess I still had the ray gun on me.

Disconcerted at my casual—and unreasonable—theft, I changed the subject.

"You still need more than reliance on a secret bookcase to protect all this." The irony of my making such a statement while having pocketed a prime piece of tech hadn't escaped me. What I couldn't understand was why I'd done it in the first place.

"Agreed. Though I suspect, for the most part, the guards will find the work boring."

"Stage random, unannounced drills to keep them on their toes. But surely there must be something you've discovered so far that would help in maintaining security."

Ryker's expression grew far-away again, as though he were checking some mental inventory. "You may be right. I like the way you think, Bishop."

As we crossed through Mr. J's room back to the main office, Ryker said, "The full services of Redclaw are available to help in your search for Dr. Knight. Don't hesitate to ask for assistance."

"Yes, sir." My answer was automatic, but I planned to find Knight on my own. The others might not trust me with their secrets or to do the work of a field agent, but I'd prove them wrong. It seemed only reasonable to keep the ray gun with me until I did.

We went back to the main area. Ryker left me to my file folder, and the office returned to its normal routine. I was grateful to be alone with Knight's file. I didn't want to think too much about the things I'd seen minutes ago, or the fact I might have shifter genes, or the gun purring in my pocket like an adopted kitten. I'd think about those things later, in the quiet of my apartment, over a box of chocolates. And maybe even a bottle of wine.

Aside from the occasional glass of wine, I'd more or less given up alcohol after my father's death, so that was saying something, indeed. Finding out my father had made an illegal fortune during Prohibition had practically turned me into a member of the Temperance Society. The events of the day, however, had been enough to tempt even the strictest teetotaler.

I opened the folder and settled myself into reading. I confess, I found Peter Knight's story compelling. It was nice to have a name to go along with the face, even as I told myself I would have to abandon my previous fantasies. In addition to the small black-and-white photo attached to the front of the record, other images caught my eye. One stood out, a color print of Knight and a beautiful woman, a stunning redhead. They stared into each other's eyes with such an expression of laughter and love on their faces it seemed impossible there was room for anyone else in their lives.

Had I ever known anything that intense? No. I didn't think a marriage should be based on anything less, either.

The enclosed file was brief, but powerful in its brevity. Knight had come to the United States during the Second World War to work with Oppenheimer's team at Los Alamos as part of the Manhattan Project. After the war, when Oppenheimer became chairman of the United States Atomic Energy

Commission, Knight had landed at Cornell, and from there had become a leading voice warning about the dangers of nuclear arms proliferation.

If only he knew....

In 1952, he married an American by the name of Margo Collins and became a U.S. citizen.

The next entry made me catch my breath. On May 3, 1953, a hit-and-run driver struck and killed Margo Knight. An attached report included a subsequent public drunk and disorderly charge against Knight, and several statements by colleagues as to the same. Obviously, Knight had not handled the death of his wife well. Given the clear attachment between them in the photograph, it wasn't surprising. Although tenured by that point, the House Committee on Un-American Activities declared Knight a Communist due to his association with Oppenheimer. As a result, Knight lost his position at Cornell and wound up blacklisted by other universities.

Then he moved out of his apartment and disappeared. Dropped out of sight. No forwarding address. No known whereabouts.

Except I had seen him last month outside the Blue Moon.

I closed the file and stood. Miss Climpson looked up as I approached her desk, a slight frown puckering her brow.

"How does this field agent thing work? If I need to be out of the office, is that a problem?"

Miss Climpson rocked back in her chair as if my question was the utter limit. Disbelief that Ryker had promoted me in such a manner dripped from every word she spoke. "Ryker assigned you a case. That's your sole priority now. If tracking down Dr. Knight takes you out of the office, so be it." She pulled her drawer open with unnecessary force and sorted through some papers to lay a stack of forms on the desk in front of me. "You need to track your expenses. You have a daily allotment of two dollars toward meals and transportation. Anything above that comes out of your own pocket and must be approved for reimbursement."

I picked up the paperwork.

"Your time is your own, but understand you're still at work, Miss Bishop. No running off to the matinee because it suits you."

"Unless, of course, my case takes me there." I met Miss Climpson's stare without blinking.

She narrowed her eyes, not liking my attempt at humor. "That would seem highly unlikely."

I shrugged. "You never know."

I returned to my desk and placed the paperwork in my drawer. I left the ray gun in my pocket. Collecting the tattered remains of my purse, along with my hat and coat, I was almost out the door when Miss Climpson raised her voice to stop me. "Where do you think you're going, Miss Bishop?"

I turned around. By her annoyed expression, it seemed Miss Climpson already thought I was taking advantage of the new rules to play hooky. I noted the dark circles under her eyes and the marked droop to her lips and decided not to be mean. "I have a lead."

Her mouth dropped open. "What? Already?"

I gave her a cheery little smile and waved as I headed out the door.

Chapter Six

As leads went, mine could have been better.

After three days of haunting the street where the Blue Moon café was located, I was stuffed to the gills with finger sandwiches and shortbread, and I never wanted another cup of tea as long as I lived.

There is only so much time an unaccompanied woman can spend in a restaurant without calling unwanted attention to herself. That first day, I lingered over coffee, dallied over marmalade and toast, and dawdled over pie I no longer had any desire to eat. When the manager fixed me with a jaundiced eye, I paid my bill and left.

Shopping was a risky venture—what if my target passed by the store while I was inside? Still, it couldn't be helped. I loitered in front of shop windows as though I couldn't decide what I wanted and then skipped inside to make a rapid purchase. Something small. A packet of needles. A thimble. A card for my mother I'd never send.

After forty-eight hours of no success and sore feet, I had to rethink my strategy. There was always the possibility Knight had come to that part of town for a specific reason and wouldn't return, but as it was the only line I had on locating him, I worked under the assumption he'd be back. Diners and bars

were my best bet. Given Knight's reported frame of mind before
he disappeared, frequenting a watering hole in the middle of the
day wasn't unthinkable. The problem was determining which
one. There were dozens of bars and grills in the immediate area,
so I began ticking them off my list.

The first one was the hardest. Obviously, a single woman
entering a bar in the middle of the day was looking for trouble.
Between the dim lighting, the hazy miasma of stale smoke, the
floors sticky with spilt beer, and the inevitable masher who tried
to put his hands on me, I had to remind myself what a coup it
would be if I found Knight. It was impossible to walk into a bar
without the patrons taking note, but I became adept at taking a
quick scan of the room for my target and making my escape
before anyone approached me. As luck would have it, no sign of
Peter Knight.

But I had hopes I might be successful yet. I still had an
ace I hadn't played.

On the third day, I showed up with a sketchbook and
drawing pencils. I'm not much of an artist, but it gave me a
splendid excuse for hanging about for hours peering out the
window as I drew the local scene. After another unsuccessful
round of bar hopping the day before, I dared not make a repeat
appearance anywhere unless I had a solid lead to pursue. For
similar reasons, I didn't try the Blue Moon again—I felt certain
the manager wouldn't have allowed me to camp out a second
time. Instead, I chose a hole-in-the-wall diner and took a seat by
the greasy window. No one seemed to care that I occupied a

table for hours, as long as I ordered something from time to time. I'm somewhat better at portraits than architecture, so I began sketching the patrons, which seemed to amuse my waitress.

But still no Dr. Knight.

I was about to give up when inspiration struck me again. With my hand flying over the pad, I sketched Knight as I remembered him from the encounter on the street, supplemented with the refresher I'd received from the photos in his folder. I drew him wearing his camel hair coat with his fedora pulled down over eyes that had seen too much. I shadowed the edge of his jaw and chiseled the elegant nose. I was putting the finishing touches on the lines pulling down the corners of his mouth when the waitress topped off my chipped mug.

"Who's that handsome devil?" She lifted her eyebrows in admiration as she poured. Her nametag read "Linda". Steam rose from my cup, bringing with it the delectable aroma of coffee.

"His name's Peter." I thought of Regina Betterton, and her "problem" our senior year of college. I let dejection fill my voice. "We used to hang out. Have some laughs, you know? Only he left me in the lurch and now I can't find him." I set the sketch pad down, pushing it in Linda's direction. Catching her eye, I added with emphasis, "I *need* to find him."

Linda made a tsking sound and picked up the pad. Pressing her lips together in concentration, she tipped her head to one side as she studied the drawing. Shaking the sketch pad, she said, "You know, I think I've seen him."

I sat up straight.

"In here?"

She nodded. "Yeah. Once or twice, though not for a while now." She squinted in thought. "Two eggs, sunny-side up. Sausage, toast, and coffee, black, no sugar. Hungover." Snapping her fingers, her eyes widened, and she pointed at the drawing. "That's right. Breakfast after a bar run. I remember now because he complained about the food there. Moneta's Bar and Grill. Over on Macintosh Street. It's not far from here, but it's not the sort of place you want to go to by yourself." Her expression was sympathetic, one woman to another that she should give up on a lost cause.

I wasn't about to go back to Redclaw empty-handed. For an instant, I thought of contacting Miss Climpson and asking for backup, but I dismissed it as unnecessary. I hadn't even spotted Knight yet. Better to wait until I was sure of my quarry.

I paid my bill and left the diner. I had just one shot at this, so I had to get it right. It was time to play my ace.

I went back to my apartment, took a long soak in the tub, and changed into something more appropriate for a night out on the town. Splurging on a taxi, I had the driver deliver me to the Moneta's Bar and Grill at nine p.m. I'd done a little research at the library in the meantime. The tavern had been a haunt of the likes of Ernest Hemingway, and that Thomas fellow, the one who wrote the poem about not going gentle into that good night.

The bar's history didn't mean it was any less of a dive than some other places I'd visited recently. Tonight, I cared less about its past occupants and more about its current.

My father once said you handled a boardroom full of hostile stockholders the same way you faced down an angry leopard: you walked into the situation as though you were in complete control.

Just because someone's bad decisions had resulted in them taking their own life didn't mean you tossed out every piece of advice they'd ever given.

An unaccompanied woman walking into a tavern at night was unseemly. But I had my ray gun secreted in my new clutch and was wearing a drop-dead gorgeous little blue number with white piping that screamed confidence. It had the added benefit of being a swing dress, and the wide, flowing skirt wouldn't restrict my movement. Smoothing my bodice, I opened the door to the pub.

Inside, it was as if I'd stepped through a portal into another world. Unlike my daytime pub crawls, the bar was full of people now. The heat was the first thing I noticed, followed by a solid wall of noise and laughter radiating off the humanity within. The air was thick with the smell of cigarette smoke and the yeasty odor of ale. The atmosphere was jovial.

I surveyed the room. A group of Brooklyn boys played darts in one corner. Several men sat a table laughing over large pints of beer. A solitary man sat at the bar itself, a crutch at his side as he hunched over his drink. Two grey-haired old men played checkers with the intensity of aficionados, the smoke from their pipes hanging over their heads like storm clouds as they studied their board. A couple of men in suits looked over in my direction, one of them nudging his friend and speaking out of the side of his mouth while never taking his eyes off me. He and his friend burst into raucous laughter, which I ignored. The few women in the joint were there with dates, which made my presence stick out like a sore thumb. I didn't see Knight.

Stalling for time, I took out my compact, using the mirror to check out various parts of the room while pretending to touch up my lipstick. According to Linda, this was Knight's usual hangout. But today's date was special: May 3rd, the second anniversary of his wife's death. My ace in the hole. The odds were high he'd be here tonight, since he was in the habit of drowning his sorrows at this particular bar. Was I too late? Or too early? I closed the compact with a snap and replaced it in my clutch.

It was then I saw him. Peter Knight. The man I'd come here to find.

I'd missed him before. He was sitting alone on a bench in a dark corner of the pub, staring down into a glass of whiskey. I straightened my dress and drew a deep breath. My heels clicked on the wooden floor as I approached his table, but Knight didn't look up. He was the sole person in the bar who wasn't eyeing me with curiosity.

I slipped into the seat across from him.

From his bleary-eyed, ruffled state, it was clear Knight had been drinking for some time. I smothered the sense of disappointment, despite knowing an anniversary of this kind would be difficult for anyone. He looked up as I sat down, blinking like a confused owl to see me in front of him.

After a brief glance at me, he dropped his gaze back to the glass cradled in his hands. On the street outside the Blue Moon, while wearing a hat, I'd assumed his hair was dark, but I saw now he had the thick thatch of sandy brown hair that so often seemed to retreat into baldness in middle age, and he hadn't shaved in a day or two. The overhead light glinted gold on his stubble, making him seem like a teenager playing at being an adult. The heavy lock of hair that hung over his forehead enhanced the impression. A rain-spattered fedora rested on the table by his hand in the manner of someone who'd intended to stop in for one drink but had lost track of the time.

I'd found him, and come hell or high water, I wasn't leaving without confirming Knight as a committed member of Redclaw.

"Dr. Peter Knight?" With careful deliberation, I pitched my voice so it was light, crisp, but friendly, and just loud enough to carry over the ambient noise in the bar.

Alcohol might have made his eyes bloodshot, but they were still as intense as I remembered. He looked up and narrowed them at my words. His dossier had listed his age as thirty-three, but he looked younger to me. His eyes gave him away. Eyes that had seen too much and lived to tell the tale. He couldn't have been out of school long when he began his war work. That alone gave testimony to his sheer intelligence.

"Who wants to know?" The accent was pure Oxford, clipped and aristocratic. And about as friendly as a door being slammed in your face.

I ignored the implicit warning to go away.

"My name is Henrietta Bishop. I have a proposition for you." I realized I should have ordered a drink to fit in. I caught the bartender's eye, and he gave me a nod before reaching under the bar for a bottle of whiskey to pour out a shot without asking what I wanted. I counted myself lucky. If I had to drink, I preferred whiskey to gin. I waited for the bartender to walk over with the glass, giving him a smile as he delivered my drink and left.

"Don't waste your time." Knight twisted his lips into a bitter mockery of politeness. "You should know you're barking up the wrong tree. You're not my type."

"How fortunate neither of us is looking to go out on a date."

There was a certain impish attractiveness to Knight's face when he smiled. The glitter to his eyes, however, suggested his smile wasn't all that nice.

"Whatever you're selling, I'm not interested. But lest you think I'm being rude, to old friends." Knight lifted his glass in a toast.

Something tightened around my throat and brought an unexpected sting of tears to my eyes. "To old friends," I said in a voice as smoky as the pub. *When in Rome.* To set Knight at ease, I took a sip of my drink and raised my eyebrows at the rich smooth flavor. It was pre-war whiskey. The good stuff. Most bars couldn't carry it these days.

Seconds ticked away on my wristwatch. Just when I was about to speak, curiosity got the better of his self-control. "Okay, I give up. What do you want with me? You aren't here to seduce me, at least, not in the straightforward Mata Hari kind of way."

An involuntary smile crept across my face at his words. "What makes you so sure I don't just want to have a drink with you?"

"You made the rookie mistake of calling me by name." Knight tapped his upper lip as he studied me with the focused concentration of a scientist examining a new, strange specimen. "If you planned to charm me with your wiles, you'd have at least pretended to meet me by accident. You passed up several men to sit with me, but have admitted you're not here on a date. I know your type. You're cut crystal and canapes with a Walther PPK in your handbag." Even under the influence, a dangerous intelligence glinted in his eyes.

"My, you must lead an exciting life. I prefer the Baby Browning. It fits in the purse better. On the other hand, the Colt .45 isn't bad for day wear." So he thought I was a spy, eh? I could work with that. "The better question might be what brings *you* here, Dr. Knight?"

"Don't you mean what keeps me here?" In a matter of seconds, the puckish grin at my rejoinder melted as though made of wax. "Ghosts. The ghosts of old friends, lost loves, and better times." He nodded at the surrounding benches, as though they were full of people only he could see. His gaze came back to rest on my face. "I'm tired, Miss Bishop. So if you don't mind, I'm not in the mood for conversation. I'd rather sit this one out." He took another long pull from his glass, his Adam's apple bobbing as he swallowed. He set the tumbler down with a decided thump.

I'd heard that argument before. Heard it and understood it intimately, knew what it felt like to be so tired, so weary of struggling that even my bones hurt. So heartsick I just wanted to go home and curl up under a blanket, but "home" was a cheap room in a boarding house for single ladies. I also knew if I wanted to see changes in my life, I was the only one who could make them happen. "If our boys had chosen to 'sit this one out' during World War II, the world would now be under Axis control."

By the way his jaw tightened, I knew I'd hit a nerve. Goodness, that glare could have been registered as a lethal weapon.

"Those days are done. My part in that is over. Ask anyone at Cornell. Washed-up Boy Genius." His words became even more slurred as he spoke, as if to reinforce the reputation.

"My boss doesn't think so. He wants to offer you a job."

Had I thought his glare lethal before? Pure hatred boiled in his eyes. He pressed his fingertips onto the table and leaned forward, his mouth twisting into a snarl. "The last man to offer me work wouldn't take no for an answer. I said no just the same. But then you know that, don't you? You know everything about me, right? You know what color my socks are and how I like my eggs cooked and the name of the cat I had when I was a child." His words crackled with hostility.

Too late, I realized I'd started something I had to see through now. I would not go back to Ryker with excuses. Nettled, I answered the part of the question I knew.

"Inky," I said. "Though if you had a cat today, I suspect you'd name it Schrodinger."

His face fell, a caricature of shock for just an instant, until the shields came down into place once more, much like a portcullis clanging shut. It was fascinating to watch his expression harden into a mask. I couldn't imagine why I'd been so bold. It had been the wrong move. Blue eyes became steel, and his mouth was tight when he spoke.

"Whoever you are, Miss Bishop, I don't want any part of you or your organization." The bench scraped across the floor as he pushed it back.

"Please," I said, reaching out in appeal. "Please sit down and hear me out."

Knight rested one hand on the table, glowering with his head lowered like a bull about to charge. He might have looked like a lost little boy sitting at the table when I walked in, but he definitely had a man's body. *Nice shoulders.* The thought was so illogical, so inappropriate, I squashed it right away.

He caught his lower lip in his teeth in a snarl. "You killed her."

His accusation took my breath away. He waved off my protest before I could get it out of my mouth, as though shooing a fly. "Oh, no, not you personally, but you and your kind. Smarmy organizations with secret agendas who want me to work for them and then murder my wife when I refuse. I suppose I'm next, eh? Well, do your worst or bugger off. You don't know how little I have left to lose."

"I'm not here to threaten you into taking a job with us." Taking a steadying breath, I picked up my glass of whiskey and turned it, staring into its depths. I'd cut myself into this game of poker. Now it was time to ante up. "I'm sorry about your wife. And I'm sorry about the dossier on you. I was showing off, and it was inappropriate. This is my first field assignment, and I'm not handling it well. Please, sit down."

My apology seemed to dampen his fury, yet he remained standing. At least he hadn't stormed out. His anger just snuffed out, like a capped candle. Dragging a fingernail in small circles on the table's surface without looking at me, when he spoke, his voice was so low I had to strain to hear him. "We used to meet here. My wife and I. Margo. Before we were married. When I was in town, that is. She was so beautiful. So fair. She was training to become a nurse. She was...." He took a moment to consider his answer. "She was an island of sanity and joy in a world gone mad. I loved her very much."

I'd spent the last few days pouring over his file, and even without the redacted statements, it was clear Redclaw had access to things beyond the standard security firm. What would working on the kinds of top-secret projects that Knight had been part of do to a man? Especially someone as young and brilliant as he'd been then. A wunderkind, they'd called him. Child genius. I struggled to find the right words—kind words—that wouldn't chase him away. "The war was no respecter of goodness, kindness, or beauty. It smashed and grabbed like some unfeeling robber, tearing apart lives without caring. You can't blame yourself for that."

His sharp glance met my eyes. "Some of us are more responsible than others."

"Yes," I agreed. I cleared my throat and held out my glass. "To the kind and good. May we live up to their legacy."

Knight's all too expressive face screwed up at this, as though he was holding back a wall of pain with his skin. But I'd gotten through to him. He took his seat and picked up his tumbler. "To the kind and good."

We clicked glasses. Knight drained the rest of his. I tossed back the entirety of mine, welcoming the slow burn as it made its way down my throat.

Ryker trusted me. I hope he was right to do so.

I was about to find out.

"Redclaw Security is an investigative firm. We find things. Artifacts. People. Information." I weighed my next words with great care, fingering the metaphorical cards before laying them on the table. I had nothing to lose. "What if I told you we could find out who killed your wife?"

Chapter Seven

For a long moment, I thought my risky gamble had failed. Knight's eyes blazed with white-hot fury before his expression faded almost into bewilderment. Somehow, that moment of confused indecision got to me more than anything else he'd said or done all evening. As he stared at the room, his face void of all expression, it was as though I'd ceased to exist. Whatever he saw, it wasn't the activity of the surrounding patrons.

At last, his gaze returned to my face. "You might already work for them."

That thought hadn't occurred to me. Catching me off guard, the accusation was almost a sucker punch, but I dismissed the possibility before the full force of his words hit me. It didn't seem Ryker-like, for want of a better word. I measured my response before speaking. "Perhaps. But if we are, you'll be able to take us down from the inside. If not, we're your best chance of finding out who was behind Margo's death."

Hearing his wife's name caused a spasm of pain to flare across his face, but his odd sense of humor soon resurfaced. "For someone just promoted out of the typing pool, you're very good at this, you know. They might have sent you simply because your ignorance makes every statement ring with the truth."

I lifted my chin. "Maybe they had a good reason for promoting me."

He snorted, eyeing the partial bottle of whiskey at his elbow. While he might be more persuadable drunk, I preferred him having most of his senses about him for this decision. When he reached for the bottle, I caught his hand in mine. He looked down at my grip in patent disbelief.

"There are others looking for you. You'd be safer with us."

"Like I care about my safety." His words vividly reminded me of the street outside the Blue Moon and a cold snow driving little needles into my skin. His attitude then made more sense now. His hand jerked in mine and pulled away.

Like before on the street corner, his defeatist attitude irritated me. I clapped down some money for my drink on the table and stood. "Fine. Let whoever killed your wife win, then."

Anger blazed in his eyes once more. It was better than apathy, even if I had to bear the brunt of it. "Who the hell do you think you are?"

I turned his tumbler upside down, the small trickle of whiskey within running down to wet the table. "Someone who hates to see good brains go to waste."

Sometimes you need to know when to throw down your cards. I turned and walked away.

I'd hoped, but hadn't expected he'd follow me. As such, I was startled by his touch on the collar of my coat as I pulled it on and then relaxed as he assisted me into it. So close to my ear that his warm breath made me shiver, he said, "'Take us down from the inside'? Fan of the movies, are we?"

Heat rushed into my cheeks, but I pretended not to notice. "'Fasten your seatbelts.'" I quoted. "'It's going to be a bumpy night.'"

His laughter warmed me more than it should have.

Once outside the bar, I realized I didn't know what to do with him. No one would be at the office this late at night. I had no means of contacting Ryker, Mr. J, or even Miss Climpson after hours, something I would need to remedy in the morning. At the very least, I needed to know where Knight was staying, and I couldn't take his word for it, either. I'd have to confirm his address before I left him for the evening. I paused on the sidewalk while I tried to determine the best way of getting the information I needed.

Knight had other ideas. "My car's along here somewhere. I'll give you a ride home."

"That's not necessary," I said in haste, before he could lead us to the car.

"You think I'm squiffy." Knight sounded insulted. "I'm perfectly capable of giving you a lift to wherever you live."

The hair went up on the back of my neck. There was a kind of breathless tension in the air around us, the quivering attention of a cat about to pounce. From a side alley to our right, I heard the faint scrape of a shoe on pavement, quickly halted.

"I think," I said, keeping my voice casual as I took his arm and forced him to walk with me, "perhaps we're not the only people interested in your services."

A car parked along the street in front of us turned on its headlights, pinning us in their glare. Knight threw his hands up to shield his eyes while I squinted and listened hard, trying to determine which direction the attack was about to come. My fingers twisted the latch on my clutch, where I'd hidden the ray gun.

Two men sprang out from the darkness on both sides, attempting to pinch us between them. One rushed me, the other tackled Knight. The man who'd grabbed my arm spun me around so hard I dropped my purse. It skittered along the sidewalk out of reach.

My attacker must have thought he could just throw me to the ground, allowing him and his cohort to concentrate on Knight. When he grasped my shoulders, I drove my heel into his instep. It was satisfying to hear his howl of pain vanish with a whoosh of air as I followed with a punch to the gut. When he doubled over, I slammed the point of my elbow into the back of his neck and he fell in a heap to the pavement. Who knew all those years of fending off drunken frat boys and handsy coworkers would pay off?

Knight scuffled with the man frog-marching him toward the car, whose back door stood open, ready to receive him. I grabbed Knight's assailant by the collar, jerking him backward. It startled the attacker long enough that Knight was able to whirl and punch him in the face. The man cursed and brought his hands up to his nose, but shook off the pain to sweep out with his leg and knock Knight off his feet. Knight went down, pin-wheeling his arms in an attempt to stop his fall.

Blood streaming down over his hand from his bloody nose, Knight's assailant faced me in the headlights framing my location. He pulled a short knife out of his pocket and lunged. I jumped back with a gasp, barely avoiding his jab. Knight was still down, but spun on his side to kick the knife-holder in the back of the knee, causing his leg to buckle. The knife went flying. I dashed in to give him a hard shove. Already off balance, the attacker tumbled over backward. His skull met the pavement with a dull thud.

It all happened in a matter of seconds. Two were down but there was at least one more in the car, with the headlights trained on us.

Knight got to his feet just as I snatched up my purse. A screech of metal announced the opening of the driver's side door. Knight grabbed me by the arm and barked a single command. "Move!"

The report of a gun went off so close the echo reverberated in my head. Something tore into my left arm, and for a moment, the sharp pain stunned me into incomprehension. Then reaction kicked in and I shoved Knight sideways, knocking him out of the headlight's beam. I dove behind him, fishing for the ray gun as I did. The shooter still had the advantage of distance on us. We were sitting ducks.

The driver of the car strode through the light cast by the headlamps, the black metal of his gun glinting in bright beams. My hand closed on the gun in my clutch, and I let the bag fall away as the warm metal molded itself to my grip.

Still too far away for the energy beam to reach him. A few more steps....

A metallic rattle forced me to look in Knight's direction. He'd snatched up a trash can lid from a nearby bin and held it like some sort of Spartan shield. I had to give him points for courage, but I doubted the lid would stop a bullet.

That wasn't what Knight had in mind, however. He rotated the lid until it was perpendicular to the ground and flung it away from him. It hurtled toward the gunman like some sort of Roman discus. With catlike reflexes, the gunman flung up his arm to block the flying lid. Roaring his rage, the gunman knocked it to one side. It fell with a clatter to the ground.

I'd already drawn a bead on the shooter. Now I depressed the trigger. The blue circles of energy erupted from the gun, striking the assailant in the middle of his chest. I held my breath as he twitched and jerked—what if the stun effect wasn't powerful enough to bring him down?

I needn't have worried. He stiffened and flung his hands up as though struck by lightning. When he fell, it was in slow motion like a tree being cut down, knees buckling first, and then pitching face first to the ground.

A wave of dizziness swept over me and I stumbled. Knight caught me by my right arm.

"You're hurt! Are you all right? What the hell did you just shoot him with? And what should we do about all this?" Knight flapped his hand at the incapacitated attackers lying all around us. "We can't just leave bodies strewn about like this, can we?"

"We need to get out of here. Damn it. You owe me a coat, Knight."

"Someone shot you and tried to kidnap me and you're worried about your coat?" His incredulity threatened to make me laugh.

"It's Balenciaga." That should explain everything.

His disgusted snort said it didn't.

My vision and hearing seemed preternaturally acute. I felt as though I could go ten rounds with Sugar Ray Robinson or climb Mount Everest. Even the initial burn of the gunshot faded into the background. I knew the high that comes from surviving something dangerous would only carry me so far, though. Knight's own heightened levels of adrenaline poured off him in waves. At least the attack had one positive side effect: Knight seemed to have sobered up. His fingers were tight on my forearm. He had no idea he would leave bruises. "Is this what working for your agency will be like? Because that was rather intense."

"No, not every day. Think of it more like hours of boredom interspersed with moments of sheer terror."

"Ah. Then not that dissimilar from some of my previous jobs."

I smiled in the darkness at the sudden sense of camaraderie. It had been a long time since I'd felt that with anyone.

The man I'd dropped to the sidewalk was out cold, if, indeed, he was still alive. I thought he might be. I hoped so—the notion I might have cracked his skull left me feeling queasy. Or maybe it was the shock of being injured. Everything had happened so fast. No one had opened a door to look out at the sound of gunfire or fighting in the street. No doubt a typical night in this part of town. I picked up my hat, previously lost in the scuffle, and noted the first attacker lifting his head. I fixed my hat in place and fired the stun beam at him for good measure. He went limp again.

We reached the abandoned car, and I turned off the headlights. After noting the registration number of the vehicle to report it to Redclaw, I closed the door. No doubt it would prove to be stolen.

"Come on. We need to get you to a doctor. My car is just down the block." Knight pointed down the street.

"Where, exactly?"

He peered about. "Er, I'm not sure. But it can't be far."

I opened my mouth to respond, only to stop at the sight of movement farther up the street. I wasn't sure what I was seeing. Something shadowy slipped in and out of the pools of light cast by the street lamps. At first, I thought it must be a stray dog heading in our direction, but then I realized it was too large. And there was more than one. A *lot* more.

The little gun quivered in my hand, almost begging me to stand and fight. I shoved it into my pocket instead. We were seriously outnumbered.

Knight must have seen the dawning look of horror on my face, for he glanced over his shoulder to see what had my attention. "What the hell is that?"

I grabbed him by the arm, even as I wrenched the door of the car open again. "Get inside. *Now*."

I shoved him into the passenger side of the front seat and climbed in behind the wheel, slamming the door as I did so. Thank God, the keys were in the ignition. Turning them, the engine caught, and I floored the gas pedal. The car peeled away from the curb with a screech of tires just as something thudded against the trunk. In the rearview mirror, multiple shadows leaped and scratched at the back window, but rolled off as the car gained speed.

"What *were* they?" Knight turned in his seat to watch the forms running behind us until they could no longer keep up. His voice rang hollow with shocked confusion.

I didn't blame him. I'd seen them with my own eyes and still felt the stunned disbelief. "Wolves. They were wolves."

Chapter Eight

I raced the car in and out of traffic, refusing to allow any sort of slowdown impede our getaway. In my haste, I shifted gears before the clutch was fully engaged, which resulted in a dreadful grinding sound. The speed at which I cornered turns made the tires squeal, and more than once Knight muttered an oath and scrabbled at the dash for support. It wasn't until I skipped the curb and took out a few trash cans that he complained aloud, however.

"I think you can slow down now." His voice sounded strained, and he splayed his fingers against the dashboard for support.

I craned my head around. "Do you see anyone behind us?"

"Eyes on the road!"

I jerked reflexively at his bellow. "You don't have to shout."

"I'm not at all certain it wouldn't be better for me to drive."

I didn't bother to dignify this with a response. My roundabout approach to my apartment made me reasonably confident we weren't being followed. Still, I didn't want to take a chance. Not with the...unusual nature of our pursuers. When I saw a taxi stand, I pulled over at the nearest side street and turned to face Knight.

"We'll leave the car here and take a cab back to my place. This one might be stolen. It's best we don't drive it much farther."

He nodded without argument, which made for a refreshing change.

As we walked toward the taxis, Knight threaded his arm through mine. I shivered a little at the warmth of his contact, taking in the familiar musky scents of pipe tobacco and cedarwood. Knight was an Old Spice man.

"Much as you like to be in charge, we'll raise fewer eyebrows and garner less attention if you let me take over from here."

Though loath to confess it, I found the strength of his arm linked with mine steadying. "Until you speak," I said. "People will remember a Brit if questioned."

"I can't imagine who you think might be questioned about us and why, but rest assured, I can do a passable American accent if necessary. Don't flip your wig."

The smooth transition into a New York accent with his final sentence made me look up in astonishment. He didn't return my glance, but he was grinning, and with his free hand, he tugged the brim of his fedora down a notch.

"You don't know my address. To tell the driver, I mean."

He flicked a sharp, speculative glance in my direction before answering. "Point taken."

I didn't know where he lived, either, and it was clear he wanted to keep it that way. But I hadn't come this far to let him slip away from me now.

When we reached the taxi stand, I gave the driver my address and slumped with relief into the back seat of the cab. Fortunately, my wool coat was black, and though the damage to the sleeve might be noticeable, blood would not. Knight noticed my movement and put his arm around my shoulders for a small squeeze.

I hissed in pain.

He removed his arm with the speed of a man who'd inadvertently shoved his hand into a furnace. His eyes gleamed in the light of a passing street lamp, worry stamped on his face. In a voice pitched too low for the driver to hear, he said, "My word, but I'm sorry."

The temptation to close my eyes and lean into him was strong, which had to be reaction setting in. I couldn't imagine expecting comfort or protection from any of my former set under similar circumstances. Tommy, offer support? He'd still be gibbering over the wolves, and no doubt blaming their appearance on the gin. And with the exception of Em, everyone else in my social circle had dropped me like a hot potato when my father went bust. As though poverty were contagious.

We pulled up outside my building. I let Knight pay the driver. Instead of taking my arm again, he guided me away from the cab with his palm on the small of my back. Even through the heavy cloth of his coat, I was acutely aware of the pressure of his hand. We walked the short distance to the entrance of my building, and then I turned to face him.

Leaning in to fuss with his collar, I murmured, "Go around back through the alley. You'll see a fire escape. I'll lower it. I'm on the third floor."

"Wait, what?" His native accent was back in full force. "I thought I was just seeing you to your door. You'll call a doctor, right? Damn it, I should have ordered the taxi to take you straight to the hospital."

My fingers tightened on his coat sleeve. If he left now, chances were we'd never see him again. "How would I explain getting shot? It raises too many questions. You're coming inside. I can't take you in the front door—this is a single ladies' residence."

He leaned back as though edging away from a dangerous dog or a crazy person. "The only place I'm going right now is home."

I swayed a little and let my voice grow faint. "Who knows what I'll find when I take my coat off? I can't bandage up my arm myself."

His resulting sigh had enough force to flutter a low curl dangling over his forehead. "You have me there. Very well. I'll meet you at the fire escape."

I waited until he'd ducked into the alley that ran along the building before I climbed the stairs to the front door. The outer door was already locked. With any luck, Mrs. King, the landlady, would be in bed, even though it couldn't be much past ten.

A single lamp glimmered in the foyer, mute testimony to Mrs. King's disapproval of anyone who came in later than she deemed proper. Even so, I tiptoed up the stairs, avoiding the riser that creaked. The last thing I wanted was Mrs. King poking her head out for an unwelcome interrogation.

Once inside my apartment, I dropped my purse on the couch and plucked at the bullet hole in my sleeve, craning my head around to examine my arm. The room spun as I did so.

How odd. I clamped my gloved hand over the ruined material of my coat and the dizziness retreated. When I lifted my fingers to peek at the wound through the cloth, the room swam again. I clamped down over the injury once more. The pain didn't made me woozy, but the sight of my own blood did. I didn't consider myself squeamish, but then again, I'd never faced my own injuries before.

I simply wouldn't look at it. Not until I had Knight's help at any rate. Provided he hadn't run off the moment I turned my back.

With that thought in mind, I gritted my teeth, peeled off my stained gloves, and hurried into the kitchen. A large window there led to the fire escape. When I put my shoulder into it, the sash opened with a wrenching groan. I froze at the sound, listening to see if anyone else in the building had noticed. A minute passed in silence before I pushed against the window frame once more. Thankfully, no one seemed to care. Once the window opened far enough, I crawled out onto the fire escape and looked down over the edge.

Thank God. Knight stood below looking up like a disgruntled Romeo. I'd have to go down to the second floor to drop the ladder where he could reach it. I toed off my heels and clambered down the metal staircase.

In order to prevent anyone from the street accessing the building, the management kept the ladder bridging the final drop to the ground stored in the locked position. The crank stuck at first, and I couldn't get it to budge onehanded, but a hard shove with my foot got it to turn. With a loud screech of metal on metal, the ladder dropped in stages, as if it had the hiccups.

Behind me, the second-floor window opened. My downstairs neighbor stood in a dressing gown observing me. Folding one arm over her chest, she used it to support her elbow as she lifted a cigarette to her lips. The tip glowed bright orange-red in the darkness of her room as she inhaled, and I could make out the ghostly wreath of smoke about her head as she exhaled.

"Well, well. If it isn't our little Miss Goody Two-Shoes."

I didn't know her name. I'm sure she didn't know mine, either. Her platinum blonde hair rivaled Jayne Mansfield's, and she had the voluptuous body to match. We seemed to keep different hours, and I did no more than nod to her on the rare occasions we met in the hallway. I didn't know what I'd done to

merit the sobriquet of "Goody Two-Shoes" unless it was my
expensive, if outdated, wardrobe.

"Pardon me?" I didn't have time to say anything more.
Knight had swarmed up the ladder with astonishing speed and
now stood beside me, slightly out of breath.

My neighbor motioned toward Knight with a flick of ash.
"You. Of all people, you're the last person I'd expect to see. With
him." She gave Knight the once-over, her slow smile showing
her approval.

I opened my mouth to protest, but Knight slid in behind
me to place his hands on my hips as if we were on the dance
floor. He half turned me to face him, pressing me against the
length of his body. Muffling a grunt as the action mashed my
wounded arm between us, I bared my teeth in what I hoped was
a fatuous smile.

"Be a pal, will ya?" Knight leaned forward to beam at my
neighbor. "You won't rat on us?"

The speed with which Knight had assessed the situation
and how he'd chosen the right approach to take with my
somewhat hostile neighbor impressed me. I also itched to slap
him silly.

She kept a cool gaze on us as she continued to blow
smoke rings. At last, she shrugged and spoke, directing her
comment to me. "You owe me."

I nodded, not trusting myself to speak.

"I knew you were a sport the minute I laid eyes on you,"
Knight said, listing a little. He gave her a sloppy grin.

"You're overdoing it," I said out of the corner of my mouth.

"You get tired of Miss High Society, I'll show you a good time." She had the effrontery to wink at Knight.

My smile felt tight when we took our leave of her. My stockinged feet slipped a little on the metal risers I made my way up the iron stairs to my window. Knight, following close behind, put a hand on my bottom, then jerked back as though he'd touched a hot coal.

My back stiffened, and I whipped around on the stairs to pin him with a glare. "Watch where you put your hands, unless you're looking for a knuckle sandwich."

"You mistake my intention." Equal parts embarrassment and offense colored his words. "I thought you might lose your balance."

"Uh-huh. If I had a dime for every time I heard that one. I suppose next you'll tell me you have a bridge in Brooklyn for sale, too?"

That did it. His back was up now. "I don't know what kind of world you live in, Miss Bishop, but a gentleman would never—"

I'm afraid my laugh wasn't very nice. "Oh, please. Gentlemen are the worst. Every secretary I know has been manhandled by a boss or coworker. At least the construction workers on the street rarely do more than catcall. Most gentlemen behave as if they have a God-given right to touch you anytime they feel like it."

I continued up to my landing and crawled through the window. Knight came in behind me, his expression thoughtful. He distanced himself from me as if I had leprosy, which had the perverse effect of annoying me. How was he going to help with my arm from six feet away?

"Please shut the window. I'm freezing." I headed off for the bathroom without looking back.

The stark lighting in the bathroom revealed dark circles under my eyes and a ghost-like pallor that startled me. I eased off my coat, hissing as the frayed material, now caked with dried blood, stuck to my dress and the skin beneath it. I let the coat fall to the floor as I tried looking at the wound through the mirror in the hope an indirect assessment wouldn't make me queasy. No luck. I closed my eyes and gripped the sink with my good hand while I waited for the spinning to stop.

When I opened my eyes again, Knight's face hovered behind mine in the mirror, and I frowned at him.

"You weren't kidding about needing help with that bandage, were you?" His crooked smile disarmed me. "And here I thought you were just trying to prevent me from ducking out on you."

"I'm not normally squeamish. But something about the sight of my own blood...." I cast a glance toward my arm. Blood had soaked through my dress sleeve, and the dark stain had that same draining effect on me as before. I locked onto his reflection instead, using his vivid blue eyes as a focal point for a world whose moorings had come unpinned. What he didn't know about my motives wouldn't hurt him.

"May I?" He indicated my arm.

Miracle of miracles, he was asking for permission to touch me. That was a first for me, and my estimation of him kicked up a notch. I nodded.

I closed my eyes at his cautious, probing touch. It still burned when he lifted the stuck material from the bullet wound, and the way he sucked air through his teeth, combined with the warm seeping told me his action had started my arm bleeding again.

Doubt colored his voice. "Well, now. That's not too bad."

"Liar."

He surprised me with a chuckle. "No, really. We have to get this cleaned up and wrapped, but I don't think you need a doctor after all. It'll leave a scar, though."

"Damn. There goes my career in Hollywood."

"I wasn't trying to get fresh with you on the fire escape." His quiet words distracted me from his examination. "Not on the stairs, and not when we were talking to your neighbor, either. Or in the taxi, for that matter." He winced at the recollection. "I was playing a part. I didn't want the cabbie or your neighbor to see you'd been shot. Like you said, it would have raised questions you didn't want to answer."

I opened my eyes. "Obviously. I'm not stupid. Though I still think you play the part of a drunk a little too well."

Small bloodstains where I'd pressed into him dotted the stark white of his shirt. His shrug seemed almost half-hearted. "It's served me well in the past. Also, it's not always an act."

I met his gaze in the mirror. He'd left his hat in the kitchen, and without it, seemed much younger than before. His eyes locked with mine for a long moment. The room seemed to shrink inward as I became conscious of the heat radiating off his body and the masculine scent of his skin. For several heartbeats this sense of heightened awareness thrummed between us, and my lips parted in response. In the mirror, our pupils dilated in unison as he recognized my proximity as well. Then he dropped his gaze, and just like that, the connection fizzled out as though it had never been there.

"Let's get that arm bandaged up. Then I can be on my way." He pushed the hair out of his eyes and glanced around the bathroom, as though a first aid kit might magically appear.

"You can't go back to your apartment tonight. The people who were waiting for you outside the bar won't give up. You're not safe." I refused to let him out of my sight until I could turn him over to Ryker.

His gaze zeroed back on mine in the mirror. This time his laugh was harsh and without a trace of humor. "I might have known you had other motives for bringing me up here. Am I any safer with you?"

He seemed not to notice the sexual implication of his words nor my blush, for he continued without missing a beat. "Those people, to use the term loosely, might know where my favorite bar is—*you* did—but they intended to take me on the spot. If anyone knew where I lived, they would have grabbed me long ago."

He had a point; one I didn't want to concede. "Wolves," I reminded him. "They sent a pack of *wolves* after you. It's a matter of time before they hunt you down."

"How the devil does someone send wolves after a person?" He moved away to lean on the wall by the sink, one shoulder up against the peeling paper, his hips canted to the side as he crossed his ankles and shoved his hands in his pockets. The same lock of hair fell across his forehead again, glowing gold in the overhead's light. He sounded almost petulant. "And who is this 'they' you're talking about?"

"The people after you, of course." As soon as I'd spoken, I realized that made little sense. Why send gunmen *and* shifters after him? I wasn't thinking straight. "There might have been more than one organization behind this ambush tonight. Who were the people who tried to recruit you before?"

"Didn't you know?" His clipped accent was cold. "The government."

That took me back a bit. "You think the US Government killed your wife and had you blacklisted because you refused to work for a secret division?" Ryker's warning about the government's potential interest in Redclaw matters came to mind, but then why hadn't the dossier on Knight mentioned any of this?

"Yes." The single word could have been chipped from ice.

"I doubt the government sent a pack of wolves after you."
But Redclaw could have. Or if not them, one of the competing
organizations Ryker had mentioned.

"I suspect you're right on that one. Which begs the
question who *can* direct a pack of wolves to attack someone?
And why are you so calm? I have a feeling there's more to this
Redclaw than you're letting on. How about we dress your arm
and then you bring me up to speed?" His mood lightened once
more, altering from frigid bitterness to amused tolerance so fast
it gave me emotional whiplash.

Nodding, I put out a hand to grip the sink as an
unexpected wave of dizziness rolled over me. The edges of the
room turned dark, and I wondered if the overhead bulb was
burning out.

Behind me, the toilet lid clattered shut, and then a firm
grasp on my good arm guided me to sit down. Knight cupped
the back of my head, sliding his hand through my hair to push
me forward. "Bend over. Take a deep breath. I believe you were
about to pass out there. Thank goodness."

"Thank goodness?" My voice quavered as I leaned over
my knees and tried to focus on the black-and-white pattern of
the tiled floor. The squares shimmied at first, but gradually
stopped dancing.

"Yes." Humor laced his voice like warm honey in a
comforting cup of tea. "I'm all for modern women and all that,
but I was beginning to think you weren't entirely human."

What if I'm not?

The thought made me shoot up straight, which was a mistake. The room whirled around in circles and Knight caught me before I fell ignominiously to the floor.

"Careful." He made sure I was sitting upright before releasing my arm and backing away with his fingers splayed as though I were a house of cards that might topple at any moment. As soon as he was confident I was stable, he began rooting around in my medicine cabinet. He held up a tube of wine-red lipstick with a frown and then tossed it back in the cabinet. "Do you have any sort of first aid kit?"

"In the kitchen cabinet by the stove."

I took advantage of his departure in search of the kit to pull myself with care to my feet. No point in attempting to clean up my wound until I was out of the dress. As long as I didn't look at it, I'd be fine, right? Wincing, I undid the buttons one-handed and peeled the dress off my shoulders, letting it fall to the floor. I was reaching for my bathrobe when he came back, kit in hand.

Heaven knows what kind of image I presented, standing there in just a Merry Widow and garters. I gave a little shriek as heat blossomed in my face and I clutched the robe to my throat. Knight gaped at me for what seemed an eternity, went beet-red, and then spun to avert his gaze while at the same time leave the room. The abrupt action caused him to collide with the doorjamb.

"Hellfire and damnation," he muttered, holding his nose. He checked several times to make sure it wasn't bleeding before extending the first aid kit toward me with his gaze fixed on the ceiling. I wasn't able to take it without exposing more skin than I was willing, and I fumbled for the box.

Peeping over his shoulder to see what was taking me so long to accept the kit, he scowled at me. "This is ridiculous. Sit down before you fall down."

I sat, holding the bathrobe up to my chin.

He opened the metal box and rested it on the edge of the sink. "Let me see your arm."

Obediently, I uncovered my arm to allow him access. Tut-tutting a bit, he turned my upper arm over and inspected the wound, and then opened the taps until the water ran hot. "Washcloth? One you don't care about?"

I indicated the small closet behind the tub with a lift of my eyebrows and a nod. He poked around in the closet before holding up a washcloth over his shoulder for my approval. Once I assured him it would do, he held it under the hot water, wrung it out, and began sponging off the dried blood. I stared at the wall, my lips pressed in a tight line.

His ministrations were surprisingly gentle. I fixed my gaze straight ahead, unable to watch as he worked on cleaning my injury, pausing every minute or so to wring out the washcloth and run it under the hot water again.

"Well, that's not so bad." He inspected his handiwork. "A bit of torn flesh. The bleeding made it look worse than it is. More of a burn than anything. You were lucky, you know."

Incapable of forming words, I nodded. The rhythmic stroking of my skin with the warm cloth and the nearness of his body in the close confines of the small room, coupled with my state of undress, robbed me of speech.

"This will sting," he warned, before applying Mercurochrome.

That was an understatement. I'm afraid when the caustic antiseptic touched my wound, I said a word no Bryn Mawr graduate should even know.

Knight found this highly amusing. A faint smile touched his lips as he wrapped my arm in gauze and fixed a bandage in place. "If your downstairs neighbor could hear you now."

He met my gaze and then froze, his eyes going wide with surprise. "You're the Bread Girl."

My skin felt as though sunburned as I realized he'd remembered our first meeting outside the Blue Moon. I tried to pretend ignorance. "The what?"

"The girl. The girl who stopped me from getting run over and then smacked me with a bread roll."

I pulled the bathrobe tighter around my throat and sniffed in my best Miss Climpson fashion. "I did no such thing. I merely offered you one. I hope you didn't waste it. They're quite good."

"Bread be damned. You gave me something else to think about besides myself that day." A light of fanaticism glowed in his eyes, which was embarrassing because I had no recollection of what I'd said to him. I just remembered being annoyed he wasn't grateful to be alive.

I was still thinking of a sharp retort when a sound from the other room made us stare at each other in alarm.

Knight's gesture was peremptory as he marched out of the bathroom. "Wait here."

I had no intention of hiding meekly behind the toilet. I wished I hadn't left my purse—and the ray gun within it—in the kitchen. Nothing to be done about it now. I belted my robe around me and opened the closet. Tucked inside stood the baseball bat every unmarried woman kept in her apartment for just this sort of thing.

When I rushed into the kitchen, Knight stood like a statue facing the window. An eerie glow from the fire escape cast flickering shadows on the ceiling and walls, and for a moment, I thought the building was on fire. Then I caught sight of what held Knight transfixed in the middle of my kitchen.

At the window, a large bird hovered, as big as a man, flapping its wings in a slow, measured beat to keep it airborne. As if the man-sized bird wasn't startling enough, flames engulfed it. An orange-yellow limbus of light emanated off the bird, extending into a halo of blue and lavender fire. It was both beautiful and terrifying. Together we gasped as it landed on the fire escape and approached the window.

Knight slipped his hand in mine and squeezed tight. I squeezed back and hefted the bat.

Chapter Nine

The flaming bird hopped a step closer to the window and cocked its head sideways, as though to get a better look at us through the glass.

"Okay, now I feel like a worm in the presence of a giant chicken." The sourness in Knight's voice made me give a nervous snort, despite the gravity of the situation.

"A giant *flaming* chicken," I reminded him.

He snapped his fingers and said, "I've got it! Not a chicken—a Phoenix!"

That dowsed the humor in both of us.

"This can't be good. First, we're beset by a pack of wolves in the middle of the city, and now a mythological creature is trying to break in the window? We should make a run for it." Knight tugged my arm as he eased a step toward the door. I inched back with him. The Phoenix shook itself in the manner of a big dog and tapped on the window with its beak.

We froze and then exchanged a wary glance.

"I don't think the bad guys would knock, do you?" Knight asked.

"Maybe it's a trap. Maybe he's relying on our innate good manners to open the window and then he'll flame us to death."

The Phoenix gave a heavy sigh and then the flames went
out. The body of the bird shimmered and changed into a man. A
naked man. One I recognized.

My boss.

"Good heavens!" I exclaimed, rushing toward the window
to open it.

"Thank you." Ryker's voice was crisp as he climbed in
from the fire escape. "It's chilly out here."

I tried to look anywhere except at him when he climbed
into my apartment.

Ryker pulled the sash down behind him and
straightened, undaunted by his naked state. "Bishop," he said in
a voice still etched with frost. "I take it this is Dr. Knight?"

Knight turned incredulous eyes on me.

"You *know* the flaming chi—I mean, this man?"

"He's my boss," I said in a small voice. "Ryker. Er, Mr.
Ryker. Head of Redclaw Security." I stared off to the left of
Ryker's bare shoulder. "May I present Dr. Knight?"

"Charmed, I'm sure." Knight's voice dripped with
sarcasm. "Let me guess—you have to shed your clothes when
you change into a Phoenix so they won't go up in flames."

"Among other reasons." Ryker fixed a cool stare on me. "I
think some explanations are in order, Miss Bishop."

I winced at the resurrection of the "Miss" when
addressing me. If that wasn't bad enough, the way I was
dressed, Ryker could leap to the wrong conclusion as to why I'd
brought Knight back to my apartment. "Um, just a minute."

I bolted for my bedroom, where I pulled on a cheap housedress and returned to the kitchen. Ryker and Knight stood squared off like two alley cats unwilling to back down enough to let the other pass. Unable to meet Ryker's eye, I held out my bathrobe while keeping my eyes averted. "Sir. If you don't mind...?"

Ryker snatched the proffered robe from my hand with poor grace. It was too short, but at least I could look at him without blushing now.

"How did you know to find us here, sir?"

He finished belting the robe and folded his arms across his chest. "Imagine my surprise when reports came in of shots fired and a pack of wolves roaming the streets outside the Moneta Bar and Grill this evening. Someone reported a woman matching your description fleeing the scene with a man, which is how I knew to seek you here at your apartment. Since you've been out of the office pursuing a lead that ended in an attack, it seemed possible you'd discovered Dr. Knight's whereabouts and yet failed to share that information. Would you care to explain?"

I did my best, recounting my impression that I'd run into Knight on the street toward the day of my Redclaw interview, and the steps I'd taken to track him down. I felt Knight's eyes boring holes into me as I glossed over that first encounter, and then again when I fudged over the details of getting Knight to agree to come with me this evening. No doubt, Knight was steamed over the realization I hadn't been completely forthcoming about who and what Redclaw served. I left out the bit about getting shot—and using the ray gun in defense—when describing the attack and our escape.

"So you mean to tell me you knew where Dr. Knight would be this evening, and yet you took it upon yourself to not only approach him, but to bring him in without telling anyone else? With no backup of any kind?" Ryker's arms fell to his sides and his nostrils flared in mounting anger. The action was rendered ridiculous by his wearing a frilly bathrobe, but any thoughts of smiling withered and died. Bitter bile rose in my throat and I swallowed hard.

"You asked me to find him. I did." I didn't understand why he was so mad with me. I got results, didn't I?

"You didn't think she'd find me!" Knight's sudden contribution to the conversation caught us both off-guard. "You promoted her to field agent, and told her to find me, but you didn't actually think she would, did you?"

"I thought she'd have the good sense to report your location to someone with a little more experience in the matter." Ryker fixed me in his glare once more. "Why didn't you use the pin I gave you to call for assistance?"

The pin. I'd forgotten about the ladybug pin. I'd attached it to the inside of my clutch, thinking I'd have it if needed, and then, like an idiot, forgot it even existed.

"Everything happened so fast." Even though I was telling the truth, my excuses sounded weak to my ears. "The attacks happened as we left the bar. First, by armed men in a car, and then by the, er, wolves."

"Yes, and if it hadn't been for Miss Bishop here, I'd be an unwilling captive or dinner for the dogs. They were waiting for me—the men with guns, that is. No doubt relying on my known habit of frequenting that bar and taking ruthless advantage of my history. Miss Bishop got shot protecting me, you know."

Too late, Knight caught sight of the chopping motion I made with my hand.

"What? You *did* get injured in the line of duty tonight. He saw the bandage before you covered it up." Knight thrust his chin forward belligerently.

"Are you all right?" Ryker lifted an eyebrow in my direction.

I nodded, not trusting myself to speak.

"Well, if that's the level of concern you have for your employees, I'm not certain I want to work for you." Knight folded his arms over his chest in an insulting manner. "What's got your knickers in such a twist, anyway?"

"Knight," I cautioned, shooting him a small frown.

"Am I supposed to be frightened because he can morph into a giant self-combusting bird that might turn me into a charred cinder? In the last hour a secret organization has offered me a job, someone tried to kidnap me, I watched a little slip of a girl coolly drop a man in the alley with Buck Rogers' blaster, and I got chased by what is, in all probability, a pack of supernatural wolves." He wiped a hand over his mouth, looking somewhat dazed. "Really, I don't think I've had enough to drink tonight."

"You took the ray gun out of the office?" Ryker's head snapped in my direction before he closed his eyes and pinched the bridge of his nose as if he were counting to ten. When he opened his eyes again, I saw little flames banked within. "I thought I made it clear to you Redclaw's purpose and the nature of our mission. What possessed you to remove a dangerous artifact from storage and take it back out on the streets with you? Really, Miss Bishop, I am most disappointed."

"Am I fired?" I blurted out.

Ryker inhaled sharply. "I don't know. It seems I made a serious mistake in sharing confidential information and technology with you. This is a grievous strike against your record."

"Did you forbid her to remove the weapon from your place of business?" Knight asked in a deceptively mild tone.

Scowling, Ryker stared at him a long moment before speaking. "No."

"So let me get this straight. You didn't give her exact parameters for finding me and bringing me in, and after showing her this advanced technology, you never explicitly said she couldn't use it. In other words, you left her to wing it. Under those circumstances, I think she did quite well, don't you?"

I wheeled on Knight. "I don't need you to fight my battles for me."

He took a step sideways, hands up in the air in a gesture of peace. "Given the way you took out the men attacking us this evening, I'd heartily agree with that sentiment."

Ryker narrowed his eyes at Knight and then flicked a glance in my direction. For a moment he had the oddest expression on his face, and then he wiped it away, to replace it with furrowed brows and stern authority. "It's late and none of us are at our best at the moment. Dr. Knight, I've arranged for someone to meet you downstairs and take you to a safe place overnight. I'll wait with you until they arrive. Bishop, I want to see you in my office in the morning."

Knight gave an audible sniff. "I'm not so sure I want to go with you people if this is the way you run your organization."

"I assure you, the mistakes Bishop made—"

"As far as I can tell, she's the only one who did anything right." Knight cut Ryker off with a dismissive gesture that caused Ryker to raise an eyebrow in response. "And rest assured, she didn't give any of your secrets away. *You* did that when you appeared on the fire escape. So tell me, why should I leave with you and go to work for this Redclaw?"

Ryker frowned, though at Knight's attitude or question I couldn't tell. "What did Bishop say to persuade you to come with her?"

"That's between me and Bishop." Knight had the effrontery to wink at me. "I'm asking you. Why should I come work for you?"

"You may have noticed there are several groups interested in your services." Ryker's manner was as stiff as a poker.

"If we're assuming the people who came after me tonight aren't the same ones who tried to recruit me two years ago, and if the—and I can't believe I'm saying this—*wolves* who chased us belong to an unknown third party, then yes. Your statement is correct."

"Then it should be obvious to a man of your intelligence you're in danger. Redclaw can protect you, among other things. But equally important, we need you. Though I hadn't intended to demonstrate the fact in quite such a fashion, you've seen the ray gun. We're collecting and cataloging such technology every day. We need someone of your background to help us understand how this tech works and what its ultimate purpose might be."

"The appeal to my vanity is a nice touch." Knight cocked his head sideways. "But I daresay this technology is beyond anything I've ever worked on."

Ryker's posture relaxed. "It's beyond everyone's experience. That's why we need someone like you. What did Bishop tell you?"

Knight shot a quick glance in my direction. I gave a little shrug.

"She said you—that is, Redclaw—find things. You're some sort of secret investigative firm."

"I never said it was a secret organization. You're the one who leapt to that conclusion."

The look Knight gave me was one of profound pity for my stunted intellect. "My dear, you didn't have to spell it out. I knew the moment you sat down. Besides, your boss turns into a flaming chicken."

"Not a chicken." Ryker was indignant. "I'll have you know—"

Knight cut him off with an upraised hand. "Yes, yes. You change into some kind of mythological beast. No doubt from a proud and distinguished family of the same. My point being, nothing about this evening has been what you would call normal. I'm still not convinced I won't discover in the morning this is all the result of too much bad whiskey." He rubbed his temples. "However calmly I seem to be taking this situation, know it results from my astounding intelligence and the desensitizing power of overindulgence."

"Keep overindulging and soon your intellectual capacity will be on par with the rest of us mere mortals." I'd had enough. "If you don't go with Ryker, I doubt you'll last twenty-four hours on your own. It's your funeral." I turned toward my boss. "You'll have my full report in the morning. I'm making myself a cup of coffee. You may both leave now."

The two men gaped at me in astonishment, as though a cocker spaniel had spoken a coherent sentence. Ignoring them, I crossed to the counter and filled the percolator with coffee. My actions were mechanical, working in the low lighting by feel and habit. I dumped coffee granules into the pot with a little more force than usual and then flung the measuring spoon into the sink with a clatter. My unwelcome guests seemed to take the hint.

"As I said earlier, we should shelve this discussion for the evening. Are you coming with me or not, Dr. Knight?"

No doubt Knight attempted to burn holes in my back with his glare, but I refused to turn around, instead busying myself by taking a cup and saucer out of the cabinet. Hopefully, neither man noticed the tremor in my hands. My injured arm started to throb, pounding with every heartbeat.

"Bishop has pointed out I shouldn't go back to my apartment." Knight spoke as though considering his options aloud. I doubt he even noticed he'd adopted Ryker's name for me. "But I don't trust you."

I turned at this.

Knight pointed at me with an index finger. "Her, I trust." He met Ryker's gaze head on. "Not you. I don't know you."

"Oh, for heaven's sake." I started to place my fists on my hips, but the action woke the sleeping dragon of pain, and I hastily dropped my arms to my sides. "I trust Ryker, even if you don't. If you trust me, then you should trust him. Just go, will you?" To my horror, my voice broke on the final words. I would *not* burst into tears in front of either of them.

"Are you going to be all right?" The concern in Knight's voice almost undid me. The last thing I wanted was sympathy right then. I gave a short, sharp nod instead of replying.

Ryker went to the window and lifted the sash. Sweeping one arm with a mocking flourish in front of him, he said, "Dr. Knight?"

Knight heaved a much put-upon sigh. "Very well. It's clear you need someone of my intelligence in your research and design department." He joined Ryker at the window.

"What do you mean by that?" Ryker asked as Knight climbed out onto the fire escape.

"If you had someone with their wits about them working for you, someone would have solved this 'I can't change form without running around naked' problem long ago. Not that it seems to bother you. Still, it can't be convenient to wind up miles away from your clothing."

"I see." Ryker seemed to recall he was wearing my bathrobe and started to take it off.

I shook my head vehemently. "Keep it."

"My office." Ryker reminded me as he crawled out the window, the robe parting to show a greater degree of bare leg than I was comfortable seeing of my employer. "First thing in the morning."

After he closed the window, I crossed to the sash and locked it. At least he didn't take the ray gun, which I sensed hiding in my clutch on the counter. Its presence was small comfort. I had a terrible feeling that ordinary bullets wouldn't stop the kinds of people who'd attacked us this evening. Worse, I'd hung a big bull's eye on my back with some pretty nasty customers.

Now that Ryker and Knight had left, I unplugged the percolator. Coffee wasn't what I wanted or needed just now. I wanted to punch things. Ladies weren't supposed to get angry.

We were supposed to swallow our emotions like bitter medicine and smile no matter the provocation. To pretend nothing bothered us.

The hell with that.

The coffee mug shattered against the far wall with a satisfying crash. *That* made me smile.

I'd angered my boss. Okay, so I'd taken a weapon out of the office without authorization, and had proceeded on my merry way to hunt down Knight without updating anyone as to my progress or plans. Ryker had even provided the means to call for help and I'd forgotten to use it until it was too late. But despite that, we'd successfully fought off three attackers and a wolf pack. Not too shabby for a socialite and a scientist. And if I hadn't taken the ray gun, I'd be dead and the attackers would have taken Knight prisoner.

Who did Knight think he was anyway, jumping to my defense like that, as if I couldn't speak for myself? As if I were incapable of standing up to Ryker. Knight had taken the words right out of my mouth, spiking my guns and leaving me with no argument of my own. Anything I'd added at that point would have sounded like I was parroting him.

I gave one of the kitchen chairs a hard shove. The cheap wooden chair knocked up against the table, sending both scudding across the floor. Moments later, my downstairs neighbor thumped her ceiling in the age-old signal for me to keep it down. I envisioned her, cigarette hanging from her lips, rapping the ceiling with a broom handle.

I took a deep breath. Yes, by all means, keep it down. Hold it in, smile even though your stomach boils with acid at the effort.

Banging open the cabinet containing my cleaning supplies, I took out the dustpan and a small broom. Kneeling to sweep up the glass shards, my mind replayed the events of the evening. Had the wolf pack and the attackers been working together or were they in competition to kidnap Knight? And were either of them associated with the group that had tried to recruit him before—and killed his wife in retaliation? There was no way to know.

I knew one thing, however. Whoever was behind the kidnapping attempt wouldn't stop now.

Chapter Ten

I don't see the point in self-pity. I've never seen it change anyone's circumstances. Also, crying in bed gets you nothing but tears in your ears. Exhausted, wired from the adrenaline-fueled events of the evening, and my arm throbbing, I admit, I was tempted to sit down with the carton of Borden's ice cream tucked away in my freezer and have a good cry. I settled for the ice cream alone. Certain I'd never fall asleep before dawn, I surprised myself by dropping off as soon as my head hit the pillow.

So when the banging of the radiator woke me before dawn, I got up, fortified myself with a pot of coffee, and drafted out my report on Dr. Peter Knight on a legal pad. By the time the sun sent dull red streaks across a leaden sky, I'd written out everything that had happened over the last three days leading up to my locating—and recruiting—Knight.

Satisfied, I pulled out my most authoritative outfit from the closet: a rather severe short-sleeved black dress with a narrow waist, done up with a double row of large black buttons reminiscent of a porter's uniform. Knight's bandaging job was still intact. Good. Let Ryker see visible proof of the risks I'd taken while I stated my case to him this morning.

My decent wool coat was a dead loss. I doubted my tailor could weave a patch over the damage, never mind how to explain how the bullet hole got there in the first place. Fortunately, I'd indulged myself with an impulse buy the previous month when the dreary weather had been getting me down. As an everyday coat, it was impractical for wear in the grimy city, being a deep red with laces in the back that cinched the waist to a ridiculous degree, emphasizing the wide bell-shaped bottom. Trimmed with fake black fur, the buttonholes were lined with an intricate black braid that crossed the front of the coat in a pleasing pattern, much like train tracks. It also had an enormous hood, though I preferred to wear a black conductor's cap instead. Paired with long black gloves, I looked like a Russian princess.

Practicality be damned. I felt like a million dollars.

I strode into the office with a matter-of-fact air and went straight to the coat rack, stripping off coat, hat, and gloves and arranging everything on the hook, careful of my injured arm. Then I took my seat at my desk, and with my good hand, whipped off the cover to my typewriter. I slapped the legal pad down beside it and jammed a sheet of paper in the machine. Typing proved not to be too painful, so I banged the keys with such fury they often locked, and paid no attention to the curious stares of first, Miss Climpson and Mr. J, and then, later, Russo when he dropped in with a delivery. As I finished each page, I pulled it out with a whirr of the roller and smacked it down in my outbox, to repeat the process again with the next. I was finishing the final page when the intercom buzzed.

I looked up when Miss Climpson cleared her throat. "Mr. Ryker will see you in his office now."

"Good." I stood and collated my typed report, tapping the papers on the edge of the desk until they lined up. "I'm ready to see him myself."

I marched out of the reception area and down the hallway, report in one hand and my purse tucked under the other arm. Giving the door to Ryker's office a sharp couple of raps, I waited until I heard his voice directing me to enter before doing so.

I walked straight up to his desk and placed the report in front of him.

His tone was brusque. "What's this?"

"The summation of my activities since you tasked me with locating Dr. Knight. Which I did, by the way. Something no one else had managed. Moreover, I convinced him to come speak with you. A good thing, since there were at least one, perhaps two, groups of people determined on taking him away with them last night. I don't think they cared whether he was alive or dead, either."

I remained standing, holding my purse in front of me with both hands like a tiny shield.

He met my eyes then, and I saw the same hint of banked fires within, an anger fighting for release.

He could rage all he wanted. I couldn't back down. I *wouldn't* back down.

"You informed me of your intentions to offer him a job within the agency. You tasked me with finding him. You said it might be dangerous and to call for help if needed." I lifted my chin. "I didn't need any help."

He opened his mouth, but I cut him off with a raised hand.

"I'm not finished. I had a very slim opportunity to get Knight on board before losing him, and I took it. You hired me because you liked my initiative. Well, I used it last night. I had every intention of calling Redclaw once we reached my apartment, but I realized I had no direct way of contacting you short of activating the signal pin. That needs to be rectified."

Ryker placed both hands, palm down, on the surface of his desk. "May I speak now?" His voice glittered with anger. I suspected, as a rule, no one spoke to him like this.

I gave him a stiff nod.

He inhaled sharply through his nostrils, but when he spoke, his voice was calmer. "When I assigned you the task of locating Knight, it was not, as he'd suggested, a deliberate attempt to see you fail or give you busy-work. I meant it to be a desk assignment based on research, a starter case, if you will. And it never hurts to have a fresh set of eyes on a problem. Miss Climpson tells me you had a lead from the beginning. Why didn't you inform me?"

I felt my cheeks burn, this time from embarrassment. "I wasn't sure it would pan out. There was only a slight chance it would."

"Nevertheless, had you done so, we could have placed other agents in the area, and perhaps avoided the fracas last night. For there to be shifters out there in the open, attacking people in the streets...."

I winced. "That wasn't *entirely* my fault. It never occurred to me that anyone would send shifters after us. I've been thinking about that. They couldn't have been part of the original attackers. They must have been a competing group of some sort. Of course, we don't know if their intent was to help or harm."

"True." He drummed the fingers of his right hand on the smooth desktop. "But we could have minimized the risks had we known your plans. You also took a lethal weapon out of the collection. We must keep a low profile. Your actions jeopardized that."

"The wolf-shifters didn't seem concerned about secrecy. Someone had every intention of taking Knight with them last night, even if it meant shooting me." I touched the stark white bandage on my arm. "If I'd used the Browning instead, the police might have gotten involved. No one died last night, and the people with the greatest cause for complaint are the least likely to do so." As my father liked to say, thieves didn't call the cops if they stepped in a bear trap while breaking into your property.

Ryker rocked back in his chair and passed a palm over his weary face. When he looked up at me, his manner was less angry and more resigned. "Tell me everything that happened.

You gave me a brief update last night, but I want to know everything that has happened since I gave you this assignment."

I motioned to the report on his desk, but he waved me off. "I'll read it later. Right now, I want to hear your firsthand account."

He listened without interrupting until I got to the part where I convinced Knight to come with me.

"How did you persuade him to come?"

That was one question I hadn't anticipated, though with hindsight, I should have. "I might have suggested by working with us, we could figure out who killed his wife."

Ryker blew air through his lips in an annoyed little huff. "Did you think that through? We looked into Margo Knight's death before we decided to make Knight an offer to come on board. There's nothing to indicate that her death was anything other than an accident. What do you think will happen when Knight realizes you lied to him to get him to agree to work with Redclaw?"

It hadn't occurred to me that Knight might be delusional about his wife's death. "He seemed adamant not only had someone run her down, but that Margo's murder was in retaliation for his refusal to work for some shady organization which had approached him."

"How would that have benefited said organization? I could see where the *threat* of harming his wife might make him compliant, but killing her? No one wins."

I said nothing. Knight might not have wound up working for the group who'd approached him, but after Margo died, he hadn't worked for anyone else, either.

Ryker looked as though he expected me to add something in my defense. When I didn't, his lips tightened. "So far, we have you acting on your own without support both in approaching Knight and making him an offer we can't deliver. Anything else you'd like to add?"

Resisting the urge to curl up in a little ball under the weight of his withering stare, I detailed the rest of the evening, pausing whenever I needed to answer Ryker's questions about the various people who'd attacked us, finishing up with his own arrival at my apartment. My face burned at the memory of his naked state in my kitchen and said, "You know the rest, sir."

When I finished, he sat in silence for a moment, flipping a pen through his fingers as he rocked back and forth in his chair. "Tell me, Bishop. Why did you take the gun? I told you one of Redclaw's main functions was to get such objects off the streets."

I hesitated. Of all the things I'd done, stealing the ray gun was the most indefensible. "Sir, I can't explain my actions. I wish I could." I turned both palms upward with a helpless shrug. "It's like the gun bewitched me. I found myself thinking it would be just the thing. With the stun feature, I could defend myself without hurting anyone, and no one would be the wiser. I'd like to tell you I considered the risks of using such a weapon in public. Or that I assumed no one would believe a witness blathering about ray guns that shot paralyzing beams. I never got that far. I simply wanted the gun. I had to have it."

"I'm afraid that argument won't hold water with me. You sound like a jewel thief speaking of a ring so beautiful he felt compelled to take it." Frowning, Ryker held out his hand. "I should like to have the gun back, please."

With inexplicable reluctance, I opened the clasp and attempted to fish the gun out of my bag. Wedged in the bottom of the clutch, it resisted all efforts to extract it, like a cat bracing its feet against the walls of a carrier it didn't want to exit. I shot Ryker a feeble smile and tugged harder, tearing the interior lining in the process of pulling out the gun. As I handed the gun over, it slipped through my fingers and flew into my lap. For some reason, I couldn't get purchase on the slick barrel, and it flipped around like a fish on a boat dock.

I looked up, ready to apologize for my clumsiness, when I saw Ryker staring at me with both eyebrows raised.

"A moment, if you will." He stood up and came around to my chair. "If I may?"

I rested both hands on the sides of the chair and leaned back so he had clear access to my lap.

He reached for the gun. It slithered away from him, and I clapped my knees together to keep the little gun from escaping my lap and landing on the floor.

"Fascinating." He gave the gun a narrow-eyed glare before meeting my embarrassed gaze.

"I'm not doing this." I tipped my head at the gun which seemed to have stopped moving for the moment.

"I didn't think you were. I wonder—" He made a sudden grab for the weapon. A crackle of blue-green energy erupted in a tiny lightning bolt and struck his hand. He jerked it back with a yelp. I started to my feet, and the gun tumbled to the floor, sliding up under his desk.

I gaped at Ryker, who stood shaking his hand. He inspected his fingers before meeting my eye. "Apparently, it doesn't like me. If you would corral your weapon, please?"

I dropped to my knees and peered under the desk. The gun was on the far side, and to my eyes, it seemed to be quivering. It skittered farther out of reach when I put out my hand. "Come on," I crooned. "No one will hurt you."

Though I'd spoken to it as though it were a frightened colt, I honestly didn't think it would respond. Surely, all its previous actions were because of built-up energy of some sort. So my eyebrow lifted and my lips formed a little O of surprise when the gun crept toward me across the carpet. It slid into my grip, and I stood to stare at it in bemusement.

"It came to me." I offered it out to Ryker, holding it with firmness this time.

"I suspect it's yours now." Ryker's voice was as dry as the Sahara and almost as forbidding. It startled me when he continued speaking as though to an unseen party. "Should I allow Bishop to keep the ray gun?"

He pointed to the 8 Ball on his desk. "Pick it up."

I turned the black ball over until the printed words floated up to the surface of the bottom chamber. "The stars are in alignment," I read.

With a heavy sigh, Ryker returned to his chair, but he remained standing behind his desk. "It would seem the weapon has imprinted on you. For the time being, I'll allow you to keep it."

Seeing as he couldn't take it away, this seemed like a wise decision. I gave the 8 Ball a wary glance before speaking. "I'm not fired, then?"

"No. But you're on probation while I rethink your position here at Redclaw. You're on desk duty again for the time being, and I want you to report for that testing we discussed last week. Dr. Botha has been delayed but he will arrive in the country soon. Your affinity for this particular weapon—and it for you—suggests my theory about recessive genes may be correct. Hopefully, the tests will confirm that. In the meantime, you'll get your assignments from Miss Climpson, as before."

"I should still have your phone number."

"You won't need it. You'll be staying in the office until further notice." His response was crushingly dry.

"And no one has ever needed to reach you urgently—say, in the event of a breach in office security?"

The firm press of his lips implied he either didn't like my attitude or the reminder of the previous attempted break-in, but he wrote his personal number on the back of one his cards in bold, sharp strokes and held it out to me.

I committed the number to memory as I waved the card, waiting for the ink to dry before tucking into my bag.

"That will be all, Bishop."

I took the reversion to the use of my last name as a good sign. At least, I hoped it was.

It wasn't easy going back to my desk and meekly settling down to the kind of work I'd been doing before the promotion. I wanted to ask how Knight was faring, but wasn't sure anyone would tell me. I saw no sign of him, which made me wonder if they had him sequestered somewhere off the premises or if he was holed up in the bowels of the building. I did the assigned work as fast as I could and wondered what Dr. Botha's testing would reveal. Would one jolt from a radioactive substance turn me into a creature from a B-rated science fiction movie? It seemed prudent to avoid such exposure just in case, and I made a note to research the possibility of purchasing a Geiger counter for personal use.

When a case involving the disappearance of a young woman—reading between the lines, presumably because of the activation of her shifter genes—came across my desk for typing, I requested leave to go to the library and check out back issues of newspapers, looking for anything that might support the case. Miss Climpson scanned me with suspicious eyes as I stood in front of her desk with my request, but when her phone rang, she waved me off and turned her attention to the caller.

Relieved, I donned my red coat and made my escape. The bus ride took longer than I'd hoped, so I skipped lunch and headed straight for the library reading room. After exhausting what limited information I could uncover about the missing woman, I delved into the older files surrounding the death of Margo Knight. The hit-and-run had made the local papers at the time, but without any leads, the story soon died. Since I was already there, I searched for any reference to mysterious occurrences, local or otherwise. The number of stories was overwhelming, though most were published in disreputable newspapers. Still, the sheer variety of conspiracy theories, sightings, and descriptions of strange 'man-beasts' was enough to give one pause. There were more shifters out there than I dreamed possible, though I had to wonder how many of the 'reports' were fake plants to discredit the real stories.

So absorbed, I allowed far too many hours to pass before I decided I would not find anything useful to help me with Margo's death. My stomach growling, I popped into a small deli to purchase a sandwich for the ride home when I spotted a police officer walking along the street. Realizing I wasn't all that far from the precinct that should have investigated Margo's death, I grabbed my sandwich and bolted to catch the next bus.

I was doomed to disappointment, however. After waiting an interminable time in the police station, observing the interactions of the colorful personages there, a uniformed officer informed me the detective who had covered the case was not in.

"Please have him contact me at his soonest convenience." I handed the officer my card with great dignity.

He flicked a glance from the top of my smart black hat to the bottom of my red coat and back up again before reading the card. "Redclaw Security, eh? What's that? Some kind of insurance company?"

"Of a sort," I replied.

"Right you are, Miss Climpson. I'll inform Detective Horowitz you wish to speak with him."

"Thank you." I'd crossed out the agency phone number and penned in my own when I'd swiped the card from Climmy's desk earlier that day. I hoped the detective would call the number I'd provided instead of Redclaw itself. To hedge my bet in case he did, I added with authority, "Be sure to ask for my assistant, Miss Bishop."

Chapter Eleven

To my surprise, just after nine p.m. a peremptory rap sounded at my door. Sliding the ray gun into the pocket of my silk kimono, where it lay like the inert object it was meant to be, I opened the door and peeked out from behind the chain.

A disapproving Mrs. King stood in the hallway. "Telephone call for you downstairs. It's the police."

The way she emphasized the word *police* implied not only had I done something to warrant the attention of the authorities, but that she'd known it was just a matter of time.

I let my brow clear before responding. "Oh, good. It must be about my missing purse. I'll be right down, thank you."

I closed the door before she could say anything else and grabbed my slippers. Though I wanted to hurry down the stairs, I took my time so I would neither appear too anxious nor catch up with Mrs. King.

Just the same, she watched from the entrance to her apartment when I entered the little cubicle for the phone. I gave her a bright smile and pulled the folding door to the compartment shut.

"This is Miss Bishop," I said in clipped tones, inserting a degree of supercilious efficiency into my voice.

"Detective Horowitz, ma'am. My sergeant said you stopped by this afternoon?" The man sounded bored or perhaps tired. Given the unusual hour, I bet on tired.

"That was Miss Climpson. I'm her assistant."

I heard papers being shuffled in the background, and then the detective spoke again. "Right you are. Sorry to disturb you this late, but I've been out of the station all day. I believe Miss Climpson was seeking additional information regarding the Knight hit-and-run?"

"Yes. Has there been any further development in the case?" I was reasonably sure no one could overhear my conversation even if I'd seen anyone lingering about, but I lowered my voice just the same.

"May I ask what your interest in the matter is?"

I detected a hint of wariness in his voice, so I trotted out the cover story I'd drafted on my way home. "I don't know all the details myself, but it appears there's an insurance policy after all. My employers are following up."

"Well, good luck with that. No new leads. It's a cold case."

I thought for a moment, then added, "So you don't suspect Dr. Knight himself?"

"The husband is the primary suspect if we believe there's foul play. We don't. Unlucky accident. Besides, the guy was pretty cut up about it. Drove us nuts for a long time, then disappeared. I hear he lost his job too. How much was the policy for?"

"Five hundred dollars. It was meant to cover funeral expenses."

Horowitz gave an audible sniff. "Hardly worth killing somebody for. Even if he wanted to get rid of his wife, which by all accounts, Knight did not."

"Well, I'm sure that's all my employer needs to know." I spoke briskly, hoping to sound like someone doing her job and somewhat annoyed at being bothered on her down time. "So they ruled it an accidental death and there's no current investigation?"

"Your employer is the first person other than Knight who's shown any interest in the last couple of years."

A dead end. Still, it wouldn't hurt to see the actual police report for myself. "I would appreciate it if you could send a copy of the report to our office. Mark it to my attention, please." I gave him the address. "Thank you for your time. Please contact me if anything changes."

He gave a soft laugh. "Sure, though it won't. But it's your dime."

I tried not to be disappointed as I disconnected the call. I'd hoped speaking with the detective would provide some shred of evidence that the hit-and-run was a deliberate attempt at murder. Perhaps it was just an accident, as Detective Horowitz said. That didn't mean I couldn't keep looking—someone who ran down a woman with his car still deserved jail time—but it didn't seem possible I would identify said person after all this time. After all, the police hadn't.

The first time I'd met Knight, he'd almost walked in front of a taxi. Having been there on the spot, I could honestly say he hadn't been paying attention. Had that been the case with Margo too?

Memory of promising Knight something I couldn't deliver made me squirm a bit in the telephone seat.

With a sigh, I pushed open the folding panels to the phone booth and headed back upstairs, noting the way Mrs. King's door closed with a click as I passed. If she'd been a witness of Margo Knight's death, the driver of the car would be in jail already.

Back in my apartment, I rolled my hair up in curlers, not an easy task when I couldn't raise my left arm as high as I'd like. Though it no longer throbbed, it was abominably sore. An early night with a good book was what I needed after the excitement and drama of the last twenty-four hours. Unfortunately, I couldn't get into the Nero Wolfe novel I'd selected, and was rummaging through my bookshelves for something more engaging when I heard a noise coming from the kitchen.

The ray gun lay on the coffee table where I'd placed it on returning to the apartment. It had been suspiciously quiet after its antics in Ryker's office earlier, almost as if it wanted me to forget its presence, but now it seemed to slide into my hand as I picked it up and crept up to the entrance of the kitchen. The light there was off, and I didn't turn it on, not wanting to alert anyone to my presence.

The sound repeated, a combination of a scratch and a tap. I peered around the doorjamb. Despite steeling myself for a possible intruder, I still jumped at the sight of Knight standing on the fire escape.

He ducked his head and waggled his fingers, as though he'd arrived late for a party and forgotten his invitation.

I hurried to the window, unlocked it, and wrenched it upward. Thanks to an earlier application of silicon spray, the window opened with ease. "What are you doing here?"

Knight climbed across the sill without waiting for me to invite him in. "What do you think I'm doing here? I didn't see you at Redclaw today." His fedora rode the back of his head, and he made a striking picture as he stood there in the kitchen, fists on his hips as he stared at me. "How's the arm?"

There was no point in dashing for a kerchief to cover my curlers. It was obvious I'd taken my makeup off, and there was no way to disguise the current state of my hair. Flustered, I dropped the gun in my pocket and retied the belt to my robe. "Healing. Sore. You must have been in the lab section. I didn't go down there today. I had an interview with Ryker, and then I left to do some research."

He leaned against my counter, the barest hint of a smirk lurking around his lips as he crossed his legs at the ankles. The movement drew my eye to the long length of his legs, and the sharp crease of his trousers down the center of his pants. Who was pressing his laundry? For someone who'd let his life fall

apart, Knight was a natty dresser. "So I gathered, when I spoke
with Detective Horowitz."

"How could he know how to find you? No one knew
where you were."

His shoulders moved up and down. "I always call him
around this time of year."

Around the anniversary of his wife's death. Right.

"Well, then you know I'm attempting to uphold my end
of the deal."

"The answers aren't out there. The man responsible for
Margo's death will never turn up, nor will you find any evidence
leading back to him. I'm more interested in the *forces* behind
her death."

"You mean the government." I wasn't so sure myself, but
then I'd never worked for the government the way Knight had.

He tapped the side of his nose. "Bingo."

I suppressed a smile at his theatrical response. "That
might be difficult to prove."

He pushed himself upright. Plucking his hat from his
head, he chucked it toward the counter where it landed with a
skid. "You're the one who made the promises, not me. Have you
got anything to eat?"

His abrupt change of subject startled me. "What? No.
And you never answered my question. Why are you here? How
did you get up the fire escape?" It was my turn to place my fists
on my hips and glare as he began opening and closing my
cabinets.

He flicked a quick glance at me over his shoulder on his way to the refrigerator. Standing in front of the open door, he peered inside. The glow from the interior light caught his puckish expression as he raided the contents of the fridge. "I already told you. I didn't see you today, and I wasn't sure if you'd been canned or not. If so, I wasn't inclined to stick around, cool toys or not. When do you go shopping next? You're almost out of everything."

Wrinkling his nose over the bottle of milk, he put it back and selected the egg carton instead. Without asking, he rummaged around beneath the stove and pulled out a frying pan. The gas whooshed to life as he turned on the burner and then adjusted it to a low flame. The nimble way he cracked several eggs into a bowl one-handed spoke of his skill in the kitchen, one that far exceeded my own.

"Being rather generous with my butter, there, aren't you?" I watched as he cut healthy portions from the slab and tapped the knife against the pan.

"Got any tomatoes?" He was back at the fridge to replace the eggs. "Ooooh. Ham. And a bit of cheese, too." He removed the plate of food I'd been saving and set it on the counter.

"That's for my lunch this week."

My protests were in vain.

"What, this? Not enough to make a decent sandwich. But perfect for an omelet." He chopped the meat into bite-sized pieces with brisk authority and whisked both meat and cheese into the eggs. Within seconds, he was stirring the mixture into the hot pan, and a delicious odor filled the air. "It will be ready in a jiff. I'll split it with you."

"I'm not eating this late at night. I'll never get to sleep."

My stomach gurgled embarrassingly loud in the quiet apartment. He lifted a sardonic eyebrow in my direction. "Really? Then you're doing it wrong. Food, drink, mindless hours of imbecilic entertainment—those are the things you need for true oblivion. Mark my words: ten years from now, virtually every home in America will have a television, and we'll all be slaves to it. Pity they stop programing at eleven p.m. Just think, if they aired television shows all night long, a whole generation of insomniacs would find some sort of bleary-eyed peace."

"Are you an insomniac?"

He flipped the omelet with expertise, poking it gently with the spatula as it sizzled in the butter. "Often." Deftly, he changed the subject. "Say, why does everyone at Redclaw call the boss 'Ryker'? Do you think that's his first or last name? Or does he just go by one name only, like that flamboyant piano player? Whatshisname. Liberace."

The mouthwatering aroma of frying food won me over. Sighing, I went to the cabinet and took down two plates, then opened the drawer beside the stove to collect silverware. "I don't know. Why don't you ask Ryker that the next time you see him? Salt and pepper are on the table."

I sat down at the small table pushed up against the wall. He divided the omelet and slid my portion onto a plate with the spatula before he seated himself. The first bite was sheer heaven, as the melted cheese and hot ham complemented the lightly browned egg. He took a bite of his own portion, made a face, and shook pepper over his half.

"Should have added it before cooking." He stabbed at his egg with his fork.

"I think it's fine as it is." I took another bite, finished chewing, and tried again. "So why are you here in my kitchen, consuming my food at this hour of the evening? Where are you supposed to be right now?"

"Ah, there's the rub." His grin became mischievous as our eyes met across the table. "Redclaw seems to think I'm a specimen they need to collect and store, like their precious artifacts. They set me up with a cot in a windowless room down in the basement. Rather like a monk's cell."

I paused with my fork halfway to my mouth. "Then no one knows where you are right now? Don't you think that will create a stink when they realize you're gone?"

"They have to notice I'm gone, first." His enigmatic smile suggested he was keeping something from me. He dug into his omelet with gusto, finishing it in about three bites. It was a bit like watching a vacuum cleaner salesman in action. "Do you have anything to drink? I had to give my whiskey to your downstairs neighbor so she'd turn a blind eye again as I climbed the escape."

Without waiting for a response, he sprang up and began rooting in the cabinets again.

"How'd you get up the fire escape, anyway? I pulled the ladder up when I got home this afternoon."

"Climbed onto a trash bin. Jumped." The cabinet doors banged shut. Snapping his fingers, he made for the small pantry on the far side of the kitchen. The folding doors hid a few shelves, where I kept my dry goods.

I tried to imagine anyone jumping from a precarious perch on a trash can to the suspended ladder, which is high enough to prevent the casual man-off-the-street from climbing it. It would be an athletic feat for any man, but somehow, I pictured Knight sizing up the distance and making the leap, catching the lowest rung in his bare hands and swinging his way up the ladder.

I could also see him bribing my neighbor with liquor, an image that displeased me for some odd reason.

"Hah!" He emerged from the pantry triumphant. "Wine."

I started to warn him but he'd already uncorked the bottle and given the opening a sniff. I stifled a laugh at the contortions his face went through as he screwed one eye shut and grimaced as if in pain.

"Good God, that's not wine, it's vinegar. Pour it out, woman." He thrust the bottle at me.

With a sigh, I took it over to the sink and emptied it, taking a moment to rinse the bottle with water before setting aside on the counter. "I'm afraid I care little for alcohol."

That was an understatement, to be sure.

"I wish I cared less. Perhaps I should put you in charge of my stock." Turning away to stare out the window, he shoved his hands in his pockets, which had the effect of pulling his pants taut against his derriere. I wasn't in the habit of noticing such things as a rule, but it occurred to me at that moment this was why men performed this action. To excellent effect, I might add.

"If I wanted to mother someone, I'd have gotten married and had a passel of babies by now." My tone was sufficiently dry that had he been a plant, he would have died from lack of water.

The smile he cast over his shoulder was the same one he'd given me in the bar the night before, a touch wicked while at the same time inviting me to join in his amusement. I found I liked it better without the accompanying bleariness. "Yes, I can see that. Though if you ever become a mother, I'm sure you'll be formidable at that as well."

I rolled my eyes at him. "What do you want, Knight?"

He spread his hands wide, palms up. "Some company, some conversation, some food."

I folded my arms over my chest and tapped one foot.

"All right," he sighed. "You said you'd help me find Margo's killer. I doubt you can do that from the reception area. You need to find an excuse to come down to the labs tomorrow."

I shook my head. "I'm on probation. Desk duty. Besides, what do you think I can do down in the labs that I can't do upstairs in the office?"

"Prove Redclaw isn't behind my wife's death."

"That seems unlikely. I hardly think Redclaw is affiliated with the government."

His narrow-eyed glare was almost pitying. "You think they're not because of the whole thing about people keeping their supernatural abilities secret, and how the government would get their knickers in a twist if they knew shifters—and this technology—existed. My dear, how naive of you."

"Why on Earth would any shifter organization risk aligning themselves with the government? You yourself fell victim to the Red Scare. Can you imagine how much worse the persecution would be if the existence of shifters became public? It would make McCarthyism look like a walk in the park." I shuddered at the thought. If the shifter secret got out, the government wouldn't stop at blacklisting.

"Believe me, I know." Knight's tone was dark, his glower invoking images of dissection labs and scientists conducting tests of unspeakable cruelty. When he went on, however, I had to marvel at his cynicism. "What's the best way to protect yourself in that circumstance? Align yourself with the devil. Think about it. We're in a race now to produce bigger and badder atomic weapons so that each country can reign supreme over the world. What if one country had an army of supernatural beings on its side? Werewolves, vampires, and the like?"

"There aren't any vampires." At least, I hoped not.

"That you *know* of."

He had a point. A terrible point.

"So." I pulled the word out as if it were made of taffy. "You think I should investigate Redclaw."

"The way I see it, if Redclaw isn't behind Margo's death, then they know who is. After all, both parties want me to work for them."

I frowned. "You say it's a secret branch of the government. You're forgetting the possibility of a criminal organization."

"All the more reason for you to be down in the labs tomorrow. The answers aren't on the street. I've exhausted all those possibilities long ago."

"And you're forgetting I'm on thin ice here. Officially, I'm confined to the reception desk."

The smile came back in full force again; the sun coming out from behind a cloud. "You'll think of something. You're resourceful like that." He collected his hat and settled it on his head. "Though I'd suggest if you're planning to make a habit of investigating, think about blending into the background. Horowitz said a certain Miss Climpson came by the precinct. When he described a dishy blonde in a red coat, I knew at once it must be you."

Chagrined, I snapped back. "Perhaps I should do all my investigations dressed like this." I swept a hand up and down my form, including everything from the curlers to the bedroom slippers and the kimono in between.

"I see nothing wrong with that." His crooked smile slid across his features into a sly grin. "I think you look quite fetching."

And before I could even sputter in indignation, he had opened my window and slipped out again.

Chapter Twelve

Knight, I decided, enjoyed throwing people off balance.

His breezy flirtation of the night before had less to do with perceiving me as an attractive woman and more to do with pushing my buttons.

Little did he know a master had installed my buttons: my mother. The interesting side effect of having a master button-pusher in your life is similar to receiving that new polio vaccine. It can render you immune to the poking of others. Recognizing his actions for what they were now, I felt certain I would handle Knight better in future dealings.

As I headed into work the next morning, I gave consideration to his provoking comments about a possible relationship between the government and shifters, and how I might go about proving or disproving it.

Knight was correct about one thing—I wouldn't find the answers sitting behind a typewriter.

Unfortunately, Miss Climpson thought that's where I belonged. I entered the office to find a mound of paperwork stacked on my desk, and no sooner did I place a file in my outbox than two more appeared. I would have been suspicious she was creating busywork for me except for the fact there was a lot of traffic in and out of the office. Russo and Miss Snowden both came in several times over the course of the morning, along with an influx of other people I'd never seen before. The phone never stopped ringing, and Miss Climpson's perpetual frown deepened as she hurried in to Mr. J's office with her dictation pad. A quick glance through the open door revealed a large number of new markers on his wall map. A smaller state map of New York was festooned with enough red pins to pass for a Christmas decoration.

Because of the increased activity, I ended up with quite a bit of Climmy's overflow typing. From her pinched expression and pursed lips when she handed the files over, I could tell she wasn't happy about having to delegate, but for the most part, the information in the files was meaningless to me. A missing dog. Strange lights reported at night on a country lane. A box of valuable antiques stolen out of the back of a car. A runaway teen. A case of sudden amnesia without an obvious cause. A woman who thought a dangerous beast was living in her refrigerator. A town that experienced a total failure of all mechanical devices at one time, which sounded like an electromagnetic pulse to me. My time spent researching scientific articles in the library suggested thermonuclear reactions generated EMPs, so it seemed reasonable to expect an influx of emerging shifters from that town in the near future. If the major world governments didn't sign a weapons' testing ban soon, the day would come when shifters outnumbered the rest of us.

I still considered myself one of "us", despite Ryker's suspicions about my genetic makeup.

My probation remained in effect. Dr. Botha had yet to arrive, which meant I had no pretext for going down to the lower levels. I suspected it would annoy Knight when I didn't show up in the labs, but try as I might, I couldn't even find an excuse to leave my desk, save for my lunch break.

Miss Climpson was so stressed by the increased workload she left me alone during her own lunch break, something she patently hadn't wanted to do, given the pursed lips and sideline glances tossed in my direction as she left. Either Ryker had taken my security improvements to heart or else no one trusted me to not make off with artifacts again because now there were two guards on duty in the reception area. They were cut from the same cloth as Russo—which is to say taciturn—with a tendency to dress like greasers in jeans, white T-shirts, and leather jackets. One even sported a pompadour.

I believe they would have been inclined to be a bit chatty, but Miss Climpson must have put the fear of God in them. The guard with the pompadour gave me a grin and a wink from time to time, but both of them kept their distance, even when Climmy left for her lunch.

When the delivery man arrived with a package needing a signature from Ryker, the two guards stiffened to alertness like actual watchdogs. The delivery man cast a wary eye in their direction as he pushed both package and clipboard toward me.

I buzzed Ryker's office from Miss Climpson's desk, but there was no response. After explaining that Ryker did not appear to be in the building and I had no idea when he would return, I failed to convince the delivery man to come back later. He tapped his watch and insisted the sender had paid for express delivery.

In the end, I signed for the package. It was the first time in memory something had arrived in this manner. Always before, someone like Russo or Miss Snowden hand-delivered sensitive items. The box, wrapped in brown paper, seemed harmless enough, and the delivery man was anxious to be off, so I scratched my name on his clipboard and placed the box on the corner of my desk.

It was addressed without salutation—just "Ryker"—care of Redclaw Security. There was no return address. The label was handwritten in spiky, bold lettering. The package weighed about the same as a sweater box, and for a brief moment, I thought it might be an article of clothing from one of the retailers. I soon dismissed that notion. If it had come from a department store, the name would be on the label. Dismissing it as none of my business, I turned back to my mindless typing.

Not ten minutes later, I lifted my head to sniff around me. An acrid odor seared my nostrils. Something was burning.

"Do you smell that?" I asked the guards.

Both began testing the air, nostrils flaring as they sniffed about.

"Something's on fire. Chemical, I think," said Pompadour, only to have the other guard contradict him.

"No, electrical." He looked about uneasily, as if he could spot faulty wiring through the walls.

For all I knew, maybe he could.

"Could it be coming from the lower levels?" I pointed toward Mr. J's office.

Pompadour shook his head. "Nope. It's somewhere in this room."

All eyes turned to the box on my desk, where a small curl of smoke wafted upward from the wrapping paper.

"We need to evacuate the building." The second guard made for Mr. J's office, but I stopped him.

"Don't be silly. Maybe that's exactly what someone wants us to do." I pointed to Pompadour. "Give me your jacket."

He clutched his lapels as though I might jerk his jacket off him. "What? No!"

"You can get another one. Leather is the best thing for transporting the box. Hurry!" The smoke was thicker now, a black oily plume that made me cough.

His cohort punched him on the arm. Pompadour gave in with a heavy sigh, removed his jacket and held it out. I snatched it from his reluctant hands and tossed it over the box.

"Get the door." I waved the other guard back when he would have followed us. "You watch our backs in case this is a trick to get us out of the office."

After draping the jacket around the box, I scooped it up and hurried to the door. Intense heat now radiated through the thick leather. It felt as if I was carrying a bucket full of lava. I stumbled as I entered the hallway, and Pompadour steadied me with a hand under my left arm, causing a slight twinge of pain. I'd almost forgotten about the bullet wound.

A quick glance toward the outer door had me rethink my plans to get the box outside the building. There was no telling what would happen if the thing exploded in the street. Even if no one got hurt, it might draw the wrong kind of attention to Redclaw.

I held the box, wrapped in the jacket, stiff-armed in front of me. "To the restroom—hurry!"

Pompadour skirted around me to fling open the door to the public washroom. Hesitating just long enough to make sure the facilities were empty, I heaved the package out of the jacket and into the sink. In a flash, it burst into flames.

Pompadour and I jumped back, shielding our eyes from the furnace-like heat. Something about the color of the flames wavering in the tiny tiled room reminded me of the spectrum of light surrounding Ryker when he was in phoenix form.

As soon as the conflagration had begun, it died down. Several objects lay within the black ashes that were all that remained of the original box.

"Be careful," Pompadour cautioned as I opened the tap. The cold water sent thick, black smoke billowing up from the remnants of the package.

Within the wreckage of the box lay two items. One was a stack of folded cloth, black with an iridescent shimmer where it caught the light. The other was a small metal box about the size of a cigarette case. A cursive R emblazoned the lid.

Taking out my handkerchief, I attempted to pick up the metal container, but it was still too hot, so I left it for the time being. When I brushed my fingers over the clothing, to my surprise, the cloth was cool to the touch. Water beaded on its surface and ran off as I poked at the material.

"What is it?" Pompadour asked, sounding petulant, and yet not hurrying forward to take over the investigation.

I picked the item of clothing up by the shoulders. It almost flowed as I unfolded it. "As near as I can tell, it's a catsuit." I frowned at the offending article.

"A whatsit?" Pompadour whined.

"A catsuit. An extremely form-fitting—" I gasped when the material seemed to undulate in my hands. I let go, but the cloth curled around my wrist and hung on. I wished for my ray gun, which I'd left in my desk, and wondered how to explain having to shoot a piece of clothing.

As if sensing my distress, the cloth released its hold and collapsed in a heap among the ashes.

"Did that thing just move?" Pompadour put his hand in his pocket, as though reaching for a weapon of his own.

"Yes, but I think it's okay. Be ready to act if it should move again, though." I had a horrid vision of cloth rising to envelop and smother me, and my hand shook as I reached for the metal case.

This time it was cool enough to touch. I shook off the water and pried the lid open. Inside, was a note written in the same bold handwriting from the outer wrappings.

Ryker—

I hear you've been flitting around town on fire again. It must be inconvenient to leave your clothes behind when you're pretending to be a moral, upright citizen. The suit is made of dragoncloth, and as you can see, can withstand even your flaming temperatures. The best part is it conforms to whatever form you shift into.

Still think we shouldn't make use of the technology available to us?

The sender signed the note with a single initial, "R." The paper was brown around the edges and a little crispy to the touch, but otherwise intact.

With more assurance than I felt, I draped the catsuit over my arm. "I think it's okay to head back into the office."

Pompadour shrugged. "It's your funeral."

He followed at a slight distance behind me down the corridor. When I opened the door to the office, the second guard crossed the room to join us.

"There's something alive in your desk." Guard Two chucked his head back over his shoulder at my workstation. "I heard it moving around in one of the drawers."

The three of us went to my desk. I laid the catsuit over my chair. After a quick nod at the guards, I eased the drawer open. We stared down at the contents: a couple of legal pads, a rubber stamp and a bottle of ink, a little dish of paper clips, and my clutch. As we watched, the purse twitched and flopped.

I blew out a sigh of relief. "Oh, that's nothing. It's just my purse."

The purse holding the little ray gun, to be precise.

The guards exchanged a side glance with lifted eyebrows but said nothing as they took their former positions. I gave the clutch a comforting pat and shut the drawer, then folded the catsuit and placed it on the corner of my desk with the note on top before taking my seat at the typewriter again.

It didn't surprise me when Ryker blew into the office as though propelled on fury and caffeine. One day I would discover how he kept tabs on the office in his absence. Was he aware of Knight's nocturnal prowling? If so, why did he allow it? The thought raised all kinds of questions I couldn't answer, so I set it aside. I stayed calm, continuing to type as Ryker pulled up beside my desk.

"Package arrived for you." My comment was unnecessary, but the way his nostrils flared as he read the note rather amused me. Crumpling the paper, he placed it in his pocket and reached for the cloth.

I stopped him. "Er, a word of warning, sir. The suit has some rather *interesting* properties. It moved when I touched it."

The faintest smile touched his lips. "I'm not surprised. I take it you read the note?"

"It wasn't intentional, sir."

"Understood. Never mind. Though his methods are less than conventional and frequently alarming, I don't believe my brother would hurt me."

Before I could process the notion of Ryker having a brother, he changed the subject. "Which reminds me, Dr. Botha should be here on Friday. I'm interested to see your genetic profile. The more information we have, the better we can help others. Someone will escort you to the lab for testing when he arrives." He collected the suit and stroked it absently when the material flowed over his arm like a living creature. That hint of a smile was still on his face when he met my gaze. "Quick thinking on getting the package out of the office, Bishop."

So. Perhaps no longer in the doghouse?

I watched Ryker leave with a sigh and returned to the odious typing he'd once promised I wouldn't have to do.

Later that evening, a cold rain fell as I left the office. The thought of stopping on the way home for dinner held little appeal. Even though the score from the bullet was healing as expected, my arm ached just the same. I just wanted to get back to the apartment and settled for the evening. I needed to finish my mending. A television wasn't in the budget, otherwise I might have sat down for a half hour with *Dragnet* while I sewed. I could now see the appeal of losing one's self in mindless entertainment at the end of a long workday. At least Em's shower was this weekend. As much as I dreaded the long train ride out of the city, a change of scenery would do me some good. With any luck, the rain would stop and I could look forward to a brisk walk by the shore. I did my best thinking when walking.

I toyed once again with the idea of getting a little dog for company, but dismissed it as impractical. Mrs. King would never allow it, which meant moving, and I'd be hard-pressed to find rooms as cheap. Besides, who would let the dog out when I was at work all day?

As soon as I took my seat on the bus home, I opened the police report on Margo Knight's death that had arrived earlier that day. I'd kept it under wraps until now, not wanting to field any awkward questions about it. As I feared, the report shed no further light on the matter. Perhaps I was going about this all wrong. What if her death was the end of her story? Perhaps I should look into Margo Knight's life instead. I could ask Knight what he knew of her background, talk to her relatives, and see if there was another reason for her death we didn't know about. The thought was encouraging, and once I got home and had a quick meal of tuna salad on crackers, I felt cheered enough to paint my toenails.

I'd just put on the second coat when I heard the telltale scratching at my kitchen window. Hobbling into the kitchen with cotton balls stuffed between my toes to prevent the polish from smearing, I flipped the switch and sighed when I saw Knight outside the window. I would have to do something about the fire escape.

"What are you doing here this time?" I asked, stepping back so he could climb in the window. At least my hair wasn't in curlers.

Rain blustered in behind him, slicking his coat and making it shine in the overhead light. He removed his hat and tossed it on the counter before draping his dripping outerwear over one of the kitchen chairs. "'It ain't a fit night for man or beast'," he quoted with determined cheerfulness. "How's the arm?"

"The arm's better, thank you." Grudging gratitude tempered my irritation. Having to keep the gunshot wound secret from most acquaintances meant there was no one to offer any sympathy.

With a satisfied nod, he helped himself to my cupboards. After opening the third one and closing it again, he frowned. "What on Earth do you eat? There's no food in here."

Shrugging, I pointed to the little pantry. He opened the folding door and after a moment, turned around holding up a single can of Campbell's Chicken Noodle Soup and a packet of saltines. "That's it?" He sounded aghast.

"I wasn't expecting company." I grabbed the dishcloth from the sink and dropped it on the floor, using my heel to scoot it around to mop up the rainwater. If I smudged my polish, I would have to hit him.

"I'd run around to the Third St. Deli and pick up sandwiches, but I have nothing to pay the gatekeeper at the tollbooth again." He pointed an index finger at the apartment below. "I've given her my last bottle of hooch."

"Probably just as well."

He nodded. "I couldn't stop thinking about what you'd said the night—well, the night you picked me up from Moneta's."

"For starters, I didn't pick you up. That sounds... unsavory. Besides, what could I have said that made such an impression on you?"

He tapped his temple with an index finger. "You pointed out the rate at which I was killing brain cells. I realized you were right. I could see them dying right in front of my eyes." He made a fluttering motion with his fingers as he withdrew his hand from his head.

His little theatrics amused me. "Someone stop the presses. I can't recall the last time a man took my advice."

He lifted a sardonic eyebrow and opened the nearest drawer. Finding a can opener within, he set about opening the can of soup. "I don't know about that. Given the new security measures now in place at Redclaw, I'd have to say someone was taking your advice. Weren't they your idea? According to that little man, Jessop, it was your suggestion to beef up security."

I pulled a pot out of the cupboard, placed it on the burner, and turned on the gas. "More like they're making sure I don't leave with the silverware."

"You're just upset because you're on probation. Trust me, you won't be for long. They'd be fools not to utilize your skills."

After dumping the soup into the pan, he filled the can with water and added it to the pan.

It was a tidy, almost domestic little scene that he had to spoil with his next words.

"Are you one of those women who refuses to eat?" He raked me with his glance as he stirred the soup.

Stung, my answer was snippy. "No. I'm one of those women who lives alone. Dinner for one is hardly conducive to becoming Betty Crocker."

A sly grin stole over his face as he gave me an assessing glance. Snapping his fingers, he said, "I've got it. You *can't* cook."

The ray gun lurched within my pocket. I had to agree with it, shooting Knight seemed like a good idea to me, too. "I just don't see the point in making a huge mess in the kitchen for one person."

"No. I'm right. You don't know how to cook. Fancy that. I've discovered something Henrietta Bishop doesn't know how to do." He was entirely too gleeful at the prospect.

"It's Rhett," I said automatically.

He wrinkled his nose as if he'd caught a whiff of bad fish. "Rhett Bishop? You can't be serious. That's too close to Rhett Butler. Though frankly, I can picture you not giving a damn."

This wasn't the first time someone had alluded to my name being like that of Clark Gable's character in *Gone with the Wind*, but it was the first time anyone had compared me to

Butler himself. I sniffed. "At least you don't think I'm like Scarlett."

"I don't know about that." He stirred the soup. The aroma of chicken broth wafted up from the stove. "Tomorrow is another day for you, too. You seem pretty resilient to me."

I couldn't decide if he'd insulted or flattered me, so I said nothing, but took two bowls down from the cabinet. Regardless of my earlier snack, the soup smelled good as he ladled it into the bowls.

He just shook his head when I added crumbled saltine crackers to my portion as we sat at the table. "Why don't you just open the shaker and pour salt directly into your mouth?"

"I like crackers with my soup."

He stabbed at my bowl with his spoon. "That's more like you enjoy a little soup with your crackers. It looks revolting. Like chicken-flavored porridge."

Put that way, it *did* sound disgusting. As I eyed the sodden mess, I changed the subject. "You never said how it is you're able to leave Redclaw with no one being the wiser."

Especially in view of the added security.

He must not have been all that hungry, for he pushed the bowl of soup aside and fished something out of one of his pockets. After placing it on the table in front of him, he gave it a gentle push in my direction.

I didn't reach for it. Much like the previous devices I'd seen, this one had that same dull metallic casing, with odd markings carved on the sides. Unlike anything else I'd seen before, however, it had a raised ring in the center that cast a warm yellow glow. "What's that?"

An infectious grin lit up his face. "I call it an image-projector. I think about what I want to look like in great detail, and it projects that image over me. I'm still wearing the same clothes and everything, but if I can imagine it, I can look like it." He swept the device back toward him when I would have picked it up. "Few people question the boss when he's leaving the building."

"What if you run into the boss? That could be awkward."

He didn't seem concerned. "The odds are low. Besides, I can just as easily be an anonymous lab tech. Have you been downstairs? There's a lot going on, and as I said the other day, they're more worried about unauthorized people getting *in* than paying attention to who's getting out."

"But to what purpose?" His attitude made little sense. "You're safer inside Redclaw. Why leave?"

"Boredom." He shrugged when I raised a disbelieving eyebrow. "Okay, then. The desire for decent food."

My eyebrow went even higher as I stared pointedly at the cooling soup in front of him.

"Fine. I don't like being caged. Is that answer enough for you?"

I could see his point. And since I had him here, I asked about something that had been on my mind since the day of the mechanical spider. "What do you think is the purpose behind these artifacts?"

He leaned back in his chair to the point he risked toppling it over backward. The front legs lifted until he settled the chair back in place with a thump. "That's the sixty-four-thousand-dollar question, isn't it?" His raised eyebrow implied both curiosity and concern. The combination was frankly compelling. "Where do they come from? Who or what is behind the technology? It's beyond anything I've ever seen, and I've worked on some top-secret projects. My guess? It's not from this planet."

My mouth dropped open. "You mean...alien?" I sputtered.

He nodded in all seriousness.

"You seriously believe Martians or Moon Men or something like that is seeding our plant with their gizmos?" The shock of his statement having worn off, scorn now laced my voice.

His shrug was eloquent. "Maybe. I think it more likely an advanced race implanted these devices millennia ago, knowing at some point we'd develop nuclear technology, hence the activation of said devices now."

"But why?"

He shook his head. "A test? A trap? Who knows? Maybe the awakening tech triggered some kind of signal to the developers and even now, they're on their way to greet us."

I wondered if we would disappoint them. It was a distinctly disturbing thought. "Is this a working theory or are you just blowing smoke?"

His devilish smile made an appearance. The way it peeped out of hiding, combined with the fall of that rebellious lock of hair over his intense eyes when he leaned forward, would have charmed the pants off most women I know.

I don't charm that easily.

"My dear, I just tinker with the gizmos." He leaned back in his seat once more, his clever fingers toying with his spoon as he spoke. "I'll leave winkling out the motives of the artifact-builders to the scary people, like you and Ryker."

I straightened. "Me? Scary? What on earth have I done to give you that impression?" Ryker, I could understand. We knew so little about the shifters, how they lived, and what they could do. The way Ryker had tossed Billy around that day in the office was a fair indication he was stronger than most men, and of course, there was the rapid healing thing as well. More than that, I didn't know.

"Scarily competent."

I wrinkled my nose. "Am I supposed to thank you? That makes me sound like every other woman in the workplace. Standing behind the boss and making him look good."

His laugh caught me off guard. "No, you have it all wrong. The smart man stands behind the girl with the ray gun."

Okay. Perhaps I could be charmed a little.

Another thought occurred to me. "You must have the shifter gene."

His head snapped up at that. "What?"

"The shifter gene. In order to make the technology work. Not everyone can, you know. Only those with the gene."

Narrowing his eyes, he said, "Then you must have it too. The other night, you with the ray gun." His brows furrowed in concern. "Does that mean we'll both change into some creature when we least expect it?"

I shook my head. "I don't think so. Ryker seemed to think it's a recessive gene in my case. But that's why they're bringing in a geneticist. To test me, among other things."

His expression cleared. "Ah, yes. Botha. Yes, they wanted a sample of my blood too. That explains it."

For a split second, the question of what would happen if two people with recessive shifter genes got together and had children leapt into mind, but I dismissed it as immaterial to the discussion at hand. I would have responded to Knight's statement, but the buzzer at the front door sounded. Frowning, I lifted a finger to my lips and glared a warning at him before I plucked the cotton balls from between my toes and went to answer the door. Though it made for a lumpy bulge, I felt comforted by the weight of the ray gun in my kimono pocket.

When I opened the door, Em breezed in as though she were at a red carpet event in Hollywood. She even looked the part, wearing a cream-colored wiggle dress decorated with sequins, and a mahogany-brown mink stole that slid off one shoulder and emphasized the grace of a lush, bare arm. The sparkling diamond bracelet completed the picture of sophisticated wealth. There had been a time when dressing in this manner would have been as natural to me as breathing.

"Rhett, darling." She glanced around with a delicately arched eyebrow, as though she couldn't quite believe what she was seeing. "What a charming little place you have. Don't think I'm rude but I haven't much time. I've got a car waiting so I must get right to the point. I need your help."

I shut the door and joined her in my small living room. She flopped down in the nearest chair, opened her bag, and pulled out her cigarette case. I pushed the ashtray on the coffee table closer to her and took a seat on the settee, hoping Knight would have enough sense to stay in the kitchen and be quiet until I could get rid of Em. "Sweetie, what's wrong? Wedding planning got you down?"

She turned her lovely wide-eyed stare on me, pausing mid-strike of her match. "How did you know? Everything's a mess." She shook her head so hard her dark-brown waves bounced, despite the heavy application of hairspray. "You must come and make things right."

"I doubt they're as bad as all that. Perhaps I can make a few phone calls for you next week on my lunch break."

Lighting the cigarette, she took several deep drags before speaking. "No, I need you there on the spot. Promise me you'll come help straighten out my wedding. There's only four weeks left to fix things. Milly has been such a sad sack and has left everything up to the planners, who have gone crazy with the expenses. Mrs. Hardcastle keeps demanding lavish changes that would put the Rockefellers to shame. Daddy might be rich, but I don't want to bankrupt him with ridiculous expenditures." To my surprise, Em pulled a dainty handkerchief out of her clutch and dabbed at her eyes. "I thought these people had class! But Eddie's mother actually approved gold leaf trombones for the wedding cake."

"Trombones? What's the significance of that? And I thought Milly was just the maid of honor. How did she—or her mother—wind up authorizing the decorations like this?"

Em's chocolate-brown eyes flashed with anger when she looked up over her handkerchief. "Mrs. Hardcastle decided I had too much on my plate to plan my own wedding. The truth of the matter is she didn't trust me to do any planning, so she nominated Milly for the job. Milly abdicates every decision back to her mother, who has the most frightful taste I've ever seen. I thought society bluebloods were supposed to be classy. She's decided on a Nutcracker ballet theme. You know, ballerinas and hideous grinning toy soldiers. Who wants that hideous junk tarting up the venue?"

Stifling a snort, I patted her hand. "A place in society is no guarantee of good taste, I'm afraid. Just tell your father. I'm sure he'll put his foot down if you don't want what Mrs. Hardcastle has planned."

"He says Mrs. Hardcastle must know best and I should bow to her expert opinion." Em's voice rose to a wail as she completed her sentence.

"Then I'm not sure what you think I can do. Why don't you elope?" I kept an ear cocked for any sound from the kitchen, but all was silent there.

"I said as much to Eddie but he just roared like a hyena. He thought I was joking. Darling, I *know* you could reel them in. Come back with me tonight to the Hamptons. Since the bridal shower is this weekend, we're staying in the Hamptons until the wedding. You can sort everything out. Daddy will listen to you. He thinks you're the bee's knees."

"Honey, I can't leave my job for a whole month." I spoke gently but firmly.

"All expenses paid! I'll even hire you as a wedding consultant. You *must* come!"

I shook my head. "And then after the wedding, I'd still be out of a job."

"Maybe, maybe not. You said you wanted a job that would take advantage of your organizational skills. What about becoming a full-time wedding planner? I'm sure you'd be marvelous."

"I'm sure I would not." The thought of marshalling vendors and caterers into creating the perfect event for high-strung brides made me shudder.

"You don't know until you try. Why don't you ask your boss for the time off?" The sound of a strange voice made both of us whip our heads around.

The person standing in the kitchen doorway was the spitting image of my downstairs neighbor, complete with cigarette trailing from her lips.

The smirk on her face, however, was reminiscent of a certain scientist's.

"I didn't realize you had company." Em sat up straighter, giving my platinum-blonde 'neighbor' a narrow-eyed glare.

"She just dropped in to borrow a cup of sugar." I fixed Knight with my own glare.

"Only Rhett doesn't have any. Her cupboards are bare. Like Mother Hubbard's." Knight had my neighbor's languid drawl down pat. Just how many times had he spoken with her?

"So she was leaving." I bounced up from the settee and took Knight by the arm. I almost gave the show away by reacting to the feel of his coat sleeve—and the undeniably masculine arm beneath it—instead of the silk dressing gown I expected.

Nor had I expected Knight to be so difficult to budge. He simply refused to move a single step toward the door. I had to relinquish my grip when he shook me off and lounged in the doorway instead. My hand itched to slap the infuriating smirk off his face. Fortunately, I have excellent self-control.

"I don't know about you, but I'd love an excuse to take off to the Hamptons for a few weeks. So very la-di-da." Knight waved his own cigarette about airily, flowing past me to take a seat beside Em on the sofa. "Trixie LaSalle, at your service." He waggled his fingers in Em's direction.

I started to push the ashtray closer to him, then hesitated. Was he actually smoking a cigarette or just projecting an image of one? And would the image extend to the falling of ash or not? And how did he learn my downstairs neighbor's name, if indeed that was her real name and not some stage persona she'd adopted? No doubt during one of his *bargaining* sessions with her on the fire escape.

Em fixed him with a look that this act of friendliness hadn't deceived her, but she didn't know how to respond other than to pretend she was. Her smile was very feline as a result. "Now see, Rhett? Miss LaSalle agrees with me. What harm can it to do ask?"

"I just started this job in March. I can't ask for time off so soon, especially not a full month. I'm not exactly in good graces with the management right now, either. Perhaps I can come down a few days before the wedding, though."

"Two weeks minimum. I'll never make it through the ceremony with anything less." Em sat up straighter. "Oh! I know! You can bring your boyfriend along. There's plenty of room at the house. Tommy will be wild with jealousy. Won't that be a nice little incentive?"

I'd almost forgotten about the boyfriend I'd invented for Em's—and my—sake. I found Knight watching me with bright, interested eyes.

"Oh, do tell us about the boyfriend." He leaned back on the sofa with the air of someone settling in for the evening.

"I can't invite my date to spend a month in the Hamptons with me," I snapped, directing my annoyance toward Em. "He works at the same agency I do. We can't both leave the office at the same time."

Em's eyes turned into feline slits, and she flicked a quick glance at Knight before skewering me with her glare. "How can you both work at the same place? You hadn't even interviewed for this job when you told me about him."

Resisting the urge to slap my forehead for such an obvious error, I said stiffly, "That's how I heard about the job in the first place. Through him."

Em's brow cleared as she stood up. "Well, that might make it hard for you to both leave, then. But he could certainly come down for a few days before the wedding." She stood. "You'll ask about getting some time off, please? Two weeks."

"A long weekend. At best."

"Seven days. I'm only asking for seven days."

I smiled as I lifted my cheek for her to kiss. "I'll see what I can do, but I'm not making any promises. Call me tomorrow with a list of vendors. At the very least, I can make some phone calls and see if I can tone down the extravagance."

"I knew I could count on you." She turned to Knight. "Rhett is utterly, one hundred percent reliable. If I needed to steal a diamond necklace, or infiltrate a palace, or bury a body, I would call her."

"Em!" I choked back laughter as embarrassed heat flamed my cheeks. "What a thing to say."

"You know what I mean, darling. You're the real deal. Twenty-four carat gold." She fixed a steely gaze on Knight. "Which means I would defend her to the ends of the earth."

"To be sure," Knight murmured without the slightest trace of amusement.

Satisfied with this challenge delivered and understood, Em took her leave.

I almost jumped when I turned back from closing the door to see Knight in his usual form sitting on my couch.

"What a fascinating woman."

If there was a trace of sarcasm in his voice, I couldn't detect it. "She's taken."

"I'm not looking. But I think you are—or do you really have a boyfriend?"

I sighed. "I'm not looking either, but an old boyfriend believes he's in love with me. Em thinks the way to restore my lifestyle to its former glory is to marry well. She keeps offering Tommy as an example."

He followed me back to the kitchen. The cooling soup, with its skim of congealed chicken fat, held little appeal for either of us. I poured it into the trash.

Knight leaned in the doorway again. I was beginning to think he had issues with standing upright. "What grown man goes by the name Tommy? That's a boy's name."

"Tommy is still very much a boy. He avoided serving in the army by claiming to be an asthmatic, a condition which seems to have magically resolved with the end of the Korean War."

"Now, now." Knight's tone was almost gentle. "Perhaps he's taking that new drug—whatchamacallit—corticosteroids or something."

"Or something," I agreed. "Anyway, I'm not interested in marrying my way out of poverty and back into good social standing, so I refused. Tommy doesn't take no for an answer easily, hence the fake date to accompany me to the wedding."

Something in Knight's expression darkened and his brows drew together. "He hasn't been annoying, I hope?"

"Annoying has so many interpretations, doesn't it? Suffice to say, I can handle Tommy."

"No doubt." Knight's smile at my assurance faded. "Back into good social standing? Am I missing something?"

"This isn't 5th Avenue." My hand swept the surrounding room. When he continued to look at me with expectation, I sighed. "My father committed suicide last year, after he lost the family fortune. My mother remarried shortly thereafter. I chose not to move in with her and her new husband."

Somehow, he gleaned all he needed to know from my terse summation.

"I see." He infused those two short words with sympathetic understanding. After a pause, he continued more briskly. "If I can be of any use, I'd be honored to be your fake date for the wedding."

I must have blinked at him several times before I found my voice. "Why in Heaven's name would you do that?"

His little shrug was eloquent. "The way I see it, I owe you. I'd be a prisoner—or worse—of some organization right now if it weren't for you, and you're in bad odor with your boss as a result." He levered himself off the doorjamb and crossed to the counter to retrieve his hat on his way to the window. Placing it on his head at a jaunty angle, he flashed his brilliant smile. "Besides. I like Em. I think her wedding will be a blast."

Chapter Thirteen

My feet dragged with exhaustion when I climbed the stairs the following evening, but I knew as soon as I turned the handle to my apartment door someone was already inside.

I flinched at the convulsive movement of the ray gun in my purse and took a calming breath. "Down, boy," I said, patting my purse as I walked through the door.

From the delicious odors wafting through the living room toward me, I had a good idea of who was in my kitchen.

I wasn't wrong. Knight stood in front of the stove, shirtsleeves rolled up to bare his forearms, a dish towel draped across his shoulder as he stirred something in one pot, while steam roiled off boiling water in another. An open bottle of wine stood at his elbow, along with my best glasses—filled with a rich burgundy of some sort. From the oven came the heavenly aroma of garlic, butter, and warm bread.

His obvious comfort level and sheer competency robbed me of speech, and any words I might have said about him breaking into my apartment died with the faint rumbling of my stomach. As I watched, he grabbed a potholder and cracked open the oven to check the baking bread.

I cleared my throat. The oven door clanged shut, and he spun in my direction with a yelp.

Spying me in the doorway, he scowled and pressed a hand to his chest. "Give me a heart attack, why don't you?"

"That's what you get for sneaking into my apartment. You're lucky I didn't shoot first and ask questions later. But I assumed most burglars wouldn't cook an Italian dinner before robbing me."

The pasta on the back burner threatened to boil over. Turning off the gas, he carried the pan to the sink and poured everything into a colander sitting there. Steam billowed up. "No doubt, you're right. That goes double for nefarious gang members seeking revenge or information."

"If they offered garlic bread, I'd spill my guts."

He handed me a glass of wine and offered his in a silent toast. "But of course."

After my long day at work, I didn't even hesitate. We clinked glasses, and I sipped from mine, eyebrows lifting at the smooth, mellow flavor. Whatever the label was, it wasn't the cheap stuff. "Not that I'm complaining—and I'm not—but to what do I owe this honor?" I nodded toward the set table and the cooked meal with a wave of the glass.

"Let's eat first while everything is hot. Sit. Tell me about your day." He took the bread out of the oven and transferred it to a small bowl.

I felt the furrow creasing my brow as I took my seat. "How very... chummy of you."

He served up a plate of spaghetti in a sauce thick with chunks of tomato, onions, and meat with the flourish of an experienced chef. After placing the bread on the table between us, he sat down with his own plate. "Don't look at me like that. I don't have designs on you. Well, I do, but not your virtue."

That assurance somehow fell flat instead of providing comfort.

He rolled his spaghetti around the tines of his fork. "My reasons for being here can wait. As for why I made dinner, I was hungry. If I have to eat one more of those horrible packaged sandwiches they see fit to feed me at Redclaw...suffice to say, the wrapper is tastier. Anyway, here I am. Two birds, one stone."

His fork was halfway to his mouth when he paused, aghast. "What are you doing?"

I laid down my knife and continued with just the fork. I'd never gotten the hang of twirling pasta and I wasn't about to drop food all over the tablecloth. "Cutting my pasta. What does it look like?"

He shook his head in mock sorrow. "Philistine. Any Italian mother worth her salt would slap you on the spot before kicking you out of her house. Anyway, how are things going in the rarefied atmosphere in reception? Though they let you out for a little bit, didn't they? I take it you saw Dr. Botha."

"I did." On his arrival, Dr. Botha had summoned me to the lower levels for the requested blood samples, and I'd seen for the first time the extensive underground layout. The new security measures were in place there as well. They'd cleared the room behind the bookcase and now the area contained only a guard behind a desk. One also had to enter a code on keypad to open the door at the far end of the room leading to the subterranean chambers.

"And?" Knight prompted, tearing off a hunk of buttered bread.

I shrugged. "And nothing. The doctor drew several tubes of blood, asked me some questions, and had me pick up a few devices to see if I could activate them."

"Same here. Gallons of blood. I'm sure I'm quite anemic now." The smile he gave me over his wineglass was friendly enough, but then his eyes narrowed. "Have you made any progress regarding Margo's death?"

By now I'd adapted to his rapid changes of both mood and subject, so I shook my head. "I'm sorry. Miss Climpson has me bogged down in paperwork. At the moment, I'm privy to little information aside from what comes across my desk. Speaking of which...." I realized I'd never told him about the strange package from the day before and its mysterious, flammable contents, so I did.

His eyes gleamed when I described the properties of the suit. "Fascinating. And sent by Ryker's brother. Funny how we've not met the man. Dragoncloth, you say? That must be a fancy name for—" He shook his head. "No, it can't be. You don't think...?"

"Dragons really exist? I hardly think so. Wouldn't they be sort of hard to hide?"

His index finger moved back and forth in agreement. "Right. Good point. Though we can't really be sure, now can we?" He squirmed in his seat.

I didn't blame him. The possibility that *dragoncloth* wasn't just a colorful descriptive term weighed heavily in the air between us. The logical argument, "There are no such things as dragons" didn't hold much water when your coworkers could shift into another form. After all, wasn't my boss a Phoenix-shifter?

Knight cleaned his plate before I'd eaten a third of mine. He tore off another large chunk of bread. I eyed the rest and wondered if I would have to fight him for it.

"So then you don't know about the big hullabaloo?" Knight pinched a piece of bread off his portion and popped it in his mouth, licking the butter off his fingers.

I watched his actions somewhat distractedly, and then, feeling my cheeks burn, forced my concentration on my plate once more.

"I know something has everyone quite flustered. Lots of activity in and out of the main office, and no one looks thrilled about it."

Knight wiped the lips I'd been staring at a moment before and flung down his napkin to leap up and cross over to the counter. He held up a folded newspaper and flourished it at me in triumph.

"I presume you have something to share?"

"You presume rightly." He dragged his chair beside mine and pushed the paper in my direction. "Everyone is frosted because someone stole a cache of artifacts right out from under Redclaw's nose."

The folded paper lay between us.

"They reported it in the news?" I couldn't believe it.

"No, no. Nothing like that. Okay, seeing as you don't know, Redclaw had a holding area outside the city where they stored a bunch of these devices until someone could deliver them to the office. Apparently, some bright lad thought it a more expedient way of transferring said devices, and as I've mentioned before, they're like nothing currently in development anywhere on the planet. Anyway, someone must have been watching—or worse, there was a leak—and the truck transporting the goods was hijacked. The thieves took everything, including the manifest listing what was on the truck."

"How do you know all this?"

Knight's lips pressed into a grim line. "Both the driver and the guard were injured. I heard the lab rats in the basement talking about it, and I coerced them into spilling the beans."

For a moment, I wondered if Knight meant actual rats until I realized he was referring to the other technicians in the subterranean labs. In my defense, talking rodents wouldn't have been the most bizarre thing to have happened at Redclaw.

"So how does the newspaper come into it?"

Knight opened the paper to the society page and tapped a large photograph. "What do you see here?"

The caption on the photo read, "Summer starts early at the Poseidon Club." The image itself could have been taken at any of a dozen or so nightclubs I'd frequented before my father's death. The photographer's flash had captured his subjects in various states of merriment with broad smiles and lifted glasses of champagne. In the foreground, with her head tossed back to show off a diamond necklace and her cleavage to their best advantage, Em gazed lovingly up at Eddie, who smiled possessively back at her. Behind them, the other revelers were not as distinct, but evening gowns and tuxedos were de rigueur.

"Em and her fiancé at a dance in the Hamptons. Which reminds me, I forgot to pick up my dry cleaning." I pushed the paper back at him.

He stopped the slide of paper with his hand, causing it to buckle against fingers before he smoothed it out. "Look again. What's that on the side table? Beside the bottle of champagne."

Frowning, I drew the paper closer. Though that part of the room wasn't lit by the flash, I made out what appeared to be a man's wristwatch lying on the table. Instead of a dial, however, the object had a familiar design with a raised triangle in the center. "What is it?"

"I don't know but it's one of ours, you can bet on that. I've seen enough of these babies now to spot one."

I studied the photograph in more detail. "Just because you think you see an artifact in this image doesn't mean the whole cache of missing devices is in the Hamptons. It may be something someone discovered without knowing what it is. Or it could even be some kind of new Swiss watch."

Knight leaned in to look at the paper with me. "I might be inclined to believe that except for this guy." He pointed to the photograph.

A handsome man stood behind Eddie, an enigmatic smile on his face as he held a glass of champagne.

My pulse quickened when I realized I'd seen him before. "Who is he?"

"Don't you know? That's Rian Sterling. Up and coming industrialist. Rich inventor. He's in the papers all the time." The little sniff Knight made suggested a degree of jealousy there.

"He was in the office the day I went in for my interview." I'd know those intense eyes and that tousled dark hair with the curious streak of silver anywhere.

"Was he now? Interesting." Knight stroked his chin as though he were a college professor considering an esoteric theory. "I'd say that makes it even more likely there's something going on in the lovely Hamptons. Aren't you supposed to go down there for a party or something this weekend?"

"Tomorrow. Bridal shower. I'm taking the train. Em will send someone to pick me up at the station."

"Call her right now. Tell her we're coming down tonight."

"We?" I supposed I sounded sharp, for Knight gave me his most charming smile.

"Yes, we. I rescued my car from outside Moneta's. We can be there in a few hours and it might be useful to have our own transportation. You have the perfect excuse for checking this out. We *have* to go."

"And just how do you plan to keep your absence a secret? I think someone will notice if you're gone from Redclaw all weekend."

"I may have done some tinkering with one of the devices I've been working on. Fascinating little thing. I've been able to record images of myself eating, sleeping, reading and so forth in my monk's cell and put it on a loop. The device can project a three-dimensional image into the room. It's better than television, if you can believe that. It's like watching a play. There are only a couple of guards on the weekends. Unless someone tries to speak to me, they'll never notice I'm gone."

"As impressive as your aptitude with the artifacts may be, I'm already on thin ice as it is." Folding the paper, I thrust it aside.

"Hey, you'll be there on the spot regardless. If you happen to stumble upon their missing do-dads while you're there, what can they say? You can always tell them you noticed an artifact and thought it warranted a closer look. If anyone will get in trouble, it'll be me. They won't fire me. I'm not on the payroll anyway."

"Perhaps keeping you in seclusion—and alive—is your payment for now."

"I'm not without resources. Besides, I'll be with you."

"Precisely why I'll be the one that gets blamed if something happens."

"You can hardly be held responsible for my actions."

He had a point, but I doubted Ryker would see it that way. "There's no reason for you to come. I don't need you."

"I'm cut to the quick." He laid a hand over his heart in mock wounding. "And here I am, your date for the wedding, too. Never mind, Miss Independent. I'd like to point out I'm the resident genius when it comes to these artifacts. I'm going with or without you."

The grin that accompanied his statement went a long way toward persuading me to accept his way of thinking. I had serious doubts it would go down the way he predicted, but he was right. I'd be right there on the spot. It would be impossible not to poke around. "Resident genius, my foot. You've been at Redclaw, what? Three days now?"

"I'm a quick study."

The bright intelligence in his eyes was hard to resist. "Very well. If you'll pull out my suitcase from the bedroom closet, I'll go downstairs and phone Em so she can expect us."

"Brilliant." Knight bounced up and out of the room.

I picked up the newspaper. So the man with the topaz eyes had a name. Rian Sterling. The day of the break-in, Ryker had accused Billy of working for someone named Rian. And Ryker had a brother who was an inventor whose name began with an R. Someone who may or may not be working against Redclaw's interests.

The sensible thing to do would be to contact Ryker and let him know what was going on. If the device in the photo was part of the missing shipment, then I should let him know. If said device was merely a new artifact someone had discovered, then someone needed to collect and catalog it anyway. But if Rian Sterling was involved, Ryker would most certainly want to know—especially if Rian was his brother.

The Hamptons were my old stomping grounds. No one would challenge my presence; it was expected. Even if Ryker gave me leave to look around, he'd never agree to Knight coming with me on Redclaw's behalf. No doubt Ryker would provide me with some agent to act as my fake boyfriend for the weekend, but the notion of pretending to date Pompadour or his cohort made me shudder. I not only needed someone I could trust, I needed someone who would blend in at the country club. Someone no one would question as my date.

Knight and I had a good working relationship. Despite his rogue tendency to buck authority, Knight had proven himself adaptive and able to think on his feet.

If I found the hoard of missing artifacts and the people behind their theft, I'd prove beyond all doubt my worth to Redclaw. If it turned out to be a wild goose chase and we got caught acting without authorization, my goose would be truly cooked.

So we wouldn't get caught.

Chapter Fourteen

The car's tires crunched on gravel, jolting me awake. I lifted my head as Knight nudged me into an upright position with his free hand. He kept the other on the steering wheel, turning the car with ease to follow the drive. As the car pulled up in front of the mansion, the headlights cut across an expanse of grassy lawn that faded away across a black emptiness I knew to be the ocean, before swinging back to the brightly lit exterior of the house. When the car came to a stop, Knight switched off the engine.

"According to your directions, we've arrived." In the darkness, his voice was like that of a fine cello, and amusement was the bow drawn across the strings. The scent of pipe tobacco lingered about him, though there was no pipe in sight. I recalled the red glow coming from the bowl, the stem clamped between his lips, and the rich aroma of tobacco, as we'd sped down the highway. At some point, I must have fallen asleep.

I wiped moisture from the corner of my mouth and suspected there was a corresponding damp spot on his shoulder. Stifling a yawn, I adjusted my hat. "My apologies. I didn't mean to doze off."

"Pity I didn't have a camera. No one would believe the formidable Miss Bishop would curl up like a cat for a nap."

"I don't know why you do that." I said crossly, swinging my feet off the bench seat and smoothing my skirt.

"Do what?"

From the house lights, I saw him looking at me, his fedora pushed back as he scratched his head.

"Make fun of me like that. 'Formidable', indeed."

"You *are* formidable, my dear. I wouldn't have it any other way."

Without waiting for a response, he stepped out of the car, stretched, and walked around behind the car. I got out before he could open my door, breathing in the hint of salt in the air. If I concentrated, I could hear the murmur of waves coming from the other side of the fairway. We were definitely in the Hamptons, where golf and tennis were King, and cocktails were Queen. Taking the hat boxes and makeup case, I left him to carry the suitcases. With a small bag under one arm, and a suitcase in each hand, Knight listed to one side under the weight of my larger case as we made our way up the stairs to the front door.

"What do you have in this thing, rocks?" The Big Bad Wolf couldn't have huffed any harder.

"You know very well what's in there. You saw me pack it yourself."

"Yes, I did. Four evening gowns, one of which was decidedly slinky. Two day dresses. Two cocktail dresses. Hats, gloves, and shoes to go with them all. It's a wonder you didn't insist on a trunk."

"Whereas your bag has seen better days." I glanced down at the battered leather case in his grip. "I'm not sure Halling will let you in with such disreputable luggage. Which reminds me, what did *you* pack?"

He set the suitcases down. "Worried I'll embarrass you? Never fear. I'll have the clothes I need and the luggage to go with it, too."

As I stared, the cracked leather case transformed into a monogrammed bag of gleaming cowhide.

"Nice trick. But when the footman carries it upstairs, won't he find it odd that it changes back into your old case? Just how long is the range on your image projector, anyway?"

The suitcase shimmered back into its former shape. "You're so practical. That's not necessarily a compliment, just so you know." He tapped his temple. "Anyway, I have all the clothing I need, even formal wear, up here."

Thinking back to his natty dressing on previous visits to my apartment, I now had a sneaking suspicion who his tailor really was. "No doubt an excuse to avoid laundry. Please tell me you wash your real clothes from time to time."

His sputtering response was lost when the door opened, blinding us with the dazzling light from within.

"Good evening, Miss Henrietta. A pleasure to see you again." Halling gave a stiff little nod in Knight's direction. "Sir."

"Thank you, Halling. This is my date for the weekend. Er...Mr. Richard Day."

"Miss Emmaline gave instructions for the two of you to be made comfortable. She and Mr. Edgar are at the club this evening. The rest of the family are at a bridge party." Halling stepped back to let us through the front door. A small gesture from him directed two footmen forward to take our bags. "Would you care for some refreshments after your trip?"

"I'm good, thank you. And you, Richard?" I batted my lashes at Knight, whose sour expression would give lemons a run for their money.

"None for me, Henrietta, dear."

His emphasis on my given name was pronounced enough to be pointed.

"I believe we'll just go to our rooms and change. It's early yet, and we'd like to catch up with Em and Eddie."

"Very good, miss."

Halling retreated, allowing me and Knight to follow the footmen up the stairs.

"Richard Day?" Knight's low growl and the warmth of his breath against my earlobe sent a shiver through me.

Ahead of us, the footmen carried the luggage at a polite distance. Sympathy prickled at my conscience when I saw how the servant carrying my bags labored. Making sure they were out of earshot, I spoke out of the side of my mouth. "It occurred to me your name might be known in some circles here. Best not to raise questions we can't answer."

"Unlikely, but I gathered your point when you introduced me to the butler downstairs. I don't fault your logic. I object to your choice of names."

Puzzled, I risked a glance at him.

"My dear woman. Richard Day? Really?"

I failed to see why he was so insulted. It wasn't half-bad for a spur-of-the-moment decision and it was a name we could remember. "Word association. Not the same kind of night, of course—"

Mock indignation rolled off him in waves. "You named me *Dick Day*."

An uncontrollable giggle burst out of me, growing louder when he rolled his eyes. The glint of amusement in his expression made me snort, and laughter lightened his voice when he took me by the elbow. "Just for that, you'll be Henrietta all weekend."

"No, I won't. Em would know right away something was wrong. No one calls me Henrietta." No one but my mother, that is. Just the thought dampened my humor.

"The butler did."

"He knows me from old. You do not."

"Ah, but you're so besotted, you allow me terrible liberties."

I opened my mouth to fire back a suitably snappy retort, but stared at him with heated cheeks. For a brief instant, the kinds of liberties I might allow presented a distracting image, and from the tightening of Knight's grip on my arm, I suspected he envisioned some as well.

The fire gleaming in his eyes banked, and he reddened. "Speaking of liberties, if I'm pretending to be your boyfriend this weekend, a certain amount of, er, touching is to be expected during the course of public activities." He choked over the last words and coughed into his hand.

I drawled in my best Mae West fashion, "If you're asking for permission to touch me this weekend, the answer is yes."

I snorted when he stumbled on the riser.

We reached the landing. The footman carrying my cases breathed a little sigh of relief. I expected our ways to part at this juncture, with Knight being ushered to one wing while my footman escorted me to the other, but to my surprise, both servants went in the same direction.

Em, it would seem, was ever-hopeful about my new boyfriend. Our rooms turned out to be side-by-side. With an adjoining door. Which I promptly locked as soon as I was alone with my bags. Which Knight rapped with his knuckles moments later.

To my utter annoyance, he was 'wearing' evening clothes and a smirk. Both suited him well, though I'd never admit it. Some men were born to wear a tuxedo. Knight was one of them. The sleek lines emphasized his lean form and elegant features, and the tux fit him as if someone had poured him into it. Which is, of course, how he imagined it.

"Some of us actually need to get dressed before going out." I shut the door in his face.

Fifteen minutes later, I opened it, then crossed back to the vanity to adjust my earrings as Knight entered my room. I'd chosen my emerald sheath, the one that fit like a glove and shimmered in the light like some exotic snakeskin. The capped sleeves also had the benefit of hiding my healing bullet wound, which was still an angry red score along my flesh. I was switching out my sturdy little Timex for the dressier diamond Cartier watch when Knight spoke.

"You look nice."

"Thank you." I touched up my lipstick with a bold red and dropped the tube into my clutch. The metal casing clinked against the ray gun. I took out the ladybug Ryker had given me and pinned it along the top of my dress. Hopefully, anyone spying it would assume it was a quixotic decoration. I'd committed Ryker's personal phone number to memory. If I had something to report, I'd call that first. But I wasn't going to repeat my mistake of not activating the pin if I needed it.

"Yes, well, the marks on your cheek where you were mashed up against me in the car have faded, and the color of your dress keeps you from being washed out."

I glanced up at him through the mirror, but he was staring at the floor, his hands shoved into his tuxedo pockets, much like a small boy forced to dress up for a party. Uncertain as to the cause of his change of mood this time, I said through gritted teeth, "You look nice as well. Good luck with maintaining that sartorial image throughout the whole of the evening."

I had the satisfaction of seeing him look aghast as we left the room. Hadn't thought of that when he'd decided his entire wardrobe could be imaginary, had he?

He drove in silence with frowning concentration to the clubhouse. When we arrived, instead of pulling up for valet parking, he parked the car himself. "Do me a favor," he said as he killed the engine. "Get out and tell me what you see."

Smothering a sigh, I did as he asked, making a slow circle around the car, crossing the beams cast by the headlights to come to the driver's side door. He rolled down the window.

"If you're hoping for a souped-up hot rod, I hate to break it to you, but you're still driving the same old junker as before."

"I was aiming for something classier than that. A Mercedes or a Jaguar. Something that would let us blend in. Look as though we belonged." He thumped the steering wheel. "Oh, well. At least we have a better idea of the limits of the image projector."

"Not necessarily. It might not be a function of distance as much as workload. You're already asking it to dress you. Maybe it can't do extended projections because it's a power problem. Anyway, it's not as if you would have been able to maintain the illusion once we went inside, anyway." I stepped back as the door swung open and he got out. "I'll let you in on a little secret about this crowd. No one is as flush as they'd like you to believe. People buy cars on credit. Memberships are offered on reputation. The most important thing is to not show the slightest bit of embarrassment or mortification no matter what the insult. Merely raise an eyebrow and look amused. Respond with that supercilious air you do so well. The one thing no one can bear is being looked down upon. If you don't care what others think, you'll be fine."

He offered his arm when I almost turned an ankle as my heels sank into the soft grass. "Supercilious, eh?"

Although we were well into spring and summer was just around the corner, the night air was still cool. I was grateful for the warmth of his arm threaded through mine. "Yes. Just like that. Speaking of which—"

It was my turn to frown. I stopped, angling him so the moonlight struck his face. The strong white light threw his cheekbones into sharp relief and touched his hair with silver. His pupils dilated into inky pools that hid the true color of his eyes. He could have been carved from marble, Michelangelo's David, even down to the shape of his nose. "Richard Day shouldn't look anything like Peter Knight. Can you do something about that?" I waggled my fingers at him. "Make your nose less sharp, somehow?"

He released me to finger the appendage in question. "First you give me a ridiculous name and then you disparage my appearance. I didn't realize you disliked me so much."

"Don't be silly. Your nose is just fine. It's a very nice nose. But it *is* a defining characteristic for you. I'd make it wider if you can. And do something about your chin."

"My chin?" If he'd been faking the haughtiness before, he'd perfected it now.

"Yes. Since you jut it out so much why not give it a slight cleft? And change your eye color, too. Those ice-blue eyes are too piercing. I'd go with a nice, common brown. Same with your hair."

"Perhaps a wooden leg and a parrot on my shoulder while I'm at it?" Sarcasm leached into his voice but his features shifted with the modifications I'd suggested. A fleeting sense of disorientation swept over me as I watched the man before me become someone I didn't know, but still seemed somewhat familiar. "There, now. Am I the man of your dreams?"

"What?" My response was somewhat breathless, as his question confused me.

"You've made me over into a movie star. I look like Cary Grant now, don't I?"

I peered at him in the dark. "I believe you do. Except for the sulky expression."

He withdrew from my perusal with a huff. "Let's get this over with. I can't maintain this forever. Between the clothes and the face, I'm already getting a headache. And what about your friends? Am I supposed to be Cary Grant all weekend?"

It did present difficulties.

"We can dye your hair if necessary. And no one at Em's is likely to remember you in the morning—it was dark when we arrived and you were wearing your hat." I was stretching it a bit, I knew. Halling would no doubt remember the man I'd arrived with. It was second nature to him. But it was also second nature for him to turn a blind eye to the goings-on of guests. If the man I introduced as Richard Day on arrival didn't look the same as the Richard Day who came down to breakfast in the morning, he would say nothing as long as my actions didn't affect the family. "As for everyone at the club tonight, they're well on their way to being drunk. If we have to, you can fake an illness and use the projector for limited periods. That might work out well for us if you want to do some snooping while I'm at the bridal shower. We'll worry about tomorrow when it arrives."

"I knew there was a bit of Scarlett in you." He took my arm again, and we strode up to the clubhouse like the party couldn't start without us.

We paused at the entrance of the ballroom to take in the crowd. A small stringed orchestra played on a stage at the end of the room. Couples dawdling over a late dinner drank champagne at tables pushed back to make room for the dancers. Conversation and music struck us like a wall of sound, with the occasional high-pitched laughter breaking through. The dancers moved on the floor in a glittering swirl of color while waiters in black slipped silently among the tables.

It was hard to believe this was once my element.

"We'll never find what we're looking for here."

"Chin up, my dear." Knight beamed at me as he snagged a glass of champagne off a tray from a passing waiter.

I punched him in the ribs with my elbow, almost spilling the glass he lifted it to his lips. "You need to keep a clear head to maintain your disguise. And *stop* mimicking Cary Grant."

Brown eyes twinkled at me as he made a crossing motion over his heart. "Just blending in. I won't get drunk, I promise. But you're right about the crowd. Shall we split up? We can cover more ground that way."

I saw both pros and cons to his suggestion, but given the fact we were just here for the weekend and we had a lot of things to check out, his plan seemed like the best one. "Agreed. We'll make our own circuit about the club and meet back here in thirty minutes."

He raised his glass in a mock toast and walked off, humming Dean Martin's "That's Amore". I couldn't help but notice the line of his tuxedo fit him exceedingly well. I do like a man with broad shoulders.

I hadn't taken two steps into the room when someone shrieked out my name. I turned to see one of my old classmates swooping down on me to kiss the air on either side of my cheeks.

"Rhett, dearest! So good to see you again. What have you been doing with yourself? No one's seen you in ages." Mary Davenport smiled like a cat flexing its claws on spotting a helpless mouse. She encompassed my appearance with a quick glance up and down. "Darling, you're so fortunate you can wear the older styles. Not everyone has the right shape to pull off a sheath."

Smiling at the unspoken implication that only a woman with the body of an immature boy could wear such a formfitting gown, I returned the compliment. "What a darling outfit. All those clever folds. The ruching is exquisite. So flattering to every form." I let my eyes sweep over hips much wider than my own.

"Givenchy. He's pure genius." Seeing as she'd failed to dent my armor, she launched another salvo. "I was so very sorry to hear about your father. Such a tragedy. I understand your mother has remarried?"

I lifted a flute of champagne from a passing waiter. "Yes. Old family friend. Came to comfort her, don't you know? And a childhood love rekindled." I took a sip from my glass, wishing it was whiskey. It had been a long time since I'd longed for hard liquor.

Really, I didn't have time for this foolishness.

"How romantic." Mary's coo was decidedly arch. "But I heard she's moved back to Idaho? Or is it Montana?"

"Wyoming. Back to the cattle ranch. They own a ridiculous amount of land. The skiing is marvelous, and the views are to die for."

Mary's smile grew tight around the edges. She leaned in with a conspiratorial whisper. "I don't know if you're aware, given that you haven't been around lately, but Tommy Stanford is enamored with someone else these days. In fact, you'll probably run into them this weekend. A luscious brunette, a little older than him, but she could give Jane Russell a run for her money, if you know what I mean."

"Thank God."

My heartfelt relief took Mary by surprise, given the way her eyebrows disappeared into her hairline. I hastened to explain. "I was hoping Tommy had forgotten all about me. I'm here with someone else."

"Oh, really?"

The patent disbelief in her voice was infuriating, which is why I couldn't help myself. "Yes. Richard's around here somewhere. He went off in search of something to eat. If you see him, send him my way. He looks a bit like a young Cary Grant."

I allowed myself a small smirk as I left her, moving off into the crowd once more. Let her chew on that.

Squeezing through clusters of revelers, I made my way around the ballroom, pausing to speak with old friends and acquaintances, keeping my eyes peeled for any sign of the device depicted in the newspaper, or anything else suspicious, for that matter. I was just about to give it up for a lost cause and head off to check out some other rooms, when a knot of dancers parted, and I found myself face to face with Rian Stirling.

Smiling, he stepped forward with his hand outstretched. Plucking my clutch out of my grip, he set it aside at one of the dining tables. "Fancy meeting you here. May I have this dance?"

What else could I say but yes? I cast a backward glance at my purse, where my trusty ray gun resided, and then let him sweep me out onto the floor.

Chapter Fifteen

The band struck up a foxtrot as we stepped into the center of the room. It was fortunate the club catered to an older crowd as well as the younger set, for a swing number wouldn't have suited my purposes. It's possible to have a conversation during a foxtrot.

"I could start with the usual questions as to how you ended up in the Hamptons, but obviously, you know people here. So let's skip to the more interesting part of the interrogation: what's a Bright Young Thing like you doing working for Redclaw?" Stirling deftly spun me in a twirl.

"As long as you realize interrogations work both ways." I found myself face-to-face with him again, staring into those tawny eyes. The resemblance between him and Ryker was uncanny. They had to be related. They had the same high cheekbones and a similar slant and shape to their eyes. But while Ryker's eyes and hair were brown, Rian Stirling's sable hair was almost black, which made the silver streak and the gold hazel of his eye color even more striking.

He lifted one eyebrow and his smile took a sardonic curve. "I can see why Ryker hired you. He likes spunk." Before I could respond, he added, "Aren't you a bit out of your depth here?"

I stiffened in his arms. Tempting as it was to storm off, I tamped down the flare of temper. He was my best lead so far. "I had my debut the same as most of the other women here. Graduated with honors from Bryn Mawr. My mother is one of the Wyoming Cartrights. My father might have lost all our money and blown his brains out, but I know the dance steps as well as anyone here."

"My dear girl." Stirling looked disconcerted. "I wasn't referring to your social standing."

"Oh." My cheeks flamed so much they practically itched. I kept my eyes focused on his white bow tie. "What did you mean, then?"

We glided around the floor, skirting other couples in time to the music. "I was referring to you being here for the same reasons I am."

"The Prentiss bridal shower?"

He laughed, as I thought he might. "Are you telling me you're not here as a representative of Redclaw?"

"Are you telling me you're here as an agent in competition with Redclaw?"

To his credit, he didn't fumble a step, but his fingers tightened at my waist.

"Just what exactly do you know about me?" A purring quality to his voice made me look up. Though he looked as calm, with a pleasant smile on his face, the fine hair on the back of my neck lifted in response to that silky undertone.

This time, I met his gaze without backing down. "You're Rian Stirling, a wealthy industrialist with a talent for creating unusual products, like the suit you sent to the office. You're also Ryker's brother. You used to work with Redclaw, but you don't anymore. The rupture between you and Redclaw has strained your relationship with Ryker, but you still care about one another."

I found myself pulled into his chest. Startled, I almost stepped on his toes. The intensity of his expression was that of an eagle spotting a mouse, and I swallowed hard.

"Half-brother, just to be clear. Ryker didn't tell you any of this."

It wasn't a question.

"No." My pulse pounded in my throat. Surely, he could hear it.

"Who's been gossiping about me at Redclaw?" Speculation flared in his narrowed eyes, and I could almost see him running through the names of the staff in his mind.

"No one. Actually, they don't speak of you at all."

"Ah." Without any indication of intent, we were somehow dancing again. "Then you know this how?"

I shrugged. "Observation. Speculation. A reasoned analysis of the information at hand."

The song ended, and he escorted me back to the table. I was relieved to see my purse where I'd left it. He pulled out a chair for me, and a waiter appeared as if by magic with two glasses of champagne on a tray. Stirling accepted them with a silent nod and sat down beside me, handing me a glass in the process.

I set it on the table untouched.

"And what does your reasoned analysis tell you?" he asked with casual good humor. Somehow, I'd avoided a landmine.

I rested my hand on the clutch. The ray gun wasn't shaking or trying to climb out of the bag. I wasn't in any immediate danger. Or was I? Perhaps the little gun was playing possum to avoid Stirling's attention.

"That you and Redclaw are at cross-purposes now. Your brother would like to trust you, but doesn't—at least, not when it comes to the artifacts."

His shrug was Gallic in nature, down to the sideways tip of his head and the purse of his lips. "Ryker and I don't see eye to eye over the artifacts. I believe they exist for a reason, and since they require the shifter gene to work, they should be available to those who can use them. Not locked away in vaults where no one can make use of the technical advantages they bring."

"Such as wealthy industrialists."

He leaned back in his chair with a smile. "That's how some industrialists *become* wealthy. But yes."

Under the guise of lifting the champagne flute for a sip, I drew my clutch closer. "Given the fact only certain members of the population can—ah—make use of said devices, doesn't that also mean going public with the existence of such people?"

Stirling's lip curled, as though in remembrance of another conversation. "That's another area where my brother and I disagree. Though I understand his point about not outing anyone who prefers to keep their abilities secret at this time. And since announcing that *any* shifters exist would in effect reveal the presence of shifters in general, secrecy remains in effect. How much has he told you, anyway?"

"I'm not sure how to answer that. This whole discussion feels a bit like consorting with the enemy."

"Dear child, if I were your enemy, we wouldn't be having this conversation. I don't think you realize the degree to which you're in over your head here." Only the amusement in his voice kept his words from chilling me to the bone. He picked an imaginary piece of lint off of his immaculate jacket and flicked it aside with a smile.

I did see his point, even if I didn't like it. Casting a glance to either side to make sure no one overheard us, I leaned in and lowered my voice. "The appearance of the artifacts and the creation of new shifters is connected to the development of nuclear weapons. Redclaw serves to collect and study the artifacts while handling matters involving the shifter world."

Stirling snorted. "That's the company line. And the Council's, for that matter. The older enclaves, the ones that pre-date the use of nuclear weapons, made a strong case for remaining hidden, and since they wield most of the money and power within the community, their word was law. Most of the new shifters are still trying to figure out their place in that community and our numbers are growing. Secrets get out sooner or later. I think it's better we control the spin rather than let everyone think the worst and try to respond to their reaction. What do your famous powers of observation tell you?"

I chose my next words with great care, remembering my initial reaction when Ryker shared Redclaw's mission with me. "Concentrating that much power, that great a technological advantage, in the hands of one organization has the potential to be disastrous if an honest man isn't in charge. I believe your brother to be such a man, but he won't always be head of Redclaw. At some point, he'll retire. Then what?"

"Absolute power corrupts absolutely." Stirling's lips held the suggestion of a smirk. "Lord Acton was right."

"I'm familiar with the quotation. You make it sound as if you were there when it was first used." I smiled to indicate I was joking, but something in his wry expression gave me pause.

Just how long did shifters live, anyway?

This conversation was getting me nowhere. Time to change my approach. "So tell me, Mr. Stirling, where does one purchase dragoncloth?"

"One doesn't." My question delighted him if his broad smile was any sign. "It's a rare commodity that's usually gifted to someone. I happen to have friends...in high places."

Again, his statement felt as though it had a secondary meaning known only to him, which was annoying. I tackled the bull by the horns. "My powers of observation also tell me you're here because of the missing shipment of artifacts. Someone here has them, don't they?"

"Not just a pretty face then."

I refrained from rolling my eyes, but he must have been able to tell from my expression I'd thought about it.

He continued smoothly. "And not just here for a bridal shower." He set aside his half-emptied glass still bubbling with champagne, his eyes going flat and devoid of humor. "Let's put our cards on the table, shall we? This isn't a Nancy Drew mystery for you to solve. I meant it when I said you're in over your head. Also, this is just a guess, but does my dear brother know you're here?"

I was certain I didn't react, but his next words proved me wrong.

"I thought not. It's not like him to send someone as green as you off on a mission by themselves. I like you, Miss Bishop. Here's some free advice. Redclaw isn't the only agency interested in recovering those artifacts, and some of the people involved aren't as nice as I am. I'm here for the artifacts. There's quite the bidding war going on at the moment. Attend your friend's shower and go home. This is none of your affair. Consider this your final warning."

He rose to give me a little bow before moving off without a backward glance. I released my breath in a gush of air and grabbed my flute of champagne for a healthy swig. Maybe Stirling was right. Maybe I was in over my head. The smartest thing to do would be to find Knight and contact Ryker to let him know what was going on. Nodding to myself, I scooped up my clutch and started to rise when a familiar voice trilled my name behind me. Perfume enveloped me when plump, gleaming arms wrapped themselves around my shoulders.

"Oh, Rhett. You came!"

Twisting in my chair, I smiled weakly up at Em. "Wouldn't have missed it for the world."

She threw herself into the chair beside me and looked up to gaze with adoration at Eddie, who stood at her shoulder. "Be a pet and find someone with a tray of canapes. I'm famished, darling."

Eddie unbent enough to give her a sappy smile and hurried off to do her bidding.

"A veritable knight in shining armor. He should wear your colors or something." I watched Eddie's progress across the ballroom, all the while keeping an eye out for Knight. It wasn't long before our scheduled rendezvous. Now that I'd confirmed the artifacts were in the area, I needed to contact Ryker and let him decide how best to handle it.

"Oh, la." Em waggled her fingers and blew a kiss at Eddie when he looked back over his shoulder. He mimed catching the kiss and putting it in the breast pocket of his tuxedo. "Eddie and I will get along famously. We understand each other. It's the rest of the family I'm worried about. To be specific, the Hardcastle women. Tell me you'll stay until the wedding. You can turn this thing around. I know you can."

The wobble in her voice made me take a good look at her. To my surprise, her luminous eyes glinted with a hint of tears. I took her hand. "Em, what is it?"

She squeezed my hand but released it to dab at her eyes with a lace handkerchief. "I told you already. Eddie's mother and sister are making a hash of the whole wedding. You can fix this, Rhett. You fix everything."

"If you knew how much I've botched things lately, you wouldn't say that." Where was Knight, anyway? The room wasn't so large that I shouldn't have been able to spot him at least once.

"Looking for someone?" The dryness of Em's tone forced my attention back on her again.

"I'm sorry. I've misplaced my date." I sneaked a glance at my watch by reaching for my champagne flute.

"He exists! I was beginning to wonder. Not a very subtle move, Bishop. I saw you checking your watch."

I shot her a grin. "We're supposed to meet up in a few minutes. Speaking of subtle, Prentiss, was it your idea to put us in adjoining rooms, or did Halling think it was easier on the house guests not to have to traverse the mansion in the middle of the night?" It felt good to sit here with Em like this, bantering the way we used to in college.

Em's answering smile brought out the dimple in her cheek and a wicked gleam in her eye. "Merely thinking of the mater and pater, don't you know. I'd hate for one of you to run into dear Papa in the wee hours of the morning."

"You needn't worry about that. Kn—er, Richard, promised to be on his best behavior this weekend. So no midnight dalliances, thank you very much."

"You disappoint me. I was hoping to live vicariously through you this weekend. Mother has put quite the kibosh on my spending too much time with Eddie before the wedding. It's the only thing she's put her foot down about. She doesn't want the Hardcastles to get a bad opinion of me. I hate to tell her it's too late for that."

It wasn't fair. Em had the most adorable pout. The same expression would look quite silly on me.

"They don't hate you."

"Hate's not a strong enough word." Em tucked her handkerchief back in her clutch. "They *despise* me. I'm not classy enough for their son. That's why you have to take over the wedding arrangements." She leaned forward and grasped my free hand. "Promise me you will. Hurry, before Eddie comes back."

I gently disengaged my hand. "I can't do that, sweetie. I'm just here for the weekend. Besides, you don't need me. You've got all the class you need."

Eddie's sleek brown head bobbed among the dancers as he made his way back to the table, a waiter bearing a full tray of appetizers following in his wake like a tugboat chasing a luxury liner.

"They'll never approve of me." Em wilted in her seat. "*You* they'd accept in a heartbeat."

"Now you listen to me. I'm going to say this just once. You're more than good enough for Edgar Stanley Hardcastle the Third. He thought well enough of you to ask you to marry him, after all." I cut off her automatic outburst with a raised hand. "I'm not finished. You want to fix this? You need to go forward as you mean to go on in this marriage. It's not just the ceremony—it's the rest of your life. If you let them cow you now, make you feel small and insignificant, incapable of planning your own wedding, they'll make your life miserable from here on out. You have impeccable taste, Em. Show them what you're made of."

Something I said lit a fire in her eyes. She narrowed them and nodded in firm agreement. "You know what? You're absolutely right."

"Of course I am."

Em looked up at Eddie's approach and offered him a hand with the languid grace of a satisfied cat. "Darling, how you spoil me."

"Nothing less than you deserve, my dear." Eddie took a seat beside Em and let the waiter place small plates filled with finger foods before us. As soon as he emptied his tray, the waiter departed.

"Exactly what I was just saying to her." I cast a benevolent smile on Eddie.

His expression tightened around the lips as he smiled back, and he leaned over and whispered something in Em's ear.

"Oh, yes. I'd almost forgotten." Em paused in the act of lifting a canape to her mouth. "Eddie just reminded me. I only found out this evening. You know Tommy Stanford is seeing someone else, don't you?"

Eddie winced and sent me an apologetic glance.

I waved my glass in an airy fashion. "Not to worry, so am I."

The tension oozed out of Eddie's posture, and then a small frown puckered his brow. "It's not that fellow you were dancing with earlier, I hope?"

"Who was that, dear?" Em bit into the canape, careful not to mar her lipstick.

"Rian Stirling. And no, he's not my date. He just asked me to dance."

"Pity." Em gave me a feline smile. "You know what I told you about rich boys versus poor ones."

Eddie flicked a startled glance at her, but she just patted his hand. His brow cleared. "Well, that's all right, then." He helped himself to some hors d'oeuvres. "As long as it's not Stirling. He doesn't have the best reputation."

"Is that so?" I took a puffed pastry shell myself. Dinner seemed a long time ago.

Frowning, Eddie nodded. "He's known for being a ruthless businessman."

"He makes the most divine things, though. Really clever gadgets that are so useful around the house. Remember that corkscrew we got as a wedding present?" Em pushed Eddie playfully on the arm. "You just attach it to the top of the bottle and it clamps down on and sucks out the cork all by itself. Simply marvelous."

I could imagine the conniptions Ryker must have gone through when that little item hit the mass market. Or how much money Stirling must make on such an innocuous use of the technology he'd recovered. And how had he adapted it for use by non-shifters? I'd have to ask him the next time I saw him.

"I'd still stay away from Stirling if I were you, Rhett. He makes Father uneasy, and there aren't many people who can do that." Eddie blinked at me in all seriousness. I could picture him ten years from now, looking like a sage owl on the board of his father's company.

His concern for me was oddly touching.

Where was Knight? I'd seen neither hide nor hair of him since we'd parted. I checked my watch again. I should head to our rendezvous point, but there was something I had to do first. I rose and made my way to the other side of the table, pausing to give Eddie a peck on the cheek. "You're really a dear old thing to be worrying about me. Don't. I'll be fine."

Eddie blushed to his roots. Men of his class rarely show concern for those around them.

"Speaking of dates, I need to find mine. Catch up with you later?"

"If not here, then at the house in the morning." Em reached for Eddie's hand without looking in his direction, certain he would meet her halfway for a clasp of fingers.

He did.

"He's a keeper, Em. Don't let that one get away."

She beamed at me. I suppose I hadn't been as approving of her decision to marry—and specifically to marry Eddie—as I might have been. She'd been right, though. They made a good couple. As much as Eddie would never be my idea of the perfect husband, a sudden spurt of envy struck me.

It wasn't the fancy wedding or the country club life I envied. It was knowing someone would stand at your side, watch your back, and be prepared to lift you up or fall down with you. That's what I desired more than anything else.

But the wistful thoughts of a schoolgirl had no place in the mind of a Redclaw agent. And I needed to find Knight so we could contact Ryker right away.

Chapter Sixteen

After waiting by the entrance for almost fifteen minutes, I gave up and went searching for Knight. Remembering his bleary-eyed state that first night at Moneta's, I feared the worst. No doubt the free-flowing champagne had gotten the better of him.

Disappointment fumed just below the surface. Knight's actions shouldn't have surprised me. Even though he'd given me the impression these last few days of a man sobering up and moving on, no doubt it was because Redclaw had been keeping him on a short leash.

What did I expect? Since the end of the war, everyone in my set seemed to be of the opinion they should play hard and drink hard, for tomorrow we might die. Fast cars, hard drink, smoking like chimneys, and washing down fistfuls of "Mother's Little Helpers" was how most of the people in my circle lived. I grew up seeing with my own eyes the lengths people would go to keep drinking, and the lies they would tell themselves and others. Namely, that they could quit anytime they liked. It had been foolish to think I could rely on Knight. I'd have to handle everything myself—as usual—and hope he didn't screw things up with any drunken antics.

There was no sign of Knight on the dance floor or with the other diners. The billiard room, perhaps? Or out on the terrace? One of the private rooms? I'd have to go door-to-door to find him. "When I get my hands on him...." I muttered as I headed down the corridor.

Something of my anger must have shone in my eyes, as the staff member who stepped up to offer yet another glass of champagne wheeled and headed in the other direction. I gave a little snort of satisfaction as he skedaddled. The hallway contained more people than I expected. A couple of women fanned themselves, overcome with the heat in the ballroom. Two men in evening dress, their ties askew, weaved their way out onto the terrace. A woman, smiling as she smoked from an ebony cigarette holder, listened with rapt attention to a man as they stood to one side of a marble-topped table against the wall.

I almost passed them both, intent on heading to one of the private rooms off the hallway, when I realized the handsome man with the movie-star features was wearing bedroom slippers. He was also Knight. I'd forgotten about the disguise.

"There you are. I've been looking everywhere for you." Holding my clutch, I slipped my arm through his, and aimed a bright smile at the woman.

"Is it that time already?" Knight squinted first at me, and then his watch, which had the unfortunate effect of drawing all eyes toward his feet. "I'm sorry. I've got the most frightful headache."

His pained expression, which I'd taken for drunkenness at first glance, sent a pang of guilt through me. He'd complained of a headache earlier, and his control over his image was obviously slipping. Who knew what the effect of prolonged use of the image-enhancer might be?

"I was just telling Peter here I wish I'd had the good sense to bring my own mules with me. My feet are killing me." Knight's new friend tipped one foot sideways, the better to display her trim ankles.

Knight had already forgotten his fake name.

"I see. Yes. We need to get *Richard* back to his room, don't we, darling?" I placed additional emphasis on the name, and with my free hand, circled my temple with an index finger. I gave Pretty Ankles a meaningful glance.

"Pooh," she said inelegantly, stubbing out her cigarette in the ashtray. "All the nice ones are taken, pink, or nuts. Never mind, Peter, or Richard, or whatever your name is. I think you're the only sensible person here."

She patted Knight on the cheek with a smile, trailing her fingers across his skin as she withdrew. She went down the hallway back toward the ballroom, swinging her purse in a little circle by its strap.

"What was that all about?" Knight peered down the hall after her.

"Didn't you notice?" I pointed to his feet.

He wiggled his toes within the slippers, moving the tips up and down. "Ah. Bedroom shoes. I was just thinking about how nice it would be to get comfortable, and there they were."

"Are you all right?" I placed a hand on his arm, causing him to look up at my face again.

He rubbed his temple. "Not really. I wasn't joking about the headache. Feels like someone's stabbing an ice pick through my eye."

I was about to suggest we should leave so he could drop his disguise when the doors to the terrace opened, sending a welcome current of cool air into the heated hallway. Over Knight's shoulder, I saw two people come in from outdoors. I recognized the man right away. It took me a second longer to place the woman's face, but when I did, the shock of it was like being plunged into an icy stream. A quick glance at Knight showed he was losing his ability to maintain *any* part of his disguise. Even as I blanked on what to say to him, his face slowly morphed back into his own.

I had no time to think it through. I just acted, grabbing Knight by the back of his neck and pulling him into a kiss, all the while fumbling behind me, clutch in hand, for the handle to the room beside us.

It wasn't a chaste peck on the cheek. It couldn't be, not for my purposes. I angled Knight so anyone approaching him from behind would just see his back, the passion with which we were kissing, and our desperate need to find a room where we could be alone.

His eyes flew open at the onslaught of my lips on his, and he stiffened at the contact. Nevertheless, I persisted. I pulled him in, thrusting up against him as I dragged him with me, silently begging him to pick up on my signals. After that initial moment of surprise, he closed his eyes and opened his mouth.

I'd thought I was in control of the situation but in a flash, the tables turned. No longer was I kissing him. Instead, he kissed *me*. And he was very thorough about it. My back thumped up against the door as he pressed in, and for an instant, I completely lost track of my intention to get us out of the hallway as fast as possible. I gave a sharp inhalation, and he took that as an invitation to plunge into my mouth as his hand slid down my back and his fingers tightened on my derriere. Acting on instinct now, I lifted one leg to hook my calf behind his, practically purring as I moved against him. It was perhaps just as well my dress limited movement to a degree, or else I might have seriously embarrassed myself right there in the hallway. I pushed my fingers into his hair, delighted Knight didn't rely on heavy pomades to tame it.

Until that instant, I don't think I'd ever been well and truly kissed. Don't get me wrong. I'd dated in college. But I'd never understood the emphasis most people put on kissing. It seemed a bit like holding hands. Nice, but nothing terribly exciting.

Obviously, I'd been doing it wrong. Or with the wrong person.

Knight didn't just kiss me. He *inhaled* me. He opened up and demanded I open in return. He was that forbidden bottle of whiskey I'd refused to drink but every cell had been craving. His kiss struck me with the same hot, smoky intensity of a straight shot of Glenlivet. Wasn't that a kicker? Warning bells should have gone off in my mind, but instead I gave a little whimper of relief when I grasped the door handle and felt it turn behind me. As the door opened, I dragged him into the dimly lit room without breaking contact. He kicked the door shut behind us with a slippered foot.

Only then did I have the sense to push him back. He stared in open-mouthed disbelief. A momentary pulse of perverse pride shot through me when I realized he was just as wrecked by the kiss as I was. The unexpectedness of it must have blown his concentration, for he stood before me wearing what must be his real clothes: a rumpled cotton shirt in pale blue and slacks that had seen better days. His actual shoes, it relieved me to see, were a pair of battered loafers.

"What the hell was that?" He passed a hand over his mouth and jaw, his pupils wide and dark in the low lighting.

"A kiss. If you're not sure, it's been too long since you've experienced one." Too late, I remembered the last person he'd kissed with that kind of passion had likely been Margo. Add breathlessness to that gaffe, and I'm sure my nonchalance wasn't convincing. There was no time to dwell on the matter, though. I ducked around him and cracked open the door.

As though she could sense my eyes upon her, the woman about to enter the ballroom looked back over her shoulder. I flinched away from the opening, resisting the instinct to slam the door shut. With luck, she hadn't seen me.

When I turned away from the door, I ran slap into Knight. He steadied me by grabbing my arms, a move that made me gasp due to the tenderness of my healing wound. Knight didn't notice. His nostrils flared as he growled. "You know what I mean."

I gave him a little push. My hands met the immobility of his chest—more muscular than I would have given him credit for—so I pushed again, harder. "Look, I understand you're mad, but I don't have time to be gentle with your feelings right now. The couple who just passed us in the hall—"

"What couple? I didn't see anyone."

"They came in from the terrace. Hence the kiss. You never saw their faces. More to the point, I didn't want them to see *our* faces."

"Because...?" His anger dissipated, leaving him standing too close to me as his gaze briefly dropped to my lips. When his eyes met mine, he lifted his eyebrows and gave me one of his crooked smiles.

Damn. Damn. Damn.

There was no way to do this kindly. "Because it was my old boyfriend, Tommy Stanford, with his new girlfriend." I raised a hand when Knight would have interrupted. "Your not-dead wife, Margo."

He stood in stunned silence for several seconds as the impact of what I'd said struck him. Then his eyes went flat and cold. He stepped back as though I were radioactive, and yet there was no safe distance from me. "Impossible."

Never had a single word sounded so clipped and deadly.

"Look, I've spent a lot of time staring at pictures of her lately. I know what I saw."

"You're delusional!" A pause while he breathed hard. "Or you're part of the coverup."

His words were like a slap to the face. Had I thought Knight angry before? Standing with clenched fists, he tucked his chin as his chest heaved with the force of his breathing. He reminded me of a bull behind the gate at a rodeo, just waiting for the buzzer to explode out of the holding pen. I believe if I'd been a man, he'd have punched me.

I held my ground.

"It was Margo. Her hair was different, but it was her, I'm telling you. I'm good with faces. I ran into you just once back in March and remembered you—and where I'd seen you—when I got handed your file." I gave my head a little shake. "That's not important. What matters is that Margo must have faked her death. Why would she do that, and why is she here now?"

I hadn't paid attention to the room when we'd entered. The lighting was subdued, coming from a couple of lamps positioned on tables beside several wingbacked chairs. A comfortable-looking sofa faced a small fireplace, now unlit and swept clean of ashes. Most likely a reading room, a place where people could go to get away from the other club members for a quiet conversation, or to pour themselves a drink stronger than you could get in the ballroom.

Knight spied a decanter on a side table. To my dismay, he sloshed whiskey into a tumbler and knocked it back in a single swallow. I moved to stop him, but dropped my hand to my side as he thumped the empty glass back down on the table.

"She wouldn't. She couldn't. I was *there*. She lay crumpled like a broken doll. There was blood everywhere. I can see it pooling around her, even now." He spoke without looking in my direction, gripping the sides of the table as he shook his head like a prizefighter who'd taken one too many blows but couldn't admit the fight was over.

"You were across the street when she got hit, and you weren't looking in her direction. You turned when you heard the squeal of brakes. That's what your statement to the police said. She was flung to one side, and the car sped off. Think about it. It would have been easy to throw herself against the car in passing, particularly if she knew the driver." Most likely she'd had a pouch of calf's blood, designed to rupture when she fell. Which meant she had to have accomplices when they took her away....

"Stop it." He clutched his head in both hands.

But I couldn't. "An ambulance arrives out of nowhere, but you don't know who called for it. She's taken to the nearest hospital, where she's pronounced dead. But you know as well as I do, you can't always trust your eyes." I waved a hand up and down the length of his body. "If she had similar technology, she could have faked her death."

"I buried her."

The raw sorrow in his voice gaped like a non-healing wound, and I was the one who'd ripped the bandage off. I had no choice. Now I was about to pour alcohol on his injury.

"You thought you buried her. It was a closed casket funeral." I put my hand on his arm.

"You don't know what the hell you're talking about. Shut up!" He wheeled around and took me by the shoulders. Startled, I let the force of his momentum carry us both to the door, which slammed shut as my back hit it. He gave me a little shake. "You saw a woman coming toward you from down the hall. In the span of what—two seconds?—you decide she's Margo and drag me in here. And yet you're so bloody sure you know what you saw. Because Rhett Bishop never makes a mistake, does she?"

I lifted my chin to meet his furious gaze. "Prove me wrong." Shoving him off me, I opened the door. "Let's go find her and Tommy and see what they're up to."

He would have blown past me, but I caught him by the arm. "Disguise."

His response was unprintable. I'm not even sure what some of the curses meant. Still, his clothing shimmered back into evening dress. His face lacked the detail of before, instead taking on the unformed look of a store manikin, but it would do. His own mother wouldn't have recognized him.

Or wife, either, I hoped.

I had to almost trot to keep up with him as he stormed down the hallway like General Eisenhower about to order the invasion of Normandy. We stood at the entrance of the ballroom, scanning the crowd, but our quarry had vanished. Spying Em dancing with Eddie, I motioned for Knight to wait as I threaded my way through the dancers toward them.

"Darling, have you seen Tommy?"

Em frowned, pulling Eddie to a halt. "He just came through with Eve. I think they were on their way out."

Oh, is that what Margo was calling herself these days? How appropriate. If Knight and I hurried, we might be able to catch them in the parking lot. I started to turn away, but Em caught me by the wrist.

"What do you want with Tommy? I thought you were done with him."

"I am. The best part of being done is saying so. I want to say my bit, that's all."

"That's not like you." Em glowered at me with unaccustomed speculation in her eyes. "What are you up to?"

"Nothing for you to worry about. See you back at the house?" I gave her hand a little squeeze and pulled away. Catching Knight's eye across the room, I signaled for him to meet me at the door.

"Well?" His face reminded me of a plastic doll, minus the fixed smile which was still unnerving.

"They just left. If we hurry, we can catch them—"

"They're long gone by now." He was as immobile as a statue when I tugged on his arm. "We should be looking for the artifacts, not haring off on your snipe hunt."

"I think this is *about* the artifacts."

He folded his arms across his chest. "Oh, go on. Do tell. This will be a good one."

"Why else would Margo be here? You've always believed some secret organization killed your wife when you refused to work for them. Now that we know she's not dead, it makes sense she was working for them all along—and still works for them today. There wasn't time to tell you before, but I spoke with Rian Stirling. He admitted an auction is taking place this weekend, and he's not the only party interested. It beggars belief to think it's a coincidence Margo would show up here the same weekend there's a bidding war for stolen technology. She *must* be involved."

"You're going to take the word of some rich guy you just met? Why would he share this with you, anyway?" Knight's tone could have stripped paint.

I hesitated for a fraction of a second. "I'm pretty sure he's Ryker's brother."

"I see. Well, that explains a lot." His nostrils flared wide as he inhaled sharply. He blew his breath out in several short bursts, obviously struggling to hang on to his temper. "It's Redclaw you trust over everyone else."

"And you," I snapped. "You convinced me to come here looking for artifacts. Now I have a lead and you don't want to follow it. Fine." I held out my hand. "Give me your keys. I'll go after them myself."

"I'm just—"

"Wasting my time. If you don't want to know the truth—"

"That has nothing to do with it. I just don't see any point in trying to track someone who's already gone."

"Maybe. Maybe not." I nudged Knight. "That's Tommy by the bar. Getting a refill on his flask, no doubt."

As we watched, Tommy brushed back a heavy curl of brown hair that had escaped his thick pomade and handed the bartender some cash. In return, he accepted a bottle of gin with a foolish grin. I pushed Knight toward the door as Tommy headed out. "Come on. We don't want to lose him."

Outside, Knight led the way to his car. The night air felt pleasantly cool after the overheated rooms of the club. The moon cast a silver light over parked cars, distorting their paint into shades of purple and gray. Ahead of us, Tommy's white dinner jacket stood out as though cut from marble. He went to the passenger side of a huge black Daimler and leaned in the open window. When he straightened, his hands were empty. I heard the clear tones of a cheerful whistle as he rounded the back of the car and got in behind the steering wheel.

I said nothing as Knight stalked to his car, but followed in his wake and slipped into the passenger side as he took his own seat. The engine started with a cough and a bang, causing the headlights to dim briefly before the motor caught.

"I don't suppose you brought anything from Redclaw in your bag of tricks that will help if this car breaks down?"

"Sorry, I left the flying saucer in my other pants."

Knight's cutting manner prevented me from responding with a witty comeback. "And your disguise, as well, it would seem."

"No one can see us now, and I need a break. My head's killing me."

His anger had settled into a cold fury. I could work with it.

"Don't lose them," I cautioned when Tommy's car left the parking lot with a spin of gravel.

"I won't." Knight followed Tommy out of the parking lot at a sedate pace, not reacting when the Daimler roared up the road. "The young fool will end up in a ditch the way he's driving. What exactly is your plan when we catch up with them?"

"I'll let you know when we do." My voice was as sharp as his and my anger at his refusal to believe me nearly as deep. His fury was fine with me. It would stop me from thinking about that kiss. In the last twenty minutes, Knight had gone from being a grieving widower to being a married man. In my book that made him off-limits. Somehow, we'd have to get those artifacts, and I needed his help. I hadn't the faintest idea what his reaction would be if he came face-to-face with Margo, but I hope I'd given him enough warning for him to be on guard. I know what *my* reaction would be to such an ugly betrayal of trust.

The Daimler's taillights were far ahead, occasionally disappearing as the road dipped and turned. When there'd been no visible sign of the other car for at least ten seconds, Knight anticipated my protest and floored the gas. The clunker leapt forward with a rattle. I didn't relax until I spotted the small red lights winking in and out of sight like a drunken firefly farther down the road. When the Daimler turned off the main strip, I knew its destination.

"Tommy's going to his family's estate. See there—that turning up ahead. Go past those gates and then bring the car around. We'll sneak in and see what he's up to." I twisted in my seat to look back over my shoulder as we passed the entrance to the Stanford property. Beyond the gates, I saw the flash of red taillights as the car hugged the curve of the drive.

Knight turned the car around at the next estate and we drove back along the road. As we came abreast of the entranceway, he pulled off the asphalt and parked the car. "We can hardly drive straight in."

"Good point. We'll cut across the drive and—"

Knight's icy drawl cut me off. "You realize in all probability he's come here with a little lovemaking in mind? Are you sure *you're* not the one who hasn't gotten over an old flame?"

"Oh, please." I drew back. "Tommy asked me to marry him and I refused. As if I wanted to spend the rest of my life with a drunken lout." I could have bitten my tongue as soon as the words were out of my mouth. "Not that you're a lout. I mean—"

"I understand your meaning perfectly." His tone was so chilly I developed frostbite. "Relax. I'm not offering my hand in marriage."

I was glad the darkness of the car masked how red my face must have been. Tempted as I was to point out that would make him a bigamist, I kept my mouth shut. That easy camaraderie between us had disappeared, as was the back-and-forth volley of wits that had marked our relationship thus far.

It surprised me how much that loss hurt.

When he spoke again, his words came hard and flat. "I'm here to prove you wrong. Once I do, once you realize Margo is dead and you were grossly mistaken, I'm done."

"Done?" Even though I wasn't sure what he meant, the word plummeted like a stone in my belly, leaving me a touch queasy.

"Yes. Done. I go back to my life—such as it was—and you and Redclaw leave me alone. For good."

"Peter—"

He got out of the car without another word and yanked on the door, stopping in mid-slam when I hissed a warning at him. Fine. We'd table this for now.

He followed me as we slipped through the gates and cut across the drive to kneel behind a row of bushes. The driveway in front of the house was empty.

"He must have taken the car around back to the garage," I whispered. "Come on."

Knight reserved his complaints until we'd situated ourselves outside the large building that housed the Stanford cars. "Now do you have a plan?"

I was about to inform him that his snarky attitude wasn't helping when a light clicked on in the garage, creating a rectangular patch of illumination through the window near our position. I grabbed Knight by his sleeve and pulled him back into the shadows.

I needn't have worried. The door to the garage opened, and the lights inside went off, leaving Knight and me safely hidden in the building's shadow. A flashlight illuminated the gravel path in front of the two people walking along it, the faint crunch of shoes drifting back to our ears. Knight would have moved to follow, but I stopped him with a grip on his forearm. I held him there until the light bobbled out of sight.

"What are you waiting for? We'll lose them."

He was so close, the heat from his body was a welcome respite from air that had grown chilly. Goosebumps prickled along my bare arms as the wind fluttered the fresh young leaves of the trees.

"If we follow them now, we'll be exposed as we cross the lawn. If they look back, there's nowhere for us to hide." I nodded at the retreating figures. The moonlight was so bright they didn't need the flashlight. "I suspect they're headed to a small pavilion near the headland. There's an inlet that comes in

from the sea, and a river deep enough for a motorboat. If they
head out from the pavilion by boat, we won't be able to keep up
with them, anyway. But since that's the most likely place they'll
go, if we hang back for a moment, we can sneak up on them
without risk of being spotted."

"And you know they're headed there because?"

An hour ago, his tone would have been arch and amused.
Now it could have cut glass.

"It's not just a pavilion. There's an underground system
of tunnels. Smugglers used the caves during the Revolutionary
War, and then during Prohibition, bootleggers enlarged the
hold, put in electricity, and shored up the walls. *Giordano's* is
less than ten miles from here. They ran a speakeasy during the
Twenties. It's a respectable restaurant now. Good food, too."

"So. Your ex-boyfriend's father was a bootlegger? Small
wonder he can afford such a fancy spread."

"No. Tommy's father inherited money, as will Tommy,
when his turn comes. *My* father was the bootlegger. Mr.
Stanford pretended to turn a blind eye to the deliveries and took
a cut. Come on. The coast should be clear now."

I started down the path, but Knight caught me by the
arm. "Wait. Your father was a whiskey peddler? But I thought
he—"

"Gambled away the family fortune? He did. At least, he
lost all the money he'd made as a gin runner. As much of my
mother's money he could get his hands on as well.
Unfortunately, he didn't stop there. He also lost money that

belonged to some pretty dangerous people. Hence the suicide." I was grateful the moon, for the moment, had ducked its face behind clouds, leaving mine in shadow. "We ended up liquidating everything we owned to pay off the mob. My mother moved back to Wyoming. It's debatable which she finds the most unforgivable: the shame of his suicide or the fact we're broke. As soon as she could, she married another rich man. So you see...." I gently removed my arm from his grip. "I understand betrayal by someone you love."

Knight was silent for several thunderous beats of my heart.

"And how do you know about Stanford's special place?" His breath brushed the top of my forehead and ruffled my hair.

"Tommy brings every girl he dates there at least once. It's about as special as Grand Central."

Knight offered a subdued snort, but I felt oddly triumphant for having triggered it. His next words dashed any lingering hope we'd mended our fences when he went on in a clear, cool voice. "You're thinking they've hidden the artifacts there. But if Tommy's love nest is so well-frequented, it would hardly make an ideal hiding place for a cache of—unusual—technology."

We needed to get moving. If Tommy and Margo were up to something in the pavilion, we might miss them if we didn't hurry. For some reason, my feet remained frozen in place. "Not a love nest." I murmured somewhere near Knight's shoulder. "Just a place Tommy prided himself on knowing about where he could sneak a kiss or two and pretend he was a part of it. Given the pavilion is on private property, it's probably safe enough."

My body swayed a little toward Knight, reminding me of the marked differences between the kisses I'd received from Tommy and the one from him this evening. The first had been an amusing, sandy, and somehow disappointing experience. The other made me want to repeat it right there against the side of the garage, complete with ripping clothes off and everything that went with that. Heat bloomed in places that should have been keeping their collective minds on the job at hand.

"Shall we go check out this special place, then?" Knight sounded like a college professor demanding I show proof of my math. It was like a dash of cold water, which I very much needed.

"This way. If you must speak, keep your voice down. Sound carries down here by the water."

We skirted the walkway until the graveled path curved into a wooded area and gave way to sandy dirt and pine needles. Tall oak trees closed in around us, limbs with newly unfurled leaves swaying in the freshening breeze. Clouds scudded overhead, dappling our progress with rapidly shifting shadows. The moon, when visible, bathed everything in a clear, bright light, throwing the path and the trees into sharp-edged relief that warped and bent with the moving cloud cover. As we went deeper into the wood, there was no sign of anyone ahead. The restless rustle of the branches sounded similar to the distant wash of waves rolling in and out again.

I'd played croquet on Tommy's lawn and dined alfresco at the pavilion at midnight. I'd dug for clams on the beach below, gotten sunburned, made sandcastles, and drunk bootleg gin straight from the bottle around a bonfire. I'd sailed along this shore in brilliant weather and walked alone in blustery winds as a hurricane rolled in.

It had been one of my favorite places to visit growing up. Had I married Tommy, I could have called it my own. Even so, the price on it came too high.

"We must be careful. The moonlight will work against us as much as it helps. This way."

"Still waiting to hear what your plan is."

The air of cool detachment might have suggested to someone else he'd gotten over his anger, but I knew better. There was an acidity to his tone that belied any levity.

"We'll take a peek in the hold below the pavilion and see if the artifacts are there. If so, I'll contact Ryker." My fingers brushed the ladybug pin, assuring me it was still in place. Provided Knight didn't walk away on the spot, I'd get him to take me back to the club so I could call Ryker, but it was nice to have a backup plan if I needed it. The ray gun's presence within my clutch provided an additional measure of comfort.

I half-expected Knight to comment on the apparent inadequacies of my plan, but the silence surrounding him was like one of those force fields from *War of the Worlds*. There was no penetrating it. Despite a moment of softening when he'd learned about my father, it was clear he was still furious with me over suggesting Margo was still alive. When I proved Margo the villainess of the piece, would he blame me as the bearer of bad news?

After the open expanse of lawn, the air in the woods was close, almost as if the trees themselves were holding their breath. They clawed the sky with a slight shift of wind from the sea, like old witches casting spells of doom. Even so, this part of the property still saw a landscaper's touch. The path continued through the copse of trees in a rich man's imitation of a forest.

"Where exactly is this pavilion? Who puts a building in the middle of the woods?" Knight encompassed the surrounding stand of trees with an expansive wave of his hand.

I pointed some distance ahead, where the trees opened up to reveal a flat promontory. Moonlight gleamed off white columns that marked the corners of a large roofed structure.

"Somehow, when you said pavilion, I thought you meant something about the size of a gazebo. You could host Glen Miller and his orchestra there."

His somewhat peeved reaction was both predictable and, in an odd way, soothing.

"I'm sure one time they did."

"I'm not surprised. It seems like the sort of—" Whatever else he might have said evaporated when all of the sudden he whipped his head around.

I peered into the woods behind us, but saw nothing. "What is it?"

The hair on back of my neck rose when he fished something out of his pocket. As he grabbed my wrist with his left hand, the moon came out from behind the clouds, illuminating the grim, determined look on his face. With a flicking motion of his right hand, he unfolded a knife. Moonlight glinted off the silver blade.

"Don't move." His voice was deep with urgency, and I gasped as he shoved a foot in between mine and kicked my feet into a wider stance. The knife flashed as he drove it down between my thighs into the taut material of my dress. Cloth split with a ragged, tearing sound as he hacked his way down to the bottom edge. When he sawed through the hem, the pieces of my dress fluttered in the breeze and my legs were free to move. It was an oddly liberating sensation.

Knife still in hand, he tugged me along in his wake. "Don't look back. *Run*."

As warnings go, that proved as impossible as the stricture to Lot's wife. I cast a hasty glance over my shoulder. Light poured down from above like molten silver, delineating the shadows sprinting toward us from behind. Any other time, I would have admired their beauty, the almost mechanical perfection of form, the way their legs moved like pistons as they closed the distance between us. The thudding of paws on the hard-packed soil as they ran through the forest rumbled over the low murmur of the sea.

Wolves.

Chapter Seventeen

The wolves raced through the woods like flames engulfing dry tinder. The pavilion was in sight up ahead, but the gap between us and those snarling teeth began closing with frightening speed. The excited yipping of the pack when they spotted us brought goosebumps to my skin. Their hot breath would be on the back of our necks within seconds.

"Hurry!" I yanked myself free of Knight's grip and kicked off my pumps. We'd run faster apart than holding hands. Side by side, we dashed toward the break in the trees where the pavilion stood like a little Greek temple in the moonlight. Sanctuary. But only if we got there before the wolves brought us down.

I caught my stockinged foot in a tree root and almost fell flat, but Knight grabbed my arm and pulled me along with a brutal grip. This time, he didn't let go.

With my muscles burning as we burst from the stand of trees, my breath came in sobs as we reached the headland and ran toward the wide, flat steps leading up onto the raised platform that served as a dance floor and dining area beneath the long roof.

As we sprinted up the stairs and into the pavilion, I begged whoever might be listening, *please don't have changed the lock.*

I charged up to the small stage that took up one end of the open floor plan. Behind the dais stood an ornate carving, depicting a series of scenes from Greek mythology. The moon went behind the clouds as I reached it, and I had to squint to make out the figures.

Paris holding the Apple of Discord before Aphrodite, Hera, and Athena. Hercules battling the Hydra. Perseus brandishing the slain Medusa's head. Persephone descending into the Underworld. Goat-footed Pan, playing his wooden flute.

The moon came out from the clouds and the silver light intensified, illuminating the figures in question. It also highlighted the sleek canine forms streaking across the open field toward us.

As the sounds of snarling and panting approached from behind, with a shaking hand I pressed on the apple, twisted the lyre sideways, then back in place, and pulled Medusa's head out from the wall before clicking it back where it had been. Something beneath us rumbled and groaned, and the dais slid to one side. A steep ladder led straight down into near Stygian darkness.

"Down here. Hurry!" I pushed Knight toward the opening.

"You first."

"Go, damn it," I yelled and shoved him again. I knew where the release was and he didn't; we didn't have time for his British politeness. I plunged into the dark hold, following behind Knight as close as I dared without stepping on his hands. My stockings were slippery on wooden rungs, and if I hadn't scrambled down this ladder a million times in the past, I would have taken both of us down to the ground. The yip of delight as the first wolf shoved its head through the opening and spied us prompted me to jump off the ladder with a quick prayer that I wouldn't break my ankle, and then I lunged for the lever mounted on the wall at the base of the ladder and pulled it down with both hands. Gears tumbled, and the dais slid back into place as wolves shoved and snarled at each other over the slowly closing entrance.

"Can they get in?" Knight's voice, so close to my ear, made me jump.

"We should be safe enough for the moment. They must change back into human form *and* know the sequence to open the trapdoor." I leaned against the damp wall for a moment to catch my breath and then stood up straight. "We can't stay here. They may have sent a pretty little wolf-shifter to make a play for Tommy. Anyone who's ever met him would have to know he's the weak link in any operation. In which case, there's a good chance he brought someone else here at some point. He wouldn't be able to resist showing off."

"It's a miracle young Stanford has survived this long." Knight sounded as though he'd be the first to volunteer to rectify that situation.

That thought had occurred to me as well. What had Tommy gotten himself into this time?

The hold wasn't as dark as I'd thought. Our eyes adjusted to the gloom as we walked forward. Dim light glowed from a series of ancient bulbs encased in metal cages along one wall. A motorboat rocked gently back and forth on its moorings alongside the old wooden dock, the reflected light on the water sending spangled beams along its hull. From the dock, a walkway extended into the shadows, where a tunnel led to the main cavern. Over the water, the ceiling sloped down to a narrow passage leading to a fissure some distance away, which was hard to spot from the outside. It took a boat with a skilled driver at the wheel to access that entrance. Someone had installed a heavy mesh gate over this opening since the last time I was here, and I saw no mechanism at the dock to raise it. The air was dank with the odor of dead fish and brackish water from the nearby marsh.

Above us, we heard claws scratching at the wood. I could only hope it held.

"Is there another way out of here?" Knight waved toward the boat. The stone walls threw his voice back to us in a weird echo.

I nodded and lowered my voice when I spoke. "There's a tunnel that goes all the way back to the main house. On the other side of the main hold. If it hasn't been closed off, that is."

"This just gets better and better."

At least Knight kept his voice down, too.

"Being torn apart by wolves isn't my idea of a good time, either. You realize someone probably hid the artifacts down here. The wolves wouldn't be on the scene otherwise."

And by implication, Margo must be in on the heist.

My words jolted him into recalling why we were there. The low-level lighting cast shadows under his eyes, making his face look drawn and severe. He gave a stiff nod.

"If we're quiet, we can sneak up on the main room, confirm the presence of the artifacts, and withdraw to contact Redclaw. There has to be a way to raise the gate, and if push comes to shove, I'm sure I can pilot the boat."

Knight shot me a look of frank disbelief. "Or we can just look for the gate mechanism, take the boat, and hightail it out of here to notify Redclaw."

As an alternative plan, it wasn't half-bad, but it wouldn't give me the win I needed.

"I thought the entire goal of the weekend was to find the artifacts. Do you really want to call Redclaw out here on a possible fool's errand before we know all the facts? Not to mention, taking the boat will tip our hand to whoever is behind the theft."

"That was before we knew how many players were involved. It's too risky. If we leave now, we can call Ryker and his minions and let them take over here. It's the only sensible thing to do."

Being told what was sensible or not had the same effect on me as waving a red flag in front of a bull.

"Fine," I snapped. "I'll check out the cavern. You stay here and look for a way to raise the gate. It won't take me more than a minute to see what's in the next chamber. Then we can get out of here."

"We're not splitting up." His words pelted me like unexpected hail.

I lobbed his own words back at him. "It's the *only* sensible thing to do. You're right. Figure out how to lift the gate while I check out the hold. If we need to leave in a hurry—"

"Has anyone ever told you you're too damn stubborn for your own good? You can't stop me from following you. Let's get this over with. If I have to risk my neck, I'd rather not prolong the agony. We'll confirm our suspicions and come back for the boat. We don't have a choice." He pointed toward the trapdoor above us. "It's the fastest way out of here past the wolves."

The passage to the main chamber was just wide enough for a man carrying a crate to navigate. Moisture dripped down the walls, gleaming in the faint beams cast by the periodic posting of a lightbulb, networked by a strand of electrical wire snaking down the length of the tunnel. The wall had crumbled in places, leaving piles of broken rock. I regretted the loss of my shoes. My stockings were in shreds, and I'd be lucky if I didn't turn an ankle or cut my feet on the sharp shale. As we neared the main room, the murmur of voices echoed with an odd reverberation off the walls.

The layout of the main hold hadn't changed much since the last time I'd been there. The tunnel ahead opened out into a small space behind a row of large boulders ringing the cavern, with a narrow path between them into the larger cavern. With luck, the natural rock wall would shield us to a certain extent as we scouted out the activity there. The light grew brighter as we approached, but the rocks cast long jagged shadows deep enough to hide the careful spy. At the sound of the voices, I felt around inside my clutch for the ray gun, and my hand had just closed on the smooth warmth of its barrel when I heard Knight's sharp intake of breath. His hand clamped down like a vise on my arm, but it was too late. I'd crossed the faint beam I never saw, causing a wave of green light to envelop me. And because Knight was in contact with me, the same energy washed over him as well.

I don't even remember falling.

Chapter Eighteen

I came to, head pounding, and mouth as dry as if I'd swallowed sand, worse than the worst hangover I'd ever experienced in my days as a carefree, party-going socialite. Oh, I *did* have actual sand in my mouth. Disoriented and confused, I lifted my head and whimpered against the clanging of a hammer on my skull. When I tried to wipe the gritty, damp dirt off my face, my arm refused to cooperate, flopping around like a dead fish barely connected to me. Panic-fueled adrenaline surged through my veins, and I tried to sit up. The dimly lit cavern spun with my movement. Shifting chain links clanked as the shackle around my wrist went taut and kept me from falling over on my back.

Someone had dragged us into the main chamber. My wrist was encased by an iron shackle and attached to a ring on the cave wall. We were surrounded by wooden crates, some of which opened to reveal a mishmash of contents. Silver and dull-green objects of various sizes, marked with the familiar designs I'd seen on other artifacts, lay in crates packed with straw. The confined space was ablaze with light—powerful lanterns of a design I'd never seen before supplemented the anemic illumination of the low-wattage light bulbs above. The bluish light cast by the lanterns would have made Knight's fingers itch to get his hands on them. Ryker's, too, for that matter.

The reflected light gleamed off an ornate gilded frame sticking up out of another crate, revealing a stack of oil paintings. An open jewelry box sat on a packing crate; a pearl necklace draped in an artful fashion over its lip. A pair of emerald earrings lay beside it on the rough wood, glowing in the strange light. Silver candlesticks stood next to an immaculate tea set. Tiffany, I suspected.

Curled on his side a scant two feet away from me, Knight lay unconscious, also chained to the wall.

At least, I hoped he was unconscious. No one would shackle a dead man, right?

An assessment of our situation was in order. For the moment, we appeared to be alone. I spied my clutch lying on one of the crates. Had they found the ray gun? Even if they had, it was unlikely the gun would have allowed anyone to take it. Either way, I couldn't get to the purse, so the gun might as well be on the moon for all the good it would do me.

Right. I had one hand free. The heavy iron band around my left wrist was too tight to pull over my hand, though I spent several minutes trying. I fancied with a little butter I might have been able to manage it, but my bruised and battered skin said otherwise. Likewise, I couldn't budge the chain bolted into the wall. If I had a pin, I might have been able to pick the lock....

The thought of a pin reminded me of the enameled ladybug. Relief washed through me when my fingers closed over

it, still attached to my dress. If ever anyone needed to fire off a
Bat Signal, now was the time, but how? I should have asked
Ryker before blithely assuming it would be self-evident when I
needed it. Pressing down on the center of the ladybug's back, I
heard a faint click. The wings glowed, pulsing brighter, then
fading before pulsing again. I repinned the ladybug inside my
bodice to hide the glow. I couldn't risk using it as a lock pick
now. If it worked as a homing signal, then damaging it might
prevent anyone from coming to our rescue.

Knight's stillness concerned me. I stretched as far as I
could within the confines of my chain and nudged him in the ass
with my foot. My breath whooshed out of me in gusty relief at
the groan and feeble movement. Definitely alive.

"Knight," I kept my voice low and shoved him a little
harder. "Wake up."

He shifted a leg as though he were crawling in place but
didn't respond. I went cold at the sound of movement nearby
and turned my head at the pathetic whimper that followed. A
small white dog with black ears lifted a foreleg in supplication
from inside his wood and chicken wire cage, his tail moving so
fast it blurred. He looked just like the dog in the Master's Voice
advertisement.

"Aw, what are you doing here, little buddy?"

The dog sneezed with excitement and pawed at the wire.
The name on the collar's tag read *Delilah*. Odd, because he was
clearly male.

"I'd help if I could." Lifting my hand, the heavy links of the chain clanked together like that of Marley's ghost. "But as you can see—"

Another groan preceded words rusty with disuse. "Who are you talking to?"

"There's a little dog here. Are you all right?"

"Define 'all right.'" Knight pushed himself upright in stages, to stop short when he reached the end of his chain. The metallic sound as he tested the length of his confinement seemed to emphasize his disbelief when he tugged harder. "You've got to be kidding me."

"Did you see anyone before we were...whatever it was that happened to us?"

He palmed his face, opening his eyes wide as he took in our surroundings. "No. Damn it, I owe you an apology. You were right about the cache being hidden here."

"I owe you an apology as well. You were right about the risk. Our mutual recriminations will have to wait, though. Whoever locked us up will be back soon, and we have no idea what they'll do to us when they return. Can you reach my purse?"

He stretched, first with his free hand, and then with one of his legs, angling with his toe in an attempt to knock over the crate where my clutch lay. He fell back with a wince and rubbed his wrist. "Sorry. It's too far."

A quick check of my watch relieved my mind on one point at least. We hadn't been out more than five minutes. And though things looked bad at the moment, I had activated the ladybug, and help was on the way. Most likely. Provided I'd activated the signal correctly, and it didn't have a limited range.

All we had to do was stall for time.

"Do you have any of the tech still on you?"

Knight patted his pockets and sighed. "No. Stripped clean. Knife's gone, too. How about you?"

"Same here." With a cautious glance around, I tapped my bodice where I'd hidden the pin. No point in giving away information, should a listening device be in place. Knight frowned at me a long moment before his eyebrows lifted and his expression cleared.

A low growl made me look over at the little dog staring at the tunnel behind us. His hackles lifted in a sharp-edged line down his back. The reason for his unease soon became apparent.

Voices echoed as someone approached from the dock entrance.

"We should be safe enough."

A little shiver of déjà vu ran through me as Tommy repeated my own words to Knight about the wolves.

"It doesn't matter. Even if someone gets through, the energy field will stop them, as it did with our friends here. Moving the field closer to the dock was smart. This way, the field will stop any intruders before they get this far. And if the shifters are busy trying to get in at the pavilion, they won't see us when we leave by the river." The woman's voice sounded sultry as smoke, but steel resided there too. No question who was in charge.

The look on Knight's face was that of a man who'd been shot but hadn't yet realized the wound was fatal. Shock drained the color from his skin as if a bullet had pierced his heart.

"But to raise the gate, we have to turn off the field. We should load up the boat and get out of here. Go while we can."

The urgency vibrating in Tommy's voice reminded me of other times, other escapades, when Tommy had skirted expulsion from school—or worse—because of his shenanigans. Easily manipulated by his desire to 'be a good sport,' Tommy was ever game for a lark until things got dicey. Then he cut and ran, neatly absolving himself of any responsibility.

"I'm sure you're right, darling." The woman spoke in an absent tone, her voice devoid of any true affection as she stepped into the light. "But I have a few questions first."

The gleaming fall of dark hair spilled from a side part in a soft wave across her cheekbone in the peek-a-boo style made famous by Veronica Lake. It was no doubt seductive, but a stupid affectation for someone clambering about a smuggler's cave with stolen goods. She'd changed out of the slinky dress she'd been wearing back at the club. The black catsuit was a smarter choice, but had the effect of making her look like a comicbook villainess, especially with the addition of a flared skirt that came to sharp points at knee-level, even as it accentuated her long legs.

I wondered if the material was dragoncloth.

But it wasn't *my* reaction that interested her. She dismissed me with a quick glance and turned her full attention on Knight.

He stared at her as if seeing a ghost. The sight of her rocked him back against the wall like he'd been sucker-punched, his jaw working without sound as he tried to speak. A drowning man might have gasped for air in the same manner going down for the third time. At last, he took a long, shuddering breath and mouthed, "Margo."

"Good. You're awake." An overweening air of superiority vied with amusement as she spoke.

Knight gaped at her for a long moment, and then an extraordinary change came over his face. Had I not known better I'd have said he'd used the image enhancer to slide that cool mask of indifference into place. One sardonic eyebrow lifted, and when he spoke, it was in that clear, cutting voice I knew so well. "Good. You're not dead."

Tommy, looking rumpled in his evening wear with his black tie pulled askew, divided his glances between Knight and Margo before focusing on me. The ubiquitous silver flask dangled from one hand. "What the hell are you doing here, Rhett? I never took you for the jealous type." He shook his head and waggled a finger several times in Knight's direction. "You know this man, Eve?"

Before she could respond, Knight cut in.

"Eve?" Knight curled his lip. "*Eve*? Eve as in the original temptress, bearer of the forbidden fruit? That's rich." He flicked a whiplash sharp glance at Tommy. "Yes, she knows me. I'm her *husband.* Or did she forget to mention that?"

Tommy's mouth flapped open and closed several times, making him look rather like a guppy. "You're married?" He stared at Margo with the woebegone expression of that little cartoon fawn on discovering hunters had killed his mother.

"Not to worry, Stanford. Since she's officially dead, in another four years, she'll be a free agent. Though under the circumstances, I think faking your death qualifies as extreme cruelty. I should have no problem getting a divorce. Tell me, Margo. Was any of it real?"

"Bitterness doesn't suit you, Peter. Nor does wallowing in self-pity and drunkenness, I might add. Flattering as it was, it was a little pathetic to watch."

Knight's lips flattened in a grim line as he lunged up toward her, brought short by the reach of his chain. He sank back. The torchlight drew shadows across his face, emphasizing the look of utter contempt that washed over him. "You watched me. You knew what...what your reported death put me through. Why? Why marry me? Why fake your death, disappear for two years, and then come back now?"

She took several steps closer to him and crouched down, balanced on her heels. Her smile curved in a caricature of affection. "Darling, you loved being married to me, didn't you?"

She leaned toward him; the bodice of her clinging skinsuit emphasizing her generous cleavage. "You were a business investment that failed to pan out. That's all." She laughed when Knight's mouth fell open in shock. "A costly investment of my time at the wishes of my employer. Had you accepted their offer, the organization would have absorbed you, and in good time, I would have been free to leave."

"I don't understand."

"Your understanding isn't necessary. Suffice to say when you turned down the job offer it was time to cut my losses. I knew Margo's death would destroy you and take you off the market. I was right. And your paranoia regarding the government meant you wouldn't turn to them, either." She cast a glance in my direction and when she spoke again, the steel flashed in her voice like a stiletto in the ribs. "I didn't count on you joining up with Redclaw. They don't work with...outsiders."

"I'd hardly call it joined." He replied with his typical British reserve: cool, collected, and dismissive. He was in control once more. "Merely camping out there until I identified all the parties attempting to put a period to my life. So, not the government. Some criminal organization? I should have guessed. Why else would someone like you have been interested in me? I take it you're with the gunmen who tried to pick me up outside Moneta's?"

"What makes you think I'm not with the wolf pack?" Her sultry flirtatiousness made me want to slap her.

"Because they're still outside the cave, looking for a way in."

"I do so admire a smart man." She trailed a finger down his nose and tapped his lips with mocking gentleness. "Pity you didn't take the offer from HADES before."

Tommy might be in his usual gin-soaked stupor, watching their interaction in slack-jawed confusion, but I refused to let them ignore me any longer. "HADES?"

Both Knight and Margo glared at me in surprise, as though they'd forgotten I was there.

"HADES." Knight's upper lip lifted in a slight curl. "The puffed-up name of the organization that approached me about working for them. I presume it's some sort of convoluted acronym. Like Hellfire and Damnation Essential Services. Oh wait, I know. Honestly Arrogant Dumb Expendable Stooges." He aimed his comment at Margo, but his obvious contempt just fed her amusement, and she tossed her head back with a little laugh.

She patted his cheek hard enough to make him flinch. "Let me repeat. There was never any *us*, my dear. You were a job, nothing more, nothing less. Since you weren't willing to come on board voluntarily, HADES had planned to pick you up after you were blacklisted, seeing as no one would care enough to look for you. But then you disappeared. So inconsiderate."

Knight's gaze met mine, pained apology drawing fine lines at the corners of his eyes. No one should ever hear their worth—their love—was just a business venture. And though he must be feeling guilty for getting us into this mess, no one had twisted my arm to come. I was the one who insisted on poking around when we had a chance to escape. On following Tommy and Margo in the first place. It wasn't his fault she was, as Joan Crawford would say, a word no lady would use outside a kennel.

None of this was his fault. It was mine.

"What about Rhett?" Tommy asked, and might as well have added, "and me."

"I'm not interested in your old girlfriends, sweetheart. With one exception." She turned a baleful glare in my direction. "I'm surprised you came down here unarmed. Where's that unique little weapon you had the other day? I want it."

Her demand cleared up one little thing at least. She must work with the people who tried to grab Knight outside Moneta's, or else she wouldn't know about the ray gun. But she hadn't found it? I wasn't going to question that little bit of good luck. I indicated my outfit with a sweep of my hand. "It didn't go with the dress."

Her eyes narrowed. She was distinctly unamused by my reply.

"What are we going to do with them?" Tommy's whine made me wince, and irritation spurted across Margo's features before she tamped it down.

"Go ready the boat. I won't be long."

"But it isn't loaded—"

"I said—" She took a deep breath and began again with a brittle smile. "I'm just going to pick up one or two representative objects to show our buyers. I'll join you in a moment."

"But I'll have to lower the shield. If the shifters have found the boat entrance—"

"They're too busy trying to break in from above. I'll be along in a minute."

"Tommy."

My single word caught him as he was turning away. Dark circles, almost like bruises, emphasized the puffy bags under his eyes, previewing what he'd look like in another ten or so years, if he lived that long. "Remember when Jane Reid stole her grandmother's pearls? She tried to get you to cover for her."

Tommy's brow furrowed as he searched for the memory, and then his expression cleared. "You pointed out I'd be an accessory after the fact, so I didn't."

He began to walk away. I shouted after him.

"Jane didn't love you! She was just using you. Like Eve, here. Or Margo. Or whatever name she goes by. As soon as you're no longer useful she'll cut you loose. Don't turn your back on her."

Tommy turned to look at me, indecision locking his step.

"Go now, Tommy," Margo ordered. "We don't have much time. We must catch the tide." She fixed her gaze upon him like a snake mesmerizing its prey.

Tommy stood as if being pulled between two poles, unable to move due to the equal forces tugging on him. When Margo realized his resolution wavered, she crooked her finger at him in a mockery of a come-hither gesture. "Tommy."

As if being jerked along by an invisible leash, Tommy stumbled toward her. Making sure Knight and I both were watching, Margo wound a hand in Tommy's hair and pulled him down for a kiss. From the way she ground her lips on his, she seemed hungry for him, and he responded with eagerness. When she withdrew, her lipstick was smeared. She looked like a wild animal that had been feeding at a kill. "Hurry, my love."

He made brief eye contact with me, and then ducked his head and turned away, shoulders slumped as he headed back to the boat dock. There would be no help from that quarter.

Margo watched him leave with a satisfied smile on her face. As soon as Tommy was out of sight, her demeanor changed. Gone was the pretense of attraction. She was all business again as she crossed over to the crates stacked in the middle of the cavern.

The terrier leapt at the wire with a growl, and she aimed a vicious kick at the cage in passing. From behind the crates, she lifted a satchel. Patting the side of the bag, she said, "I have everything I need here. Including back up." She undid the latches, extracted a little Beretta, and closed the bag again.

With her gun held rock-steady at Knight, she tossed him a key. "Unlock your chains. You're coming with me."

He undid the shackle, rubbing his wrist as he got unsteadily to his feet. His leg gave out from under him, and he fumbled for balance, knocking up against the nearest crate. He caught it just as it tipped over, but several objects fell to the sand, including my clutch.

Cursing, he pulled himself upright to shake out a leg and stamp it several times before bending down to pick up the fallen items and replace them on the crate. "What about the girl?"

Margo slew her glance at me sideways with a curl of her lip. "She stays."

"You're just going to leave her here? She could starve before anyone finds her."

"I wouldn't worry too much about that." Her feline smile didn't bode well for me.

Something in her tone brought Knight up short, and a note of desperation entered his voice. "At the very least, unchain her. She can leave after we go. There's no one at the main house, I have the car keys, and the nearest phone is miles away. She's no threat to your business."

"I'm going to leave her where she is. If the shifters get in here, I'd like them to have something to keep them occupied until I return."

"You can't—you wouldn't—" Knight sputtered in disbelief his pupils wide with horror.

Margo shrugged with a casual elegance. "She stays chained or I shoot her outright. Who knows, maybe the shifters won't kill her. Consider it my way of giving her a sporting chance. Either way, I won't have her following us."

"I won't go with you. Not unless she comes, too." Knight's lips pressed together as he stood clutching an armload of artifacts.

"Yes, you will. Or I'll shoot you both and be done with it. HADES might be put out, but at least you won't be working with Redclaw. My boss would like that." There wasn't a trace of hesitation as she took aim at his chest.

Knight raised his hands, dropping everything but my purse and a trinket box, looking like a nervous bank teller at a holdup.

A low-thrumming rumble vibrated around us.

"What's that?" Knight asked, arms splayed out for balance. "An earthquake?"

Margo flicked her glance toward the docking area, even as she frowned. "Tommy must have raised the gate over the boat entrance. It's too soon, the idiot."

The sound of a boat engine reached the hold. More than just a casual idle of the motor. It was the full-throated roar of a throttle being shoved forward. The little dog bounced forward in his cage, barking.

"He's leaving without us." Margo's beautiful face twisted with fury, and she wheeled toward the boat bay.

Knight flung the clutch in my direction. It landed just shy of my feet, the clasp open and the contents scattered. I didn't see any sign of the ray gun, but was pleased Knight had included the key to the shackles in his quick toss. I shifted my foot to cover it.

The movement caught Margo's attention. "What did you do?" She leveled a suspicious glare on Knight.

"You're not going to let him take the boat, are you?"

"We'll take your car. Go." She waved him toward the tunnel at the back of the cavern. When he hesitated, she swung the gun around to point at me. "Your choice. Move or she dies. And then you're next."

Something inside my clutch twitched. The bag humped forward, then flopped like a fish on a hook. The caged terrier tipped his head first one direction, and then the other. I sent a slight prayer that he wouldn't bark. Catching his gaze on me, I lifted a finger to my lips for silence, not that he could understand.

Something slithered out of the bag and made its way toward my hand, visible just by the marks it left behind in the damp sand. My fingers closed around it just as the first wolf appeared at the tunnel's opening.

Chapter Nineteen

"How did they get in here?" Margo raged at the intruders. "Get back!"

The wolves must have found the boat bay opening, and when Tommy had lowered the energy shield to raise the gate and escape with the boat, there'd been nothing to keep them out.

Margo fired several shots at the wolves skulking around the boulders lining the entrance to the cavern. The sound rang my ears in the confined space. Bullets pinged off the rocks surrounding the dark opening, sending stone chips flying. A high-pitched whine caused me to flinch and duck as something passed close by my head.

As the wolves retreated behind the pile of boulders, Knight tackled Margo, forcing her gun hand toward the ground as he shouted, "Are you insane? Haven't you ever heard of a ricochet?"

She elbowed him in the gut hard enough to make him grunt with a whoosh of air, and wrested the Beretta free. Fury stripped her face of any possible beauty as she snarled like a harpy at him.

I dropped the invisible ray gun into my lap. Margo was too far out of its range; I had to get free before I could help

Knight. I tried to pull the key into reach, but only buried it deeper in the sand. Taking a calming breath, I forced myself to relax and concentrated on grabbing the key with my toes.

Margo pointed the gun at Knight again, and I thought it quite possible she would shoot him out of sheer temper.

Knight seemed to think so, too. "Go ahead, shoot me. But I'm thinking you only have so many bullets—and then what? The wolves will be on us. Is there another way out of here?" Knight cracked out his questions with the voice of someone used to being the smartest person in the room.

It got Margo's attention.

"Yes." She nodded toward a dark opening at the far end of the hold. "There's a tunnel out the back." She grabbed a torch off the wall and thrust it with a shower of sparks at the wolf who poked his nose around the bend. With a snarl vicious enough to match any wolf, she overturned several crates and touched the torch to them. Orange flames leapt up from the straw used for packing, burning bright. The thin dry wood of the crates burst into flame, and black smoke filled the air. "We're leaving. Now!"

It was a good thing Margo wasn't looking at me when I gripped the key with my toes. The triumphant smile would have been hard to hide. Gratitude for having ditched my shoes and for Knight having slashed my dress fueled my relief when I was able to transfer the key to my palm.

On the other side of the fire, the wolves howled in frustration as they paced back and forth behind the fire blocking their entrance; the flames casting gross, fantastical silhouettes

like demons on the rough stone surface behind them. The little
dog in his cage barked in return.

"Rhett!"

Thinking I was still trapped and defenseless, Knight
would have taken a step in my direction, but Margo shoved him
toward the tunnel.

I'll never forget the stricken look on Knight's face as she
forced him forward, abandoning me to my fate.

After pushing him inside the passage, Margo flipped a
switch by its entrance, causing a string of anemic light bulbs to
flare along its path. She paused at the opening to look back at
me, taking in my captive state and the burning boxes that would
soon prove no barrier to the wolves. I saw the moment she
decided to let things play out on their own. Being torn apart by
wolves was a far more gruesome death than a quick bullet to the
head. With a grin that would haunt my nightmares for weeks,
she ducked into the tunnel and vanished from sight.

I didn't waste any time. The key fitted into the lock on my
wrist, and with a quiet snick, the shackle fell open. The warm
metal of the ray gun fit into my hand as if designed just for me.
No sooner had my hand closed around it than the gun
materialized. Given the gun's short range, I'd have to let the
wolves get closer than I'd like, and it would take too long to
charge on stun, but just having it in my hand lent me confidence
I hadn't known I'd lost. I switched the setting from stun to kill.

Without a care as to whether I burned Redclaw property or valuable artwork, I tossed more objects into the fire, which showed signs of dying back.

The terrier emitted a bizarre yodeling cry, and I frowned at him. If I released him, would he run off or join in the melee? Surely it would be safer for him to remain confined, and yet how was that any different from Margo leaving me chained for the shifters to find? His odds seemed poor no matter what I decided. I'd at least give him a chance. I opened the door.

The terrier bounced out of the cage and shook himself with vigor before looking up at me with bright, shoe-button eyes and a tail wagging too fast to see.

"Run, little buddy." I chucked my head toward the far tunnel.

He lifted one paw in submission. His little black ears stood in sharp contrast to his white body, and his legs trembled with either fear or excitement. His excited eyes fixed on mine, as though willing me to understand something just outside my range of comprehension.

The flames were dying out. As the last box collapsed in on itself with a crack and pop, the little dog turned his head to look at it. The tag on his collar didn't shift with his movement, but remained fixed in place, the ornate lettering declaring DELILAH.

Why call a male dog Delilah? Unless....

I had no time to consider the matter further. Through the thick smoke, what seemed like dozens of gold eyes gleamed in the shadows. Several wolves came into the light, their canines gleaming as they bared their teeth. I edged behind some crates, hoping for some cover for when they attacked.

As if responding to some secret cue, wolves boiled out of the opening like angry wasps from a hive. I fired, dropping several in their tracks, but more followed. The ray gun grew hot in my hand and took longer to cycle up again with each shot fired. They'd be on me soon and would show no mercy. Of that I was certain.

When the trigger clicked several times and nothing happened, I tucked the gun in my waistband and hurled everything within reach at the rush of bodies. China plates, small boxes covered with mysterious symbols that weighed as much as gold ingots, and even the Tiffany tea set rained down on my attackers with more sound than fury. Selecting a driver from a monogrammed bag of golf clubs, I executed a textbook swing and connected with the lead wolf, who let out a high-pitched yelp and collapsed. I caught another one on the chin with the backswing, glad that all that time at the country club had paid off.

The little dog dashed in and out among the longer legs of the wolves, latching on to a flank or neck only to be flung to the side, barely avoiding the slashing of wicked teeth. He bounced up again every time as though on springs, unwilling to give up. A wolf snatched the driver out of my hands midair in his jaws and tossed it aside with a triumphant growl. I bashed him with a painting, ramming the canvas down to split over his head so he wore the frame like a gaudy necklace. The force of the impact made me stumble backward, and I landed on my back with the wind knocked out of me. The fall jarred loose the ray gun from my waistband, and it landed a few feet away.

It didn't move when I reached for it with splayed fingers.

The wolves closed in with lowered heads and lips peeled back to reveal every tooth in their mouths. A thin stream of drool trailed from the mouth of the wolf wearing the Picasso.

The terrier sprang into the middle of the circling wolves, placing himself between me and the pack.

The little dog looked back at me over his shoulder, and I felt him willing me to get it. To put together the pieces. Somehow, in that instant, I knew what to do.

"Samson," I whispered.

The tag on the terrier's collar flipped from DELILAH to SAMSON and I swear the dog grinned at me. His tongue lolled in an expression of utter delight before the skin on his face rippled in a subtle wave. His tail elongated, lashing from side to side. His snout lengthened, and then the hair on his muzzle gave way to scales as his teeth grew larger and his pupils changed from round dots to reptilian slits. Brown irises morphed into gold, and the little paws shifted into three-toed feet sporting enormous talons as his body grew in size.

The wolves collided into each other in an effort to stop their forward charge as the dog blocking their path turned into a giant, teeth-gnashing reptile. One of them shrieked like a puppy as Samson roared a defiant challenge. The hair went up along the back of my neck and arms at the sound.

I blinked as wolf-shifters turned and ran, with Samson-the-lizard in hot pursuit, knocking aside boulders as big as my head without hesitation as he scrambled out of the cavern. No. Not a lizard. I recognized his species from my Sunday afternoons at the Museum of Natural History. First identified in 1924 by Henry Field Osborne, the creature had been named *Velociraptor* by the scientist.

I'd just seen my first dog-shifter. And he was a freaking dinosaur.

Thank goodness, he appeared to be on my side. For now. But perhaps it would be best to be somewhere else upon his return.

I picked up the ray gun, which was still cool, but perhaps it needed more time to recharge.

Stepping on a sharp stone, for the first time I noticed the condition of my feet. Cut, bruised, and battered, it was a wonder I'd gotten this far without falling down. My stockings hung in tatters, doing more harm than good, and I tore them off. I needed to find something to use as a sort of makeshift slipper and go after Knight.

The torchlight sputtered and flickered, casting a beam on something that glimmered behind a large vase. A pair of ruby pumps with short, manageable heels, sturdy bows, and thousands of red sequins sparkled up at me.

Miracle of miracles, they fit. Almost as if molded to my feet. I didn't care if they were part of Redclaw's cache or stolen from one of the local estates. All that mattered was that they protected my feet.

The air was close in the narrow passage. If not for the feeble light cast from the electrical system, it would have been impossible to navigate. As it was, the walls had crumbled in places, depositing piles of rubble I had to scramble over. Margo and Knight couldn't be that far ahead, yet I heard nothing but my own ragged breathing as I fought a rising panic. The walls seemed to push in on me, and more than once, I barked my shins on an outcropping of stone, or fell against the dank walls, scraping my knuckles.

Where were they? If I didn't catch up to them before they reached Knight's car, the chances of rescuing him were slim to none.

I came to a fork in the passage, one I did not remember from my earlier rambles with Tommy. To the left, the tunnel curved around a bend toward the main house, the electric bulbs weaving in a drunken line along the rock walls as far as the eye could see. The fork to the right was black as pitch. As I stood between the two branches, a damp wind flickered in from the right, ruffling my hair and bringing with it a hint of salt air. Someone must have dug this passage since I was here last, and it opened out somewhere on the estate.

I hesitated. Creating a new tunnel had to have been a tremendous undertaking, one that took someone with a lot of resources and manpower. But if the organization Margo worked for had decided another entrance was necessary, one that didn't cross over exposed estate grounds or exit into the house library, then it wouldn't have been impossible. The Stanfords were away from the estate for much of the year. A dedicated team could get the job done in a matter of weeks. Provided Stanford Senior wasn't behind HADES in the first place.

No matter who built it or why. The real question was, which way should I go?

Logic dictated they took the lighted path, since it would come out the closest to Knight's car and have the advantage of putting a locking door between them and any followers. A breeze brushed my cheek, and I saw the fluttering movement of intact cobwebs along the lit tunnel. The almost imperceptible barrier across the passageway told me what I needed to know.

They didn't go that way.

I plunged into the dark tunnel.

Cold blackness enveloped me, threatening to smother, save for the promise of an exit ahead. Without warning, I walked straight into a large boulder. Patting the chilled stone with my hands, I found the opening off to one side and ducked within. Far ahead, a faint gleam of moonlight pointed the way out. The passage was narrow and rough-hewn. I had to navigate by touch. An eternity passed before I reached the opening, bursting through the brush covering the exit to gulp deep breaths of cool air, relieved to be above ground once more.

I'd come out behind the house, on the far side of the tennis courts. From here, anyone could reach the road bordering the estate without difficulty. No doubt Tommy had unlatched the workman's gate to allow HADES access. I hesitated. Would it be best to try to intercept Margo and Knight before they reached the car, or cut across the estate and set up an ambush where they least expected it?

A light bobbed ahead in the woods like a lovesick firefly. No longer certain I could make it back to the car before they did, I ran toward it.

I heard Knight before I caught up with them. His sarcastic griping carried over the quiet night noises. I didn't know if he intended to make it easy for someone to follow them or if he was just being his usual prickly self, but it was the sweetest sound I'd ever heard.

"You won't get away with this, you know."

"For God's sake, shut up." Margo, I was happy to hear, was out of breath. "I have the goods, and I have you. If you'd played your cards right, this could have been a partnership."

"The way you partnered with young Stanford? Forgive me, but you seem all too ready to jettison that relationship at the first opportunity. Literally."

"Tommy was a means to an end." Margo hustled Knight along. "He's no longer useful. For his sake, he'd better not cross my path again."

Through the trees, the stone wall of the estate loomed. As I'd suspected, they headed toward the workman's gate. Once they reached the road, it would be impossible for me to follow without being seen. I still didn't have a clue how I would stop Margo from driving off with Knight. At least she didn't know the ray gun wasn't working. All I needed was the element of surprise.

No sooner had I thought the words, then a series of flashlights came on all at once, pinning Margo and Knight as though they were attempting to escape from Stalag 17. I dove behind a tree, pressing into the rough bark in the hope no one had spotted me. After a moment of frozen silence, now sure no one had seen me, I peered around the edge at the scene taking place.

Margo squinted into the light, maintaining her grip on Knight's arm as she covered him with her weapon. "Who goes there? What do you want?"

"Brave words." The lazy voice sent a chill up the back of my neck. "I might ask you the same."

"Arturo. Good, you're here." To my ear, Margo sounded more nervous than relieved, but perhaps that was just wishful thinking. "Just in time."

"Funny. I was just saying the same to the boys, here. Wasn't I, boys?"

A menacing chuckle, even more threatening for the invisible sources, echoed in the woods blocking the path to the road.

"Who's the boyfriend?" Arturo lit a cigarette, the bright spurt of the match flared, highlighting a handsome, if somewhat brutish face. He drew on the gasper, causing the end to glow a bright orange-red for a moment.

"Let me introduce the no longer esteemed but still brilliant Dr. Peter Knight. I was on my way to deliver him to you, as promised."

"Really?" Knight's sneer was his supercilious best. "I was under the impression you were on your way—"

His words ended with a grunt as she shoved the gun muzzle into his ribcage.

"Let the doc talk. I'd like to hear what he has to say. A little bird told me you haven't been playing square with us, Nancy."

Nancy? Seriously, how many names did this woman have?

"You'd believe some malicious rumor over me? You *know* me." She lifted her chin in defiance, and her gun wavered from its steady press against Knight's side, angling toward the glow of the cigarette. Knight tracked the movement with his eyes and then went back to squinting straight ahead.

"That's just it. I *do* know you. Where's the goods?"

"In a safe place." Margo snapped. "Not far from here. If you'd just—"

"What's in the bag?" An ominous tone underlined Arturo's voice, a hair-raising threat that was even more chilling for its seemingly benign inquiry.

"The bag?" Margo repeated, and her free hand slid back to the shoulder strap of the duffle. "Oh. I was bringing you some samples. The best of the artifacts, so to speak."

The end of the cigarette burned redder. Arturo dropped his smoke and ground it out with his shoe. "I heard you were planning to sell to the highest bidder."

"That's ridiculous." She did a remarkable job of hiding her fear. I'll say that much. Anger masked any wobble her voice might have had. "I secured the goods. I saw an opportunity to get you Dr. Knight, and I took it. Yes, word about the artifacts must have gotten out. We ran into wolf-shifters earlier. I suspect they followed Peter." In a move so subtle I almost missed it, she rotated her hand so she aimed her gun at the spot where Arturo stood just outside the light. "But as to attempting to sell the artifacts behind your back? I wouldn't be that stupid."

"No." Arturo sounded almost regretful. "I wouldn't have thought so. What I don't understand is how you thought you'd get away with it."

Margo's hand jerked, but it was too late. The spurt of gunfire flared like little bolts of lightning from the dark stand of trees, the noise covering the involuntary gasp I made. I was certain the pounding of my heart would give my position away, even as I kept my eyes glued to the scene. Despite the seeming barrage of bullets, the unseen gunman's aim was true. Margo slumped to the ground without a sound, leaving Knight quivering where he stood. I pressed a knuckle into my mouth to quell any sound, horrified at what I'd just witnessed.

Knight's breath came in sharp huffs. His shock was plain to see as he gaped at Margo where she lay crumpled at his feet.

"Dr. Knight. If you would be so kind as to collect the bag and come with me?" Arturo spoke as if he were inviting Knight to join him for a drink on the patio. Knight stared at him a long moment before leaning down to pick up the duffle. His movements were jerky with stunned disbelief, but he complied. Really, what choice did Knight have?

I remained where I was, chest heaving with the effort of suppressing the instinct to bolt away from the clearing. Trembling, I watched as Knight tugged at the bag, removing it from beneath Margo's body with some difficulty before he joined Arturo at the line of trees.

I did nothing as Arturo's men swung their flashlights away from the scene of death and picked their way back toward the road where, no doubt, they had a car waiting.

Arturo's men grossly outnumbered me. The ray gun was dead, and even if it worked, there were serious limitations on its range that Arturo's well-armed men didn't face. There was no way I could save Knight now. As long as Knight was worth something to them, Arturo and his men would keep him alive. But why, oh why hadn't I contacted Ryker the moment I knew the artifacts were in the area? Or given Knight the ladybug pin when I had the chance? At least we'd be able to track him then. I had no choice now but to let HADES—or whatever dangerous organization employed Arturo—take Knight away and hope somehow I'd be able to find him.

I had to go for help.

I waited until there was no longer any bobbing movement of flashlights in the woods before I dashed forward into the clearing. With shaking knees, I dropped to the bed of pine needles carpeting the ground and felt around with my hands. I knew Knight wouldn't fail me. He had to know I was his only hope of escape. Once Arturo shot Margo, Knight had few options, and therefore would plan accordingly.

The moon came out from behind the clouds and bathed Margo's body in a dread, cold light. I'd never seen anyone dead up close before, not even my father. The casual violence of her murder was unnerving. It must have been even worse for Knight, who'd been standing next to her. Had he moved even a fraction of an inch he'd have been a casualty as well.

Something glinted in the leaf litter beside Margo. My grin was surely triumphant when my fingers closed on the car keys Knight had dropped during the confrontation with Arturo. No doubt hoping I was following and would stop at the sight of Margo's body. Snatching them up, I scrabbled to my feet and turned to find myself surrounded. I never even heard them coming.

Moonlight cast an eerie illumination on the odd assortment of beings facing me. A silver wolf, bigger than the ones I'd battled before. A leopard, whose spotted coat blended in with the shadows cast by the foliage. As I stared, a Great Horned Owl glided in on soundless wings at least six feet wide to land in a nearby tree. And though my heart dropped to my red ruby slippers, I held my ground as a great brown bear stepped forward, opened his massive jaws, and roared at me.

Clutching the car keys in one hand and the ray gun in the other, I said with as much calm as I could muster, "Redclaw, I presume?"

Chapter Twenty

The bear shook his head and sneezed for good measure, which I took to be agreement. I pointed toward the road. "They took Knight that way. They're armed and dangerous."

The leopard hissed, baring long teeth that gleamed in the moonlight. The owl hooted in derision, and the bear merely huffed, stamping its massive paws as it stomped up and down in place. The ray gun warmed in my grip as I waved it toward the road. "Let's go."

The owl flew off ahead of us in ghostly silence as it glided through the woods. The wolf and the leopard raced ahead, disappearing out of sight when they went in divergent directions. Even the bear, which I assumed would be slow and pondering, left me in the dust, demonstrating how those massive hindquarters could power through the brush.

I ran as fast as I could behind them.

Bursting through the workman's gate onto the road, I took stock of the raging battle before I plunged in. Shouts of dismay preceded reckless gunfire as Arturo's men retreated toward the big Cadillac parked by the side of the road. If they'd had any sense, they'd just dive into the car and drive off, but they'd waited too long. The large owl swept in to rake dangerous talons at their faces, and it was impossible for the gunmen to draw a bead on it as the bird of prey weaved in and out of the melee. The bear bounced on the hood of the car with both front feet until it caved in and the windshield cracked. I crept up on the gunman about to shoot the bear and stunned him with the ray gun, sending up silent thanks it had at least enough juice for that setting again. The leopard bowled over the man who'd been about to shoot me in retaliation, but yowled in pain when a bullet scored its flanks. That gunman went down with a gurgling scream as the wolf leapt in with slashing teeth.

Shouts and rapid gunfire drew my attention to the appearance of a giant praying mantis in the middle of the road, pulling a smile from me despite the circumstances. They never should have left Knight alone with the duffle bag. While Arturo's henchmen concentrated their fire on the illusion, I snuck up to the back of the car. If I could get close enough, I could take out the shooters with the ray gun and free Knight.

It was a good plan. It should have worked. The team from Redclaw distracted Arturo's men. Another few feet and I'd be in position. But I didn't account for the alertness of Arturo's crew, or the rapidity with which they realized the mantis was a hoax. Knight got clipped with a right hook for his trouble and went to his knees, rubbing his jaw. His eyes tracked me as I crossed the moonlit road to get into place. Some sixth sense must have alerted the man who'd hit Knight to look behind, and he shouted a warning when he saw me. Wavering blue rings of light struck him where he stood, but two other men whipped around to target me. In that split second, I knew I couldn't take them both down. I fired, holding my breath as the rings made their way through space and time toward their objective, but both men were in position to shoot, and just one collapsed. That left the other shooter poised to take me out.

A wall of heat came between me and the gunman as Ryker, in Phoenix form, descended. Wings extended to protect me, and a being of fury and light landed between me and certain death. His hooked beak opened in a cry of rage that was terrifying to behold. I imagined what the shepherds with their flocks had felt when the Angel of the Lord appeared to them. Orange, purple, and blue-tinged flames radiated off Ryker as he shielded me, and I almost fell to my knees and covered my eyes.

The gunman wasn't as reverent. With an inarticulate cry, he fired his weapon, pumping lead into Ryker's body, which jerked and shuddered. The flames went out; the Phoenix transformed back into a man wearing a skinsuit, and Ryker toppled to the ground.

"No!" The word ripped its way out of my throat. Ryker *couldn't* be dead. Not like this. Not because of me.

The wolf howled. The leopard roared. The bear snapped his teeth in fury as several bullets found their mark and he went down mid-charge at his assailant.

Knight swept his hand into the back of the shooter's knee, causing it to buckle, but the gunman maintained his footing. He pistol-whipped Knight as punishment, forcing him down on his hands and knees in the dirt.

Lips pulled back in a sneer, the gunman raised his weapon and pointed it straight at me. The owl swooped by his head, just as Knight leapt up and plowed into me, knocking me down and covering me with his body. Knight's enthusiastic tackle not only took my breath away but also caused me to drop both the keys to his car and the ray gun. I looked up into his eyes for a startled moment, certain someone else was about to die trying to save my life.

Branches cracked like rifle shots, wrenching our attention to the woods behind us as something heavy crashed through the underbrush, powering in our direction with the speed and force of a locomotive. An undulating cry clawed its way out of the forest, and the gunman jerked his weapon around to face the oncoming attack. He fired before the unseen creature even made an appearance, sending two shots in rapid succession toward the beast hurtling through the undergrowth. On the third shot, his gun clicked uselessly, and he tossed it aside with a curse.

From out of the woods burst a dinosaur the size of a large calf. Snow-white teeth gnashed in the bright moonlight as it paused beside the road, glancing from where I lay clutched in Knight's arms back to where the gunman braced himself at the open car door. Lips curling as it uttered a guttural roar, the velociraptor launched itself toward the car. The shooter dove inside with a shriek, slamming the door shut as he started the engine. Smoke boiled out of the block as the car moved off with a scream of tortured rubber. The dinosaur loped behind it on two legs like—well, like a dog chasing a car.

"Come back, you imbeciles!" Arturo shouted as his men fled in all directions, chased by the rest of the Redclaw team. "It's another fake. An illusion! I will prove it to you."

Knight pulled me to my feet as Arturo stalked toward us. "You've created your last illusion, Dr. Knight. You're more trouble than you're worth." Moonlight glinted off the barrel of his gun.

"Oh, hell." Knight cut his glance sideways at me, his voice somewhat pained. "I thought he'd be out of bullets by now."

For the last words he'd ever say to me, they were most appropriate.

The thudding of galloping feet made us look down the road, where the velociraptor approached with terrifying speed.

I said a *distinctly* unladylike word. More than one. Knight echoed me.

Arturo glanced over his shoulder as death charged straight for him. He gave a loud snort. "I am not fooled by your apparitions."

"I hate to tell you, old man," Knight said, neatly mingling apprehension with subtle regret, "but that's not one of mine."

"You lie!" Arturo snarled. "You're good, I grant you. But this is nothing but a trick, I tell you. A manipulation of the mind. A—"

He went down with a scream in a welter of blood as the velociraptor tore into him. I closed my eyes and clung to Knight as Arturo died, praying we wouldn't be next.

"Don't move." Sensing Knight was about to bolt, dragging me with him, I opened one eye. "He goes after anything that runs."

Knight's arms closed around me like bands of steel. I would discover bruises later. The dinosaur, snout still bloody, came over to us, snuffling along the ground. Though I couldn't stop trembling, I squelched a squeal when he rooted around the bottom of my ragged dress and nosed my bare legs. When he stood on his hind legs and placed his massive paws on my chest, I staggered under his weight and held my breath as he nuzzled up against me and slurped his tongue along my ear. I had to hold my breath. He stank like rotten meat.

"Delilah," I mumbled, my lips stiff with fear.

The dinosaur shook himself and seemed to collapse inward, rolling up into a little ball only to bounce back on his feet as the small terrier. He leapt up on me again, leaving behind little bloody paw prints as he licked my hand. He looked so darned adorable; I couldn't believe just moments before he'd been a killing machine.

Knight released me with an exaggerated whoosh of air, and bent over, hands on his knees. I staggered back from him a step, surveying the surrounding battlefield. What was left of Arturo's team had been decimated. Bodies—or the remains of them—lay scattered about like broken toy soldiers.

I couldn't bring myself to look at Ryker, who lay where he'd fallen, dying to protect me.

Instead, I hurried over to the moaning bear shifter, who had collapsed on his side. I knelt beside him, placing a hand on his shoulder. When I hit a wet patch of fur, I pulled my hand back to stare at it, the coating of blood looking almost black by the light of the moon. The terrier, coming up beneath my arm to sniff at the bear, sat down and whined.

"Is he—?"

I looked up at Knight. "No, but he needs help. Fast."

I put out my hand without thinking, and Knight hauled me to my feet. "We need to find your car keys. Then we can take him to…. No. We'll never get him in the car. I'll stay here. You go to the nearest phone and call for a doctor. No. A vet. No." Panic gripped my throat with icy fingers and squeezed them shut. I couldn't think. I couldn't breathe. I sucked air in, but it felt like nothing was getting into my lungs.

"Hey." Knight pulled me into his arms, the familiar scents of pipe tobacco and Old Spice wrapping around me like a comforting blanket. "Hey. It's going to be okay."

"No, it's not!" I pounded his shoulder. "I don't know what to do. I *always* know what to do."

He cupped my face in his hands and tipped up my chin to brush away my tears with his thumb. "That's one of the things I like best about you. You still know what to do. Just break it down into smaller steps."

"I killed my boss."

"No, you didn't." Knight's voice soothed, even as one hand dropped to the back of my neck and he tucked me into his shoulder. "You got Ryker—er, that is to say—Ryker died shielding you. A completely different proposition."

"You started to say I got Ryker killed." I sniffed but found myself steadied by the very Knight-ness of his attempt to comfort me.

"An unfortunate turn of phrase. Now, think. What do we need to do first?"

I appreciated the "we" there. "Find your keys. I dropped them when you tackled me. Get help. One of us should stay here. Me, since the other Redclaw agents will return soon." Against my will, my eyes began to fill with tears. What would my coworkers say when they found out about Ryker?

A growl caught our attention. The terrier stood with all hackles raised, one paw lifted as it stared intently into the mulch. There, the ray gun crept toward me. I snatched it up before the little dog attacked it. He leapt at my hands as I pulled it out of reach. "No. Bad dog! The ray gun is our friend."

The dog sat on his haunches and tilted his head from one side to the other in response.

"I must take a closer look at that weapon at some point. Clever little thing, coming back to you. Notice I'm not asking any questions about the dog just now. I take it you control the change by voice command? I have a feeling I know how you got away from the wolves in the hold. Now we just need to find the car keys. Or we could look at Margo's bag of tricks and see what else is in there. Who knows, perhaps there's some type of radio communicator?" I didn't need moonlight to know Knight had one eyebrow lifted. I heard the devilish imp in his voice.

"You're bloody brilliant."

"If I do say so myself."

Knight's crooked grin heartened me in a way I couldn't explain. I could do this. With his help.

The terrier pawed at my leg, his little claws catching me by surprise. With a yelp, I looked down at him.

He glanced over his shoulder and yipped several times.

I followed his line of sight and saw what had caught his attention. Digging my fingers into Knight's arm, I turned him to face Ryker's body. "Do you see what I see?"

There was no need for him to answer. No sooner had I spoken than the little curl of smoke rising from Ryker's prone form puffed into a bright flame. Flickers of orange licked along the edges of his body, outlining the black skin suit as it did so, the margins of the flames burning an intense blue. It reminded me of the mysterious package sent by Rian Stirling, programed to self-destruct. Without thinking, I stepped forward as though to put it out.

Knight held me fast, preventing me from getting closer, and a moment later, we both retreated, shielding our eyes from the white-hot flare. The wavering heat forced us back even further. As muscle and bone collapsed and turned into charred remains as fine as powder, the suit folded in on itself. Hot as the fire had been, it soon burned itself out. A slight breeze ruffled the pile of ash, carrying it away in a tumbling, spinning swirl of silky soot.

With wary caution, I bent over to touch the suit lying in place of Ryker's body, almost like a chalk outline at a murder scene. It was already cool.

"They'll want to know what happened. Mr. J and Miss Climpson, that is. I should take this back to the office." I lifted the suit up from the ashes intending to stuff it within the duffle.

"Well, that would be dashed awkward, seeing as it's my only article of clothing."

Knight maintains he did *not* scream, but I was there. We both yelped. And then I whipped around toward the voice, ray gun at the ready.

"Stand down, Bishop. I've already been shot once tonight." Ryker stepped out of the shadows, looking like Thorvaldsen's statue of Jason and the Golden Fleece in the moonlight.

"You're alive!" I squeaked, before averting my eyes. I held out the suit, fixing my relieved gaze on Knight all the while.

Ryker's fingers brushed mine as he accepted the suit, and I flinched at the lava-like heat radiating from them.

"Sorry." The whisper of cloth suggested he was getting dressed as he spoke. "There's always some residual warmth after a Phoenix resurrection."

"Warmth" was a rather benign word for the process, but as a Phoenix-shifter, no doubt he didn't even notice such things.

"Of course." Knight slapped his forehead. "Phoenix. Fire. Ashes. Rebirth." Knight paused, and when he continued, I could hear the frown in his voice. "You took a bullet for Bishop. Several, in fact. Does that mean you're immortal?"

"In a manner of speaking. What's our situation, Bishop?"

Ryker's cool dismissal of his death and rebirth brought me crashing back to reality. I pointed to where the bear lay. "Sir. The attacking force appears to be dead or routed, but I'll catch you up later. One of your agents is down."

Ryker crossed to the bear's side in three swift strides and knelt to assess him. "Hang in there, Russo. Help's on the way."

"Russo? That's *Russo*?" I couldn't believe it. I mean, I knew my coworkers were shifters, but somehow, I'd pictured Russo as a coyote or a raccoon. I had a hard time seeing the lean young man in the rain coat as the massive bear lying at our feet.

Rooting around in the duffle bag, Knight let out a triumphant shout and raised one of the green lanterns that had been in the cave. When he flipped a switch, the lantern bathed the entire clearing in a bluish light. Holding the lantern aloft, he brought it over so Ryker could see the extent of Russo's injuries.

They looked terrible. Blood soaked the brown fur and had pooled around him where bullets had gone in at the shoulder and sides. Russo lay on his side, head and neck outstretched, as he groaned in pain.

"Sir, Knight and I can go for help. Or, if you prefer, we can—"

"Not necessary." His tone was brisk, but not unkind. From a zippered pocket, he withdrew a watch and fastened it to his wrist. Seeing my interest, he said, "We haven't yet mastered the ability for me to wear it when I'm flying."

"That looks like Dick Tracy's two-way wrist watch radio." Knight leaned in with the lantern for a better look.

"It wouldn't be the first artifact to end up in a comic strip. Science fiction and superheroes can pave the way for the release of such technology to the general public."

Knight sat back on his heels, mouth open in admiration for a second before he grinned. "That's brilliant. Get a generation of kids thinking how cool and advanced the technology is, and then ten or fifteen years later, introduce the artifact, and voilà!" He snapped his fingers. "The population is already primed to accept it as normal."

"Something like that." Ryker pressed a button, activating the tiny screen. Mr. J appeared as though he were on a microscopic television, looking his usual frazzled self.

Ryker explained the situation, and Mr. J assured him he would relay the message to the teams already on the way, making them aware of the medical emergency. When he'd finished his call with Mr. J, Ryker withdrew a small vial from the same pocket and shook some tiny white pills into his hand. Handling the massive jaws with care, Ryker placed the pills under Russo's tongue and lowered his head to the ground once more.

"Pain meds. Dissolves under the tongue. Formulated especially for shifters by our labs. And now we wait." Ryker rested his hand on Russo's shoulder. "It won't be long now."

"But sir—Russo needs help right away. Shouldn't we—?"

Ryker shook his head. "Shifters are tougher than they look. We have accelerated healing rates when in shifter form and are resistant to most human diseases, too. Help is on the way. All of our teams have at least one agent trained in emergency shifter medicine." From another pocket, he pulled out a folded pad that he pressed against the worst of Russo's wounds to stem the loss of blood.

"But as tough as shifters are, you can still die. All except for you." There was an underlying note to Knight's statement that made it of an accusation rather than born of curiosity.

Ryker shot him a cool look I would not like to have received myself. "As you've seen for yourself, I *can* die. I just come back."

"How old are you? Are there any—"

"It's not something I care to discuss. In the meantime, perhaps you'd like to catch me up now." Steel reverberated in his voice, and a suggestion of patience wearing thin. Before I could speak, the terrier thrust his nose into Ryker's hand and licked his palm. "Who's this little guy?"

Knight opened his mouth only to snap it shut, his eyebrows crawling into his hairline as he shot me a look of horror.

Tugging the dog gently back beside me by his collar, I cleared my throat and began. "Part of the story, sir. I took advantage of the fact I had a social engagement in the area to follow a potential lead on the missing artifacts."

"We." Irritation brought out the English in Knight. "*We* followed the lead. It was my idea. Don't take all the blame for this, Bishop."

Ignoring him, I continued. "Once here, we ran into Rian Stirling, who confirmed our belief the artifacts were in the area and intimated there would be an auction to the highest bidder."

"Oh, really." Ryker's voice went dark and silky. I wondered if he knew how much he sounded like his half-brother just then, and had to hide a shiver. Was his threatening tone because of the illicit sale, the presence of his sibling, or the fact I'd spoken with Stirling? And if Ryker could come back from the dead, was his half-brother immortal too? "Go on."

"Before we could contact Redclaw and inform them of our discovery, we recognized Dr. Knight's wife among the guests, calling herself by another name."

Ryker glanced up at Knight. What he saw in Knight's face, I had no idea. To me it looked as though a portcullis had clanged shut. But Ryker's expression softened, and I heard sympathy in his voice when he spoke. "Margo Knight was here? Alive?"

"Margo Knight never existed." Liquid nitrogen couldn't be any colder than Knight's clipped voice.

I cleared my throat. "And is dead again. For real this time. But I'm telling my story out of order."

Still crouched beside Russo, Ryker rolled his hand to indicate I should continue.

I shot a look at Knight, who had his hands in his pockets and was looking off in the direction where Margo's body lay. "It seemed probable the woman who'd called herself—"

"Oh, for heaven's sake," Knight snapped, facing us once more. "Just say Margo. You sound like the protagonist from a Rider Haggard novel. Next thing you know, you'll be referring to her as She Who Must Be Obeyed."

"Very well." I swallowed any annoyance. It had been an evening of difficult revelations for Knight. I wasn't going to quibble with him. "Margo had seduced an old friend of mine. They were using an old smuggler's hideout on the property to store the stolen artifacts, as well as what appears to be valuables taken from neighboring estates." I indicated the dog. "He was there, along with artwork and jewelry. In my zeal to confirm the presence of the artifacts—"

"Great Scott." Knight pulled on his hair until it stood out over his ears in angry tufts. "This isn't a court of law, Bishop. We got captured. The man Margo tried to double-cross showed up and killed her. Then Redclaw arrived and there was a bloodbath. End of story."

"You forgot the wolves," I pointed out.

"Right you are. Yes, there was a rival gang here, too. I don't know where they've gone." Knight looked around as though they might be lingering, and I cocked my eyebrows at the terrier, though in the dim light, I doubt Knight saw my gesture.

"I see." The moon had ducked behind the clouds, or I'm sure I would have witnessed a smile twitch across Ryker's lips. "Perhaps you could fill me in on what happened after I was shot?"

"Oh." Knight shifted uncomfortably and glanced at the dog. "I'm not sure as I can say. There was so much going on."

"Knight used an artifact to create the illusion of monsters. Giant insects, that sort of thing. Arturo's men ran, and the Redclaw agents went in pursuit."

"Yes." To my ears, Knight's agreement was too swift not to sound suspicious. "That's what happened."

I jumped when the owl flew in and landed on a tree limb with a loud hoot.

I turned to Knight, but he'd moved off to one side, taking himself out of the conversation. I couldn't begin to imagine what was going through his mind. Even though I'd known betrayal by someone I loved, it wasn't the same. Regardless of how things ended, at least I'd known my father really loved me. Knight didn't even have that small comfort.

My father hadn't died right before my eyes, either.

The moon came out from behind the clouds and bathed Knight in its clear chill light. He stood with his hands shoved into his pockets, looking utterly lost.

The wolf and leopard padded up; their progress almost silent as they arrived through the woods. Yellow lights came bobbing toward us from the road, causing me to stiffen and bring the ray gun up to bear, but the relaxed postures of the surrounding predators made me realize it was the help we needed.

The cavalry was here at last.

Chapter Twenty-One

Once the medical personnel had Russo's care well in hand, Ryker delegated tasks to the various teams. Those in shifter form he left to secure the perimeters and to make sure no one from rival organizations made a move onto the property. Ryker selected four armed agents in human form to join us as we guided the team back to the hold. Ryker asked questions as we went, teasing more details from me. For some reason, Knight seemed as reluctant to spill the beans on the dog as I was, and so I was able to keep the dog's shifting abilities out of it.

The little dog looked woebegone when I made him stay at the top of the ladder into the hold, but I had no choice. I lacked the means to carry him down.

"We must be careful," I warned before we began our descent. "There've been at least two parties, other than Redclaw, interested in these items, and for all we know, they've come back."

But there wasn't anyone inside the cavern. Not even the dead. Someone had stripped bare the hold, save for a single, empty packing crate in the center of the room. Knight's handheld lantern illuminated an envelope of heavy cream-colored paper lying on top of the crate. The letters R and S were entwined like snakes on the red sealing wax. The letter was also addressed to me.

I broke the seal and pulled out the thick writing paper.

My dear Rhett, it read.

I want to thank you for leading me to this tidy haul of objects destined for Redclaw's lockdown and storage. My half-brother has no feel for the good these artifacts can do the shifter community—nor their economic value—and I think I can put them to far better use than him.

I trust you won't feel too badly about their loss. As I see it, they were lost to Redclaw already, you merely failed to recover them. I took the liberty of cleaning up the mess left behind after your altercation with the competition. I want you to know I would never have set thugs of that sort upon you, nor was it my intention to let you die at their hands. It seems you are not without resources after all, and someday, you'll have to tell me how you managed to hide a dinosaur in your clutch.

I look forward to meeting you again in the future.

Rian Stirling's bold and spiky signature sprawled across the bottom of the page.

"Let me see that." Knight snatched the paper out of my hands and held it up to the torchlight as he poured over the words. "That sleek devil. I might have known."

With a sigh, Knight handed the letter over to Ryker, who read it over.

"I see." Ryker handed the letter back to me. He didn't—quite—grind his teeth. "Damn him. He acts like this is some big game in which he's scored over me once again. He's putting me in a hell of a position. It's not just about the technology. I hope the Council—" He shook his head, as if thinking better of completing that sentence.

"It's not a total loss. M-Margo...." Knight stumbled over her name. "Margo took a bag of select artifacts with her to show her buyers. We recovered that."

"Oh." I looked down to turn an ankle sideways. "And I have these shoes. I don't know if they were part of the cache or stolen from one of the neighbors, but they were here at any rate."

"Hmph." Ryker didn't look impressed. "What about this dinosaur mentioned in the letter?"

I waved a hand. "Oh, that. Knight fiddled with his image projector and made it look as if a dinosaur was about to attack. The wolves fell for it and ran."

I'm not sure why I was so determined to keep the dog from Ryker's notice. Perhaps because I knew as an 'artifact', the little guy would spend the rest of his life caged in a secret vault inside Redclaw. It didn't seem right. Or maybe on some level, I agreed with Rian Stirling. At least as far as the dog went.

"Interesting. Despite not smelling anything of the sort?" Ryker tipped his head with a faint, disbelieving smile.

"Knight's illusions are extremely realistic." My glare dared Knight to say otherwise.

"I'd like that image projector back. I believe you've done quite enough with it, Dr. Knight."

"It got smashed in the fight." Knight shoved his hands in his pockets, looking unhappy at the thought. No doubt he realized he'd be on a short leash from now on.

"Very well. Not a total loss then." Ryker's lips twitched, doing a poor job of concealing a smile. "I'll contact the teams and send them on a search of the general area. Who knows, we might get lucky and get a line on Rian's whereabouts, though I suspect he's long gone. I'll take charge of the recovered artifacts. I trust you can make your way back to the city? I'll want a full report on my desk by Monday. That goes for you, too, Knight."

"Actually." Knight spoke in that aristocratic drawl I knew oh-so-well. "I'm not going back to Redclaw."

I refused to look over at him, no matter how much I wanted to do so.

"Oh?" When it came to haughty superiority, Ryker could match Knight vowel for vowel.

"With Margo dead, the threat to me is over. I can't see her organization—what's left of it—continuing their attempts to force me to work for them."

"I see." Ryker didn't quite stroke his beard, but I pictured him doing so just the same. "While I don't entirely agree with your reasoning, you're forgetting one important thing."

"Which is?" The irritation in Knight's voice chafed like sand in a shoe. I winced despite myself.

"Redclaw can use someone like you. At the very least, your skills won't go to waste." Ryker shrugged. "Think it over. You don't have to decide right away."

Knight didn't respond. He remained uncharacteristically silent as we left the hold and returned to the pavilion where the little dog greeted us as though we'd been gone for days. Knight's frosty silence continued after we joined the rest of the teams back at the clearing. Redclaw had removed the bodies, wiping any trace of what had happened that evening to prevent unwelcome questions from the locals. Knight's rigid lack of reaction made him hard to read. Was he upset Redclaw had disposed of Margo's body without his input? Did he still care for her, despite everything she'd done? Barring that, did he just need to say his goodbyes? Or, as I thought about the things I'd learned about my father after his death, a chance to speak his mind? Even if it was to a corpse.

Russo, still in bear form, had been loaded into the back of a van, the interior of which glowed with light and activity. Fluids dripped from a glass bottle suspended above him into a line taped to one massive leg. How the medics had found a vein under all that fur was beyond me. Stepping forward into the light spilling out of the van, I was surprised to find Betty Snowden in charge of his care. Wearing a crisp, white lab coat spotted with blood, for once she looked confident and capable as she administered an injection into the fluid line and checked his vitals. She seemed satisfied with the results when she did so, a small smile curving her lips as she replaced the syringe in her leather bag. She stroked the massive bear's head with a gentle hand.

"Is he going to be okay?"

She looked up, freezing like a rabbit on being startled. Recognizing me, the fear oozed out of her, but it was replaced with a polite disapproval. "He'll do. I was able to remove the bullets." She held up a small jar and gave it a little shake, causing the stained pieces of metal within to roll around with a clatter. "His blood pressure is back up again, and the healing is progressing nicely. A few days in bear form and he'll be right as rain."

"Good." The relief was almost too much. My lip quivered as I tried to speak. "I didn't mean...it wasn't my intention...oh hell. I'm sorry he got hurt because of me."

Betty's eyes flew open wide at my language, but then narrowed as she studied me. "If you're going to be part of a team, you have to act like it. You can't go around leaping into frying pans and expecting someone else to put out the fire."

Tears blurred my vision. "I'm so sorry. I didn't think. Or I did, but...I wanted to prove myself to Redclaw. To all of you."

She wiped her bloody hands on a cloth as she studied me. "You say you wanted to prove yourself. That's fine. I get it. You want to help. To be an ally." She tossed the cloth aside to stand with fists akimbo on her hips. "But you'll have to do more than be sorry. Listen. Learn. Educate yourself. Give more than just lip service to being part of a team."

I blinked hard. "You're right. You have every right to be upset with me. Maybe this team thing isn't for me."

She leaned out of the vehicle to pat my shoulder, showing more graciousness than I would have were our roles reversed.

"That's your choice. But there's lots of good reasons to be part of something." Seeing my distress, she straightened and relented a little. "This showdown would have happened either way, once we knew about the auction. But it's better to plan a response than react to a crisis."

She was right. Of all people, I should have known better. But I'd never known what it meant to be a part of a team. Not until now. When it was perhaps too late.

Nodding, unable to speak for fear of embarrassing myself further, I stepped back into the shadows. Ryker stood on the far side of the clearing receiving reports from several agents checking in; an odd mix of human and shifted beings. I had no idea how the shifted agents communicated with him, but no one seemed to have any trouble understanding one another. I looked around for Knight. He was in the general area where he'd tackled me, swinging his lantern back and forth above the leaf litter. The little dog trotted alongside as I approached him.

I let the keys dangle from my fingers. "Looking for these?"

With a grunt, he pocketed them. "Russo?"

"Betty says he'll be okay. As long as he remains a bear, or something like that." The terrier sat at my feet and looked up with bright attention at Knight.

"Must be nice. To heal like that. A bit hard on the grocery bill, perhaps. Do they have to raid trash cans for him or what?"

His heart wasn't in the banter, I could tell. That felt sad and wrong, but I had no idea how to fix things between us. Or even if it could be fixed. The hand in his pocket jingled the keys before he spoke again. "I'm going back to the city. I'm sure someone will give you a ride to Em's house, and she'll see you catch a train back to town on Sunday. Under the circumstances...."

"Yes. Of course." The last thing he wanted to do, no doubt, was hang around the rest of the weekend pretending to be my date while I attended a bridal shower. It was the last thing I wanted to do as well, but I couldn't let Em down. "Don't worry about me. I'll find my own way back."

"I have no doubt. Self-reliant Bishop, that's you." He took out his pipe and a small pouch of tobacco, going through the motions of filling the bowl and tamping it down before striking a match. The flare lit up his face as he drew on the stem, shading the clean lines of his face, accentuating the sharpness of his features and the shadow of stubble along his jaw.

"There's such a thing as being too self-reliant, you know." I watched him as he pulled in that first heady draw of nicotine, wishing for a moment for a cigarette myself, though I rarely smoked.

"My dear, you wouldn't be you if you were anything else." He removed the stem from his mouth, cradling the pipe in his hands as he stared down at it.

"It's a long drive back to the city. You could wait until the morning."

He made a small sound, possibly a snort, though it was hard to tell. When he looked up, his eyes were in shadow, making it difficult to read his expression. I had no difficulty reading his voice when he spoke, however. Pain and unhappiness marred his usual light tenor.

"I was in love with a monster."

I shook my head. "You were in love with a false image designed for the sole purpose of fooling you. What she did was unspeakably cruel."

"You may be right, but the fact remains that she *did* fool me. I can tell myself I was young and naïve, and know it's the truth. Until I met her, my life was my work, and my work had led me down some dark paths. But it galls me to realize someone assessed these weaknesses of mine and played on them. To recognize my judgement in these matters is terribly flawed. I'm supposed to be the smart guy, after all." His smile was painful to witness, brittle and sharp, like glass on the verge of shattering. "Working with you these last few days...I'd started to think—" He put a hand up as if to stop himself. "It doesn't matter. I can't do this right now. I have to go."

I tried to stop him. "What about...Redclaw?"

He lifted both shoulders in a helpless little shrug. "I just don't know."

He walked off without another word, without a single look back, puffing on his pipe as he went down the road toward his car.

I felt a paw on my foot and looked down. The little dog stared up at me, his whole body aquiver. Shifting the ray gun to my left hand, I knelt and ruffled his ears. "I guess it's just you and me, kid."

He licked my fingers and followed with a jaunty step as I went in search of a ride.

Chapter Twenty-Two

Although after midnight when I stepped out of a car at Em's, I still beat her and Eddie back to the house. Halling let me in without commenting on either the lateness of the hour, the state of my torn and blood-spattered dress, the absence of my date, or the fact I had a dog with me.

"Mr....er...Day...was called away on business. He won't be returning. Please have his bag brought to my room. I'll take it back to the city with me."

"Very good, miss." He hesitated, no doubt torn between professional duty and humanitarian concern. "Is everything all right, Miss Henrietta?"

I shook my head. "No, but it's not something you can fix."

He gave me a small, understanding nod. I hoped the Prentiss family knew what a treasure they had in Halling.

No footman guided me to my room. The terrier trotted up the stairs with me as if he'd been following me his entire life. I watched him in the mirror as I removed my makeup and raked the snarls out of my hair. Setting aside my brush, I called him over. "Here, you."

He looked up from where he'd been cleaning his paws and bounced across the room toward me with the odd skipping step I associated with small muscular dogs. I examined his collar. As I'd thought, it didn't come off. At least not by any means I could tell. "We'll have to get some sticking plaster or something and cover up the name. The last thing I want anyone to do is call you by your dinosaur name because of word association."

His little stub of a tail wagged furiously.

"Oh, no, you don't," I admonished when he leapt up on the bed and settled himself on my pillow. I hesitated throwing him off at first. Even as a dog, he had sharp teeth. But instead of defending the position he staked out, he went limp as a noodle when I tried to scoop him up, melting into the counterpane when I moved him. He forced me to drag him by his legs to the side of the bed so I could set him on the floor. Before I'd even turned around, he was back up in a flash.

This time, I scooted him to the foot of the bed. "Compromise, okay?"

He curled into a little ball with a sigh and tucked his nose into his paws.

The dress was a total loss. Knight's little trick with the knife had made it functional, but it would never be the same, even without the bloody paw prints—both dinosaur and terrier-sized. I wiggled my toes as I slid off the ruby slippers and tucked the shoes into my suitcase to take back with me to Redclaw on Monday. Exhaustion turned my limbs to mud as I washed my battered feet, changed into silk pajamas, and crawled into bed. When I switched off the lamp, the blackness wrapped around me as thick and enveloping as a comforter. After a moment, I spoke into the darkness. "We need to come up with another name for you."

There was no response from the foot of the bed.

"How about Buddy?"

Not even a twitch.

"Asta?" It amused me to consider calling him the name of the terrier in *The Thin Man* movies.

Nothing.

I yawned, closing my eyes. "It has to be something worthy. Suitable." The words slurred as sleep crept over me. "Captain."

He lifted his head. Padding up to my side, he sniffed around and then turned in a circle several times before settling against the back of my legs.

"Captain, it is." I smiled in the dark at the soft snore.

I fell asleep minutes behind him.

The next day, I did all the socially appropriate things. Took Captain on a long walk over the estate and down to the beach. Had brunch with Em's family. Did the bridal shower thing, playing the silly games and enthusing over the gifts. Em, I was pleased to see, had begun taking charge again, vetoing several of the more insipid proposed activities, and ordering Halling to serve mimosas. That loosened things up, even to the extent Milly laughed out loud a time or two, earning a vicious glare from her mother that didn't appear to bother Milly one iota.

It seemed the day would never end, however, and after the shower, I asked to be taken to the train station.

"Darling, are you sure? If you have a headache, perhaps you should just go lie down."

Em's kindness made me want to scream. I knew I wouldn't feel better in my dingy little apartment, but at least I wouldn't have to put on a show of enjoying myself. "No offense, dear, but I just want to go home."

"Ah." Em gave me a knowing look. "Your boyfriend didn't leave on business, did he? He left *you*."

I surprised myself by bursting into tears.

"There, there." Em patted me on the shoulder and steered me into a small parlor. "Chin up, love. There's more fish in the sea."

"But I liked this fish." I plopped down in the wingback chair and dabbed at my eyes.

"Well, *that's* a first. Which is a good sign. It means it won't be the last."

I gave her a watery smile and then relented when she offered to send me home in style via the family chauffeur. Riding in quiet luxury right up to my door beat the heck out of negotiating the train and then hailing a cab with luggage and a dog.

The sun was setting when we pulled up to my lodgings, lighting the buildings across the street with a warm, buttery glow. I left the luggage on the curb and snuck Captain up the fire escape, only to have Trixie catch me as she sat in her open window smoking a cigarette.

I paused in my climbing, with Captain tucked under one arm. "There's a bottle of gin in it for you if you didn't see the dog."

She stubbed out the cigarette and knotted her sash around her dressing gown before drifting toward us. She scratched Captain under the chin and he closed his eyes in bliss, even as a back foot jiggled in sympathetic itching. "Don't need a bribe. I like dogs. Just don't get caught."

I sighed and nodded. I'd hide Captain as long as I could, but I needed to look for another apartment, one that would allow dogs. The odds were Mrs. King would scout him out in no time, no matter how careful I was.

On Sunday, I slept late and then wrote up my report for Ryker. Captain provided a welcome distraction to the merry-go-round of thoughts that plagued me otherwise. I fashioned a collar and lead out of an old headband and one of my belts. It would do until I could go to a pet store. Had it not been for sneaking Captain out on potty breaks and figuring out what to feed him—which was pretty much anything I hadn't nailed down, since the dog had the stomach of a garbage can—I might not have left the couch.

I tried reading but couldn't concentrate on anything. Fiction just seemed too tame after the last twenty-four hours. I thought about baking cookies or something to bring with me to the office on Monday as a kind of peace offering, but I didn't want to poison my coworkers. Cooking wasn't my strong suit, no matter how easy Betty Crocker promised it could be.

Instead, I worried about my job status. Ryker would decide I was too unreliable to continue as a field agent. I'd be relegated to desk work if I kept my job at all. The others would hate me for getting Russo hurt, and for losing the stolen artifacts. Miss Climpson would sniff and glare down her nose at me, and Mr. J would look like a sad Bassett hound who'd known all along I'd be a liability and a disappointment.

And I decided I could live with all of that if Knight was there on Monday morning.

But he wasn't.

After admonishing Captain to be as quiet as a mouse in my absence, I caught the bus to work. Perhaps if I had to move, I'd find an apartment closer to work so I could slip home at lunch and let Captain out. After all, if I had a velociraptor for a dog, I wouldn't have to worry too much about the neighborhood, would I?

Attacked by a sudden case of nerves, I wiped my palms on my skirt before opening the door to Redclaw, but all the stewing and worrying had been for naught. The reception area buzzed with activity as I entered, but no one paid me much attention, save for Miss Climpson, who arched an expressive eyebrow in my direction and then went back to her phone call.

I typed up my report and took it to Ryker's office without waiting for a summons.

"Ah, there you are, Bishop," he said when I knocked on his door, as though he'd called me in anyway. "I see you have your briefing done."

"Yes, sir. Any word on Russo?"

"Recovering nicely. Grouchy as a bear, which is to be expected, under the circumstances." His smile was without censure, even if it wasn't warm.

"Perhaps some honey would be in order."

"Good idea. I'll suggest that to the staff." This time, he offered an encouraging flicker of humor.

"And Dr. Knight?"

Ryker's lids dropped partway, and he lifted one shoulder in the slightest of shrugs. "No word. But then, I expect it was a bit much to ask, given the manner in which he'd reacted to circumstances these last few years. Geniuses aren't always the most stable of intellects. In his case, however, I'd rather hoped—" He eyed me with quiet speculation.

"Sir?" I prompted.

Ryker scooped up the Magic 8 ball and leaned back in his chair to roll it idly in his hands. "You seemed to have a rapport with him. I'd hoped the two of you would work together as partners. A team."

"I'd have liked that very much, sir. But I have a lot to learn about teamwork first."

"Acknowledging your faults is the first step to correcting them. Tell me, Bishop, do you think Knight will return?"

I held my hand out for the 8 ball. When Ryker handed it over with a small smile, I thought about his question and rotated the ball so the window on the bottom faced up. The word cube floating within rolled end over end and came to a stop. "The signs are unfavorable," I read aloud.

"Ah well." Ryker reclaimed the 8 ball and set it on the corner of his desk. "You can't always rely on these things." He gave me a measuring look. "I believe I owe you an apology."

"Sir?"

"I didn't know what to make of you when you arrived in our offices that first day. What with your flimsy excuse for being there and then you showed an aptitude for the artifacts. But that left us in a quandary: were you what you claimed and had just stumbled into our office by chance, or were you a plant? And if you were a spy, who sent you?"

"If you thought I was a spy, why didn't you send me packing?"

His fingers splayed as he rolled his palm over. "Mr. Jessop asked me the same. Suffice to say I believe it's better to keep an eye on the devil you know. If you were a spy, we could limit what you had access to. If you weren't a spy, then you were someone very interesting, indeed. Despite the fact you're a terrible typist."

This time his smile lit up his eyes.

I frowned, however. "Just how is it that you know what's going on in the main office? You knew about the Slinky—and the bread rolls—as soon as they happened."

He held up the 8 ball. This time when the sphere rotated, instead of a triangle with printed words, a small image of Mr. J's office floated to the surface.

"Is that—?"

Ryker nodded. "We have cameras in several places. They feed into the 8 ball. I'm told we should have had one focused on Dr. Knight's room."

Heat bloomed in my cheeks. I didn't want to touch that statement with a ten-foot-pole. "At what point did you decide I wasn't a spy?"

He replaced the 8 ball on the corner of his desk. "You had every opportunity to poke around when left on your own, but you didn't. At least, no more than the average new employee. And both Miss Climpson and Mr. Jessop tested you from time to time. Your ignorance of both the technology and your own ability to handle it seemed genuine."

"The mechanical spider."

He nodded again. "That was an accident, but a telling point in your favor. However, it became apparent during Billy's break-in attempt you were unaware of shifters as well. Oh, I had a moment when you figured out things so quickly, I had my doubts, but that's why I decided to test you by assigning you to find Knight."

"A safe enough test because you didn't think I could."

"Not because I thought you were less than capable, but because no one had found him before. My mistake was then failing to give you any real training in what it means to be a

Redclaw agent, even after I saw your potential for independent action and thinking on your feet. I should have realized those same characteristics would have unforeseen consequences without the proper parameters."

"I just wanted to prove myself to you and the others, sir." I sat up straighter, meeting his gaze full on.

"I see that now. Starting today, I'd like you to report to the labs. Ask for Williams. He'll walk you through the protocols and see that you get off on the right foot this time. Set you up with a team for some easy retrievals, that sort of thing."

I sat down in the chair across from his desk. "You're keeping me on? As a field agent, I mean?"

"Why not? You're intelligent and capable of independent thought and action, traits we value in our field agents. You have a tremendous amount of courage and don't easily cave under pressure."

"I got you killed."

"No, you didn't. I think we've established that I don't stay dead. I chose to take bullets for you because I can."

"I disobeyed your orders to stay behind a desk. I almost got Russo killed." My voice wavered as I choked out the last bit.

Ryker nodded. "That much is true. If you owe anyone an apology, it's Russo. You're headstrong, but that's the flip side of your strengths. I suspect you've been under-utilized most of your working life. Redclaw will change that. My mistake was not fully integrating you into the team. Yours was…resisting integration. You'll need to work with other people, Bishop."

"Yes, sir. I'd like that, sir."

"That means taking orders from those in charge over you." He lifted a sardonic eyebrow, as though he thought that might be a deal-breaker. As if reading my mind, he went on, "But I guarantee we will value and appreciate your input."

I couldn't ask for better than that. Except, perhaps, for seeing Peter Knight walk in the door.

Routing several violent gangs while attempting to recover artifacts under Redclaw purview generated a lot of paperwork. After I'd filed the appropriate forms in triplicate, I went down to the labs. Williams was a dark-skinned man with gray sprinkled in his tight black curls, who first asked me to compare the list of the missing inventory with everything I'd seen or recovered from the cave. I realized I'd forgotten to bring the ruby slippers to work with me, but he dismissed my concerns when I brought them up. "Take your time bringing them back. We'll test them, but they don't sound like anything special."

He then handed me a thick notebook brimming with loose papers. "Ryker thinks we need an employee handbook. I agree. Most of the protocols and mission guidelines are outlined here. I'd like you to review them, then organize them into an accessible format. If you come across anything you have questions about, or feel we haven't covered, we want to know about that, too. Write it down."

"Me?" It seemed like I was the last person who should create employee guidelines.

Williams flashed a brilliant smile at me. "I wondered about that, too. Ryker said who better to find the holes in the fence than the fox looking to get out of the henhouse?"

I'm sure my smile in return was somewhat sour as I acknowledged the left-handed compliment. I wasn't thrilled about the additional paperwork, either, but at least Ryker was keeping his word about my expertise and input.

After that, Williams asked about the ray gun, brow furrowed in concentration as I recounted the functions and limitations it exhibited since it had been in my possession.

"It must need time to recharge when being used heavily. It's possible we might design some sort of battery pack for it. We need to run tests to determine its full capabilities." He reached for it, but the gun reared back from his grasp and emitted an ugly high-pitched whine.

"Perhaps another time," I murmured.

"Indeed." His eyebrows jumped for his hairline, as if he'd raised his hands at gunpoint. With a sigh, he added, "What we need is a scientist who can understand the mechanics of the tech we're discovering. I'm an engineer, but there are limits to my knowledge."

Redclaw needed Peter Knight.

I didn't dawdle over my assignments. When the clock struck five, I closed my typewriter and locked my folders in my desk. I wasn't sure how long a little dog could go without a potty break and I had no idea what a dog-shifter might do to my apartment in my absence. Best get home on time for once.

Captain met me at the door when I put the key in the lock, dancing on his hind legs with excitement and turning pirouettes. He took three or four steps toward the kitchen before rushing back, trying to hurry me along.

The reason why wasn't hard to discern. The mouthwatering scents of frying meat and onions, overlaid with apples and cinnamon, filled the apartment. I set my purse down on the coffee table and came to a rest in the doorway to the kitchen, leaning against the jamb to watch Knight cook.

He stood with his back to me, one of my aprons tied around his waist, covering the lower portions of a crisp Oxford cloth shirt in pale blue, paired with navy pants sporting a sharp crease. A new navy jacket hung on the back of one of the kitchen chairs. He'd set the table for two, with plates side by side. A tattered daisy leaned over in a water glass as the centerpiece. An open Bordeaux sat on the table.

He continued to stir over the frying pan, not looking up as I came in.

"You're here because?"

"Well," Knight waved a fork, spattering the stove with grease, "Once I returned to my hovel, there were no terriers turning into dinosaurs, no bears, no owls, and no blonde with snappy comebacks who shoots people with ray guns like she was born to it, and maybe she was. Life was unspeakably dull."

A slow smile tugged at my lips. "And perhaps lonely?"

One shoulder lifted in a half-shrug.

Pretending a nonchalance I didn't feel, I nodded. "Perhaps, I, too, missed a devilishly handsome Englishman who's far too smart for his britches, and who is also the master of the snappy comeback. Your suitcase is here, by the way. I didn't know where to send it."

Something in the line of his back relaxed. "Well, there you are. I'm not sure where I'll be staying at the moment. Hungry?" Casting a glance at the trembling dog who looked up at him with frank anticipation, Knight chucked a piece of bread in his direction. The dog leapt up, catching the food midair with the speed and accuracy of a striking snake.

"You shouldn't feed him like that. You'll spoil his appetite."

Knight shot me a sly glance over his shoulder before he concentrated on the cooking once more. "That, my dear, is precisely the point. I rather think full is better, don't you? If nothing else, I hope he'll remember who gave him tidbits if I ever run into him in his hungriest, angriest form."

"You have a point." There was something so right about Knight's presence in my kitchen, fixing dinner as though he hadn't walked out of my life two nights ago. Everything that had seemed wobbly and off-kilter clicked into place and turned smoothly once more. "What's for dinner?"

"I'm glad you asked." He pointed to the various pots on the stove with the spatula, giving it a little flourish as he spoke. "The obvious, Salisbury steak. Over here we have mashed potatoes, and in this pan, cooked green beans. Not, I should point out, cooked into a limp mass in the tradition of some of your Southern chefs, but as God intended, which is to say still green and somewhat crunchy. There are rolls warming in the oven, and apple crisp for dessert."

I came forward to peer over his shoulder. "You realize, of course, this little performance will seal your fate as the maker of all meals in the future, right?" I wiped a drip of cinnamon glaze off the edge of the pan holding the crisp and brought my finger up to my lips. He just missed smacking my hand with a wooden spoon as I leapt back, laughing.

"I can live with that."

His words were quiet, but I took great satisfaction in them just the same.

"I think this is done. Well, what are you waiting for? I cooked dinner. I'm not serving you, too." Despite his claim to the contrary, he took the rolls out of the oven and transferred them to a glass dish, covering them with one of my linen napkins to retain the heat.

Suppressing a grin, I filled my plate and crossed over to the table. It was then I noticed that his glass was filled with water. Startled, I glanced up, but he appeared not to notice. Eyeing the bottle of wine, I came to a decision and returned to the tap to fill my own glass with water as well. I took my seat across from him at the table.

"How was work?" He passed me the rolls. He flicked a quick glance at my glass when I set it on the table, and though he didn't make eye contact, a small smile quirked at his lips.

I closed my eyes and breathed in the warm yeasty aroma of the bread as I uncovered the rolls. Something bumped into my legs under the table, and a cold nose nudged my knee. I ignored it.

"I still have a job. In fact, they put me in charge of creating an employee handbook, which will set protocols for future training of agents, among other things. No leads on the artifacts, though. It looks like Stirling got clean away with them."

Knight pursed his lips as he buttered a roll. "My guess is six months from now, we'll see some breakthrough advances in industrial technology that will revolutionize factories, netting Stirling a fortune in sales as everyone climbs on board to do the same."

The Salisbury steak was divine. Mine always turned out as tough as shoe leather and about as tasty. I took a sip of water. "More like we'll see some inventive new toy for the homemaker. Something that automatically slices bread or cooks food in a fraction of the time. Or records your television programs so you don't have to be home when you watch them."

"Why wouldn't you be home when your favorite television show was on?"

I shrugged. "I don't know. Maybe you're out at a dance. Or a PTA meeting. Or hunting down renegade shifters." I set my glass down. "Whatever it is, it will change our lives. It will be something useful to every household, which everyone will want to buy."

"A telephone you can carry with you wherever you go." Knight paused with a forkful of mashed potatoes halfway to his mouth, his eyes going glassy as he pictured the possibilities. "Car doors that unlock or start their engines with a press of a button."

"Of course," I said with deceptive casualness, as I speared several green beans with my fork, "it would diminish some of Stirling's victory if we beat him to the punch with our own inventions."

Knight straightened and stared at me. Underneath the table, a small foot pawed at my ankle. Surreptitiously, I palmed a green bean and slipped it under the edge of the tablecloth. The odds were good the dog would eat it and the beans were crisper than I liked. Captain took the vegetable from my hand with unexpected gentleness. So far, I had found nothing he'd refuse to eat.

"Do you think Ryker would go for that? Redclaw releasing technology under specific, controlled conditions, I mean?" Knight's hopefulness encouraged me to hope as well.

"It would be a way to fund the organization while controlling the release of the technology to the public. Eventually we'll want a bigger, more secure location. That's going to cost. And it would have the advantage of taking some wind out of Stirling's sails, which wouldn't be a bad thing. You should ask Ryker tomorrow." I waved my fork in his general direction before concentrating on my plate once more.

That the thought had only just occurred to me then was not something I needed to share.

"Huh." Knight sipped his water. "I might just do that."

I steeled myself with a deep breath, not wanting to push him too far, too fast. "Truth is, I could use you around Redclaw. We work well together, don't you think?"

"I thought you preferred working alone. Being independent and all that."

I was silent a moment. "I've said that, I know. But claiming independence is another way to avoid being hurt. If I'm not relying on anyone, they can't disappoint me when they let me down. The truth of the matter is, I'm not as independent as I believe. There's Em, for starters. I know I could call her and say I need some outrageous sum of money—like five thousand dollars—and she'd say, 'Cash or check, darling?'"

"Not to mention, she'd want to help bury the body." Knight smiled as he leaned back in his chair.

"Exactly. And Trixie downstairs has become a partner-in-crime over hiding Captain."

"Captain?" Knight's eyebrow lifted as his brow furrowed, then cleared. "Is that what you're calling the dog? I guess that's as good a name as any. Smart move, covering his name tag with sticking plaster. I take it you're keeping him? You didn't turn him in to Redclaw because...?"

I shrugged. "I can't explain it. He deserves more than a life in in a cage, numbered and labeled like some exhibit in a museum."

"Tell me about it." Knight frowned, obviously recalling his confinement to Redclaw's basement.

"Then there's Redclaw itself. I activated the signal, and they came. Not only did they come, but they didn't hesitate to put their lives on the line for us. Because we're Redclaw, too. That's...powerful. I've never experienced that kind of loyalty before."

"Loyalty is important." His eyes darkened for a moment, as his thoughts turned inward.

"And then there's you," I said lightly, toying with my mashed potatoes, refusing to meet his gaze. "We make a good team. With your brains and my planning, we'd be unstoppable."

I looked up when his hand closed over mine. His eyes met mine, humor and excitement sparkling within.

"'I think this is the beginning of a beautiful friendship'," I quoted, lifting my glass up in a mock toast.

He lifted his glass in salute, but then set it down to raise my hand to his lips and brush it with a kiss. "Something like that," he murmured.

Heat suffused my cheeks, so much so I wondered if I had a fever. I didn't want to pull my hand away, and yet I didn't know how long I should sit there blushing like an idiot. To my relief, he withdrew his hand first, after giving mine a little squeeze.

"I, uh, should let you know—" His cheeks bloomed red, and I wondered if my fever was catching. He coughed into his hand and tried again. "I don't want to rush into things. With you, I mean. With us. The way everything ended with Margo—"

Having a wife who'd married you for the sole purpose of manipulating you into working for a corrupt, if not criminal organization, who faked her death and then was executed for real in your presence...Yes that would make anyone a little gun-shy.

"Completely understandable," I said with my usual briskness. "I think that's wise. It will give you time to come up with something suitable, as well. I think a side of beef will do."

"Suitable?" He pulled back to narrow his eyes at me while he cocked his head. "Why on Earth would I need a side of beef?"

"As tribute." I waited until he picked up his glass to continue, timing my next comment for when he'd taken a sip. "You'll need to do something to persuade the dog to give up his spot on the bed."

His resulting sputter was utterly perfect. As was the wicked gleam in his eye when he stopped choking. He raised his glass this time for a toast. "Here's looking at you, kid."

When I touched the rim of my glass to his, it chimed like a bell.

The Redclaw Universe:

If you enjoyed this story, please consider leaving a review in the location of your choice. Reviews help a story's visibility, and as a result, help with sales. Likewise, be sure to recommend it to your friends. Every recommendation means more than you could ever know.

You can follow McKenna Dean on her website at McKennaDeanRomance.com. All her social media links are there, or you can follow her on Facebook, Instagram, and on Twitter. If you want to make her day, tell her how much you love her stories by contacting her at mckennadeanromance@gmail.com

Be sure to sign up for her newsletter too! You'll receive a link for a free copy of *Snowfall*, a short story set in the Redclaw universe!

All the stories in the Redclaw Security series can be read as standalones, and feature a different couple in each story. The Redclaw Origins and Better off Red series are sequential series stories, featuring a main couple and recurring characters in each novel.

Made in the USA
Columbia, SC
30 September 2020